THE DEADLY DOG SHOW

BY JEROLD LAST

ACKNOWLEDGEMENTS

Even more so than usual, my wife Elaine made lots of useful suggestions and constructive criticisms, and helped with editing several drafts of the manuscript. Elaine also shared memories of her and our time spent at several dog shows in the region, as well as her extensive experience as a handler, owner, and breeder of German Shorthaired Pointers. I'd also like to thank Kerry McKallip for her careful and thorough editing of a late draft of the book. Thanks to Kerry's efforts there are fewer run-on sentences, as well as fewer usages of "that" sprinkled like parsley at random, throughout this book. Special thanks are offered to our own Jolie (Grand Champion V. D. Nacht's Classic Beaujolais, SH, CGC) for serving as the inspiration and model for Juliet. She's always been a special dog who tries her hardest to please us, and Juliet can only be a small part of the real thing.

Rockefeller University looks like I describe it in Chapter 6, or at least it did when I spent a year there as a post-doctoral fellow. Suzanne and I both liked that rug in the Abby Aldrich Rockefeller Auditorium a lot. Roger and I share a common love of hot pastrami sandwiches. Two of my sons attended college at the University of California at San Diego, in La Jolla. That gave us a lot of excuses to become familiar with the area, including Delmar and Carlsbad in the North County. Carlsbad Ranch is a little-known jewel to include in your travel plans if you ever get there, and the dog beach is exactly where I described it.

This book has its roots in frequent requests from Elaine and several of her friends for me to move my characters from the world of the Mercosur region of South America to the world of dogs and dog shows, at least temporarily. There is a brief scene in the book in Chapter 10 where Bruce makes a clumsy effort to show Juliet for the first time in a dog show and makes several mistakes in the ring, with predictable results. For some reason as we worked out the details of Bruce's misadventures in his first experience in the ring, Elaine felt obligated to remind me of the only time I ever tried to show one of her dogs, a long time ago at a major show in Sacramento at the Cal Expo facility. Elaine was 8+ months pregnant with Matthew and I was completely unprepared when she told me it was my turn to show our dog Fliegen while she was going to relax and have a few Braxton-Hicks contractions. I can tell you from personal experience, when you don't know exactly what to do and you haven't practiced beforehand with the dog, it's a lot harder than it looks to step in there and make everything go correctly, even with a well trained and experienced show dog. I've been told that the comic relief in my performance was very welcome, and that several of the old timers still remember the moment fondly.

To the best of my ability I avoided the temptation in this book to base any of the dog show characters on real people we knew. Several of the people Roger and Bruce meet on the show circuit are deliberate caricatures of real dog show types and have one or more looks or behaviors taken from real life to give a bit of authenticity to the scene, but any resemblance to real people living or dead is purely coincidental. The only dog-related character in the story modeled after a real person is Sherry Wyne, who has several elements of my wife Elaine in the integrity of her breeding program and in her attitude towards dogs as beloved pets as well as featured performers in beauty contests.

TABLE OF CONTENTS

Chapter1.The client

The initial offer came from Sherry Wyne, the western regional representative of the American Kennel Club, on a bright sunny day in October without a trace of smog in a cloudless sky. The kind of day the Los Angeles Chamber of Commerce tries to convince tourists to believe happens every day in Southern California. She came into my office in Century City in Los Angeles, exactly on time for her appointment. After standing in the doorway and removing her sunglasses she put them into a case in her purse and gave her eyes a moment to adjust. I motioned towards the client chair across from my desk.

Sherry walked over to the comfortably worn leather client chair, arranged it to her liking in front of my desk, and sat down gracefully. She glanced around the office from her seat. My large mahogany partners desk had a computer monitor on top, the computer tower and a laser printer under the desk could only be seen by their reflection in the large mirror hanging high on the wall behind my desk, and against the wall were a couple of file cabinets. All of these furnishings were remnants from my previous life as a patent attorney. A partially filled coffee pot stood in an electric coffee maker on top of one of the cabinets. The opposite wall featured a large window with a great view of the Tehachapi Mountains to the north, and several of my various martial arts competition trophies sat in mahogany bookcases lining the remaining wall space. The office lacked any trace of recent elegance. It was functional and the furniture lacked a decorator's touch, but it had a nice view. The ambiance implied I should be attracted to the offer of a big case.

Her voice had a hint of Western Canadian ancestry left far behind. I could hear it mainly as a hint of something different in her speech cadence, which was slower than typical for Los Angeles. An occasional British usage was detected in a few words that were pronounced differently, like "aboot" for "about". "Good morning. Are you Roger Bowman, the investigator?"

I looked directly at a well-dressed woman in her early forties, very attractive with a suntan and an outdoorsy appearance despite wearing a typical dark gray business suit. "Yes, I am. How can I help you today? You didn't tell me very much about what you needed done on the phone when we made this appointment."

Sherry returned my direct look. Unlike 99% of the people who sat in that client chair, she looked very much at ease. "I'm here today on behalf of The American Kennel Club. Do you know anything aboot the organization?"

I wanted to say something like "Cut to the chase," but knew from long experience that letting the client tell it the way they wanted is faster in the long run than trying to get to the point immediately. So I settled for stating, "They run dog shows and define the rules for how pure-bred dogs get to be champions who are recognized as high quality animals. They also maintain the registry for purebred dogs in the United States."

My potential new client smiled. "Close enough for starters," replied Sherry. "We, and by we I mean the AKC, have a problem that we think you could help us with. But before I tell you what the problem is, I need to ask about your availability for a very complicated case. If you're interested in our case and can make the time to do it, I think I can promise you a very unusual, but positive, change in your life style over the next few years."

I smiled back at her. "You're starting to intrigue me, Ms. Wyne. Tell me about this case. May I offer you a cup of coffee? It's fresh ground from a blend I like a lot. I plan on having one myself."

She sat back in the chair and crossed her legs, assuming a very relaxed position. "Yes, thank you, Mr. Bowman. Black will be just fine."

I poured two ceramic mugs of coffee, handed her one and kept the other, sat down behind my desk, put my feet up on the top of the lower drawer so I could look very relaxed too, leaned back, and appeared to listen attentively.

Sherry shifted effortlessly from the role of client to her all-business persona. Her body language said that she was now going to take charge of our meeting. She sipped a bit of coffee then set the cup down on her side of my desk and began her story. "Let's start with your schedule for the next couple of weeks, Mr. Bowman. I would need your commitment to fly to New York City in the next week to meet with the AKC executives who will tell you the details I don't know and basically vet you for the job. If either you or they decide you're not the right investigator for what they need, you'll get all of your travel expenses reimbursed and you may bill the AKC your regular fees for the time you've spent traveling and interviewing. In addition, if you are willing to explore this job further you may keep whatever money is left over from the $5,000 retainer I've been instructed to pay you today. Will your current schedule allow you to visit our corporate headquarters in New York City that soon, Mr. Bowman?"

From the standpoint of how much money I'd be paid, this case sounded like it might turn out to be, by far, my biggest case ever. So, I took it pretty much as it was offered to me. "Yeah, my schedule is flexible for the next few weeks. I can telecommute or delegate everything that needs to be done in the office and fly to New York in the next week. What else can you tell me now?"

She uncrossed her legs and leaned forward towards me while speaking earnestly. "If the AKC decision makers like you, and I'm pretty sure they will, they're going to make some strange requests. They haven't told me what they plan to offer in return for your agreement to these requests, but I'd be glad to make a few suggestions if you're interested."

This interview was getting more and more intriguing. Sherry Wyne was very good at her job and had me completely hooked. "Sure, why not?"

Sherry leaned even further towards me, deliberately changing the mood from her interviewing me for the job to soliciting my complicity in a plot. "First, they'll ask you if you like dogs. The correct answer to that question is a strong yes. Do you like dogs, Mr. Bowman?"

"Yeah, I do."

"Do you have a favorite breed, Mr. Bowman?"

"Yes. If I were buying a dog I'd get a German Shorthaired Pointer."

"That's a perfect answer, Mr. Bowman. May I call you Roger?"

I can play the body language game too. I leaned towards Sherry and became a co-conspirator. "Sure."

Sherry's voice became more enthusiastic. "I don't know if you checked me out and knew the right answer to my question or whether the stars are aligned perfectly and the gods favor you as our lead investigator on this case, but I don't think it matters. In addition to being the AKC regional representative for the western region, which means I attend all of the AKC-sanctioned dog shows in the region and handle any problems that might arise on behalf of the organization, I breed, show, and hunt dogs. I'm based in Sacramento, California and breed some of the best German Shorthaired Pointers in Northern California. Part of the deal the AKC is going to want is for you to get a dog and start showing it at most of the western regional shows. Can I make a suggestion here?"

If I had a tail I'd have wagged it here. I didn't have the tail, so I settled for an earnest expression. "Your suggestion would be most welcome."

Sherry stood up and started to walk over to the window, looking out at the Tehachapi Mountains to the north. "You may have to do some tough negotiating when you meet Harold Carswell in New York City because this is going to cost the AKC a lot of money, but if I were you, I'd demand first that you need a dog that can win at these dog shows. You'll want to borrow one of my finished champions for the duration of this job. I'd suggest Juliet. They'll know which bitch I mean; she has the potential to become a top ten winning bitch in the country. As your cover for going to all of these dog shows, you can be the rich dilettante sponsoring a winning dog who wants to show Juliet as a special, so she qualifies for the Eukanuba and Westminster Kennel Club shows. As a rich and not too bright sponsor you'll be able to get away with asking the kinds of naive leading questions that would be considered rude if an experienced dog person asked the same thing. Dog-show people love to gossip, especially when they're promoting dogs they own or their own breeding programs. If they think you might be willing to sponsor their next champion dog you should be able to get away with asking them anything, even personal questions they normally wouldn't answer."

She paused a few seconds to let that all sink in, then continued. "If the AKC agrees to proceed on the basis of that arrangement you should ask them to cover all of your costs: entry fees, handling fees, and transportation and lodging to and from each show for you, your family, and your professional handler. I'd also ask them aboot covering the cost of a puppy which you and I would choose from Juliet's next litter so you can maintain your cover as a dog fancier if the AKC ever needs your services in the future."

I whistled appreciatively. She was talking about a lot of money here. Sherry continued, "As you can guess from what I just told you, the AKC is going to want to hire you for the entire upcoming cycle of Western regional dog shows. On the west coast, that means almost the entire year, with a break between Thanksgiving and mid-January. This could be a part-time or full-time job depending on your needs, since the dog shows are generally on the weekends, but can run from Thursday to Sunday or Monday. The AKC can afford to pay you whatever you ask, so before you get to that interview, you may want to think aboot what works best for you in terms of part-time versus full-time work for at least a year, maybe longer."

I looked pensively at the mountains through the window behind my potential new client. "Can you tell me what this case is all about, Sherry?"

She walked back from the window and sat down in the client chair while finishing her cup of coffee. "You make very good coffee, Roger. I apologize in advance for this answer, but no. I'm not being coy here; I honestly don't know. I know that something is wrong on our western show circuit, but it's just a feeling I have and that I've discussed with the AKC corporate folks. I don't know how much more they might know than I've been told."

I fiddled with some papers on my desktop. "Why me, Sherry? How did you find your way to me as a possible detective? Surely the AKC hires private detectives from all over the United States routinely for security jobs."

She leaned towards me again. Her body language, as well as her words, said that we were co-conspirators in this discussion. "The AKC decided that whoever we hired had to be an outsider who lived in the region, preferably in California, and who nobody on the local dog show circuit knew anything aboot. They wanted someone who wouldn't be recognized as an investigator and couldn't possibly be involved in whatever is going on, so they asked me to find someone who fit those requirements. I found you by chance, partially because your wife Suzanne had made some inquiries from me about buying a dog last year and partially because your name came up when I asked for suggestions from a police investigator I know in Los Angeles, Charles Brown. You apparently met him on a murder case you both worked in Los Angeles last year. It was as simple as that. I had a highly recommended private investigator whose wife was interested in one of my dogs. Your name jumped up to the top of my list. And here we are."

This was getting more and more interesting. I tried to rein in my enthusiasm until our little negotiation was completed. "What do you mean by feeling something is wrong on your dog show circuit, Sherry?"

Sherry got up from the client chair again and started to pace. "I don't really know. We breeders have a pretty good idea about which dogs in the group are structurally and temperamentally the best and which dogs should win if they're handled properly in the show ring. Different judges are idiosyncratic and look for different styles of dogs to pick as winners, so you can never know for sure which specific animal will win on any given day, but a good breeder can usually guess which dogs will win most of the time. The wrong dogs have been winning too often in several of the different breeds. Not so often that it's obvious, but often enough for me to feel that something isn't right."

She paced back and forth, slowly and deliberately. "Another thing is that all dog handlers are not created equal, some are better than others. Those top handlers tend to get the best dogs to handle. The wrong handlers are winning too often as well. If I were going to cheat at a dog show, I'd bribe the judge to select my dog to get the points. The AKC is especially concerned there's never any reason for a rumor to start about a judge being corrupted, or the integrity of any AKC dog show being to compromised on that basis."

We talked for another 30 minutes about timing, logistics, and the whole dog show lifestyle. The more Sherry told me, the more I liked the whole idea. Suzanne would be easy to sell on it; she wanted our son Robert to grow up with a pet dog in the house, the sooner the better. The problem for me would be finding time to go to a dozen or more shows, and for our busy family to find time to go to any dog shows together. I also wasn't so sure about Robert's nanny, Bruce, who would have to do most of the training, dog walking, and poop scooping. That might turn out to be a hard sell.

Sherry gave me a business card with her personal cell phone number written by hand on the back, shook hands good-bye, and told me she would be in touch with details of when and where my meeting with the AKC management would be held.

I called my top detective and good friend Vincent Romero into the office. Vincent was an ex-CIA agent. I first met him when my wife and I were chasing the serial killer we called the Surreal Killer through Peru and Chile. Vincent subsequently moved from his job as a university professor in Iquique, Chile to Los Angeles and took a job with me. Although he is about 50 years old, he is in excellent shape for his age. He's got a permanent tan from his many years in the Atacama Desert of Chile, and is very, very good looking according to Suzanne. At almost 6 feet tall and wide across the shoulders he looks the part of a bodyguard, and in Hollywood where image is often more important than substance he brings both image and substance to his job as a P.I. Vincent handles all of our bodyguard work, and manages the agency in my absence.

Vincent hit the proper keys to save the report he was writing on his computer, came into my office, and sat in the client's chair while I filled him in on the possibilities of the job Sherry's bosses might be offering.

"What do you think, Vincent? It would be a big change from what we usually do and we'd have a large and very wealthy corporate client who might continue to throw business at us for the rest of our careers. But, I might need your help at some of the dog shows and you'd have to handle most of the routine stuff here at the office on your own for as long as a year. Are you up for that level of responsibility?"

Vincent looked thoughtful. He cleared his throat and fidgeted a bit. He had an odd conversational quirk. Like most South Americans, he more or less randomly sprinkled his speech with the word "claro", which means "sure" or "OK" in South American Spanish. In the context he used it, it was the classic parsley word, which looked good when added to the mixture but had no meaning and just lay there like a garnish. "Claro. It sounds good to me, especially if we can renegotiate my salary and job description a bit to recognize the increased responsibilities I'd have. That would seem to be fair to me."

I tried to look stern and act like a boss. It was hard; I like Vincent as a friend as well as a colleague and that was the answer I wanted to hear. "I suspect they'll have me out to New York City early next week and they'll dither around for the rest of the week before they make any offer. Why don't you come up with a detailed proposal by the end of the week, outlining what it would take for you to say yes to backing me up up on this case while we wait to see if all of this is real?

"By the way, Sherry Wyne gave me a few suggestions on how best to negotiate with her bosses, particularly about the dollar amount I think would be fair if they offered me the job. I think I'll do the same here. While you're thinking about what's fair if you take on more responsibility with the agency, you might want to think about what the agency would look like if we were partners rather than an employer and employee."

Vincent looked stunned. With a shocked expression he mumbled something I didn't understand completely about not expecting this, stood up, and walked over to his office to get back to work.

Chapter2.At home

    I went home at the usual hour for quality family time with Suzanne and Robert while Robert's live-in nanny Bruce prepared dinner for all four of us. As it happened, we had a perfect living situation for becoming dog owners on short notice. When her father was killed in Salta, Argentina, Suzanne inherited a large house in Beverly Hills, which she owned free and clear. I guess we, or more correctly our family trust, owned it now under California's community property laws. The two-story house had probably been built in the 1920s. It was large, gorgeous, and being on the end of a block had only one immediate neighbor. There were plenty of shrubs and trees between the houses to prevent the noise from a few dog barks from becoming a problem. Most of our neighbors had their own dogs or cats and we got along well with them, and so I didn't anticipate any problems on that score either. The outside of the house was white stucco with lots of windows. It stood on a well-manicured lot with a broad front lawn, gardens, mature trees, a small fenced-in swimming pool in back, and privacy from the street ensured by high shrubs and six foot high stucco walls with a gate for entrance.

    Suzanne and I made a good team for solving the oddball murders we always seemed to get involved in when we visited South America. My strengths tend towards the deductive. I can analyze problems logically and do a pretty good imitation of Sherlock Holmes every now and then. Suzanne is also a strongly logical problem solver, but her strengths include a tilt towards the intuitive. She can look at the same facts as everyone else and make quantum leaps forward by some sort of internal logic that most of us don't have. A few months ago, we finished one of our more complicated cases in Montevideo where we'd found a dead body in the bed in our hotel room. Now back at home, we settled down to our normal routines. We both worked out in our respective martial arts training a couple of nights a week at a local dojo. Suzanne was completely into karate while I preferred to mix Brazilian Jiu Jitsu with my karate. We were both pretty advanced in our respective forms and it kept us physically fit.

My business had been quiet since our return from Montevideo, not enough clients to keep me as busy as I liked. On the other hand, Vincent Romero was very busy, making money for us hand over fist handling the bodyguard portion of our detective agency. I guarded bodies with him enough to feel I was doing my share, but was always looking forward to a new, big case or two. Suzanne was hard at work on research, teaching, and grant writing at the UCLA Medical School where she was a Professor of Biochemistry, but took pains to get home early enough to enjoy some time with our now 9-month-old son Robert.

When I arrived home today, Suzanne and Robert were playing together on the floor of our open family room off the kitchen. They sat directly opposite each other in the middle of a large, old oriental carpet, completely surrounded by colorful wooden blocks Suzanne was using to build different shaped structures as fast as she could. Robert was knocking them down as fast as Suzanne could build them up, accompanied by much laughter from both of them.

I walked over, careful to avoid stepping on any of the blocks. "Suzanne, how would you feel about getting a dog? I know we've talked about it lots of times, but I mean getting a dog now, while Robert is still an infant."

Pausing in her block construction to look up at me, Suzanne let a big smile play over her face. "Good timing Roger. Bruce and I have been discussing how we feel about dogs a lot lately. We've even looked into what might be involved in buying a purebred hunting dog. It turns out that Bruce, our nanny of many talents, has another skill set we weren't aware of, but is relevant here. Bruce, why don't you tell him how you feel about a new dog?"

Bruce, who was enjoying a well-deserved break from the immediate responsibility of childcare, had been politely pretending not to be listening and smiled. "As you both know, I was a Navy SEAL before becoming a Nanny. One of the jobs I had in the Navy was to train and handle the dogs our squad used on our missions. I'm a very good dog handler and an excellent dog trainer. I love dogs!" he exclaimed with completely uncharacteristic enthusiasm.

He walked closer to the pediatric construction site and continued. "It would be a lot of fun to train a hunting dog for you, and even to show the dog if its got the right bloodlines, temperament, and conformation to compete in dog shows. It should be pretty easy for me to make the jump over into training your dog for hunt tests, too. But, and it's a big but, Robert's still too young to start with a brand new puppy right now. A puppy would demand too much time and energy for me to be able to spend the necessary one-on-one time Robert should have at this age. Next year a puppy would be perfect, but if you want a dog right now, I'd recommend an adult that's already well trained and who has lived with a family. I believe an adult would fit right in here, if there was any way you could find such a dog."

Suzanne jumped back into the conversation with both feet. "I feel exactly the same way as Bruce," she added enthusiastically. "As a matter of fact I've actually contacted a few breeders and have a pretty good idea about the specific breeders and bloodlines I'd like you to look at when we start dog hunting."

I turned back to look directly at her. "I spoke to a potential new client today that had a case that ought to interest both of you. Can we talk about it now?"

Suzanne looked disappointed. "Are we changing the subject from dogs on purpose, Roger?"

I bent over to pick up a block that looked like it would fit into the top floor of the house she was building with Robert and handed it to her. "No, we're not. The case is related to the subject. Does the name Sherry Wyne ring any bells with you?"

Suzanne took the block and tested it out. It fit perfectly. "Sherry Wyne. Isn't she the GSP breeder from Sacramento who owns and shows my favorite dog of all I've seen so far, Juliet?"

"Yeah, that's exactly who she is." I went on to tell Suzanne and Bruce all about our potential new clients, Sherry and the AKC, and the possibility of getting Juliet as a family member for a year or more, plus one of her puppies after that.

Both loved the idea, as well as the idea of my working for the AKC as a dog show detective, and possibly Bruce volunteering his services both as an assistant detective and a professional handler. As long as the AKC decided it wanted to hire me, the family could make this work.

With a big smile, Suzanne made me an offer I couldn't refuse. "If I volunteer to pack your suitcase and keep our luggage fitting into just one carry-on bag each, can I accompany you on the trip to New York? A short getaway together would be lots of fun and I have someone there I need to visit."

"Is that OK with you, Bruce? Suzanne and I promised each other (omit) some quality time for (just) the two of us to spend together, and this could be a good start."

"I'll be glad to look after Robert for a couple of days. You two guys deserve to have a couple of days of vacation. Glad I can help."

It seemed clear to me that if the AKC folks wanted me for this job I'd be an extremely enthusiastic employee, even if I was an expensive one, especially if they were willing to meet all of the conditions Sherry had suggested. All of the adults were up for expanding the family by one dog, and I suspected that if Robert had a vote, he would make it unanimous.

Chapter3.New York, New York

The lyrics to a popular old show tune go something like "New York, New York, It's a wonderful town. The Bronx is up and the Battery's down".

A more modern version might go something like "New York, New York, It's not really a wonderful town. The cost of just about everything is up and the service is way, way down!" New York City emulated this modern version from the moment we got off the plane.

We arrived on our direct flight from LAX to JFK Airport about an hour late. Fortunately all of our baggage was carry-on, as we heard numerous complaints about lost and stolen suitcases from fellow passengers waiting in line for a taxi into the City. We finally got to the front of the line and into a taxi, which ever so slowly fought its way through traffic on the Long Island Expressway, through the Queens-Midtown Tunnel, and into Manhattan to our hotel. The flat fare was supposed to be $52. The cab driver asked for $100 with a perfectly straight face. Through the years I've learned not to put up with crap like this. I responded by pulling out my wallet, flashing my badge and credentials, handing him two $20, one $10, and two $1 bills, and telling him I was letting him go this time for his tip. However, if it ever happened again he'd be going to jail and losing his taxi medallion. The cabbie didn't like it, but knew better than to argue as we walked into the hotel. The doorman and two bellhops witnessed the entire exchange and smiled at me with their approval.

Our airplane tickets and hotel reservations, and my itinerary for tomorrow from 9 AM until after dinner, had all been arranged for me. The only thing not scheduled in advance down to the nearest minute was a bathroom break, or perhaps I wasn't going to be allowed any. Suzanne would be on her own until dinner, when she would join us at a trendy and very expensive

French restaurant a block or two from the building that housed the AKC offices.

Tonight, Suzanne and I were free to have dinner alone. This was an opportunity to introduce Suzanne to what I considered one of life's greatest pleasures, something exotic and only available in New York. Not trendy, not as expensive as standard yuppie fare in The Big Apple, but a neighborhood hole-in-the-wall Kosher-style delicatessen serving hot pastrami and corned beef sandwiches on fresh deli rye bread with half-sour pickles as well as other local ethnic odds and ends. These could all be found in Los Angeles, but just didn't taste the same as the authentic versions in New York City. I'd done this previously in my earlier life, and had been dreaming of sharing the experience for her first time with Suzanne.

We entered the crowded restaurant to a sensory assault of sights, smells, and sounds. The air was hot and steamy, the steam originating from huge chunks of meat, cooked to perfection and being sliced behind a glass counter by busy chefs with large knives and electric slicing machines. The smells were a symphony of spiced meat, sharp pickles, and spicy mustard. The sounds originated from smiling customers stuffing their mouths with overstuffed sandwiches, shouting meat slicers calling frantic waiters to pick up each of the sandwich plates as it was prepared, and surly waiters snarling at impatient customers who ate too slowly for a new group to be seated promptly.

"Take dat table," snarled a gnome dressed like a waiter. The gnome was in his 70s, had sparse patches of gray hair scattered at random over his pink scalp, was barely 5 feet tall, and skinny enough to look like he hated food, or maybe he just couldn't afford to eat here and was surviving on the rich smells. The old gnome's face had a perpetually sour expression, to make sure we understood that like all native New Yorkers he hated tourists, especially customers.

"Fasta lady, I ain't got all day," he exhorted Suzanne as he scooted through nooks and crannies between the tightly clustered tables and chairs. Normal sized people like us had to bump and push our way through the aisles that the old waiter navigated quickly and efficiently.

We looked at other diners' plates on tables as we alternately scampered and sidled through the crowded dining room to the far wall. The overwhelming majority of diners sat in front of large plates containing sandwiches heaped with layers of pink meat, pastrami or corned beef. The overstuffed sandwiches were held together with toothpicks, one in each half sandwich, topped with a variety of colorful, fancy ribbons of plastic. Sliced dill pickles and pickled green tomatoes filled whatever space remained on the plates. The occasional nonconformist had blintzes, potato pancakes, or kreplach decorated with sour cream on their scrupulously meatless platters. Carnivores and herbivores alike both drank glasses of cream soda to avoid mixing meat and dairy products.

"Siddown," he said rudely when we got to our little micro-table, barely large enough to hold two dinner plates, slamming a couple of menus down to emphasize we had reached our destination. The tiny table held a dispenser with slots for the salt and pepper, napkins, and the menus. We were against a wall on one side, had chairs across from each other, back-to-back with other diners sitting at similar micro-tables, and a third, empty chair on the fourth side creating an aisle so narrow we had to enter and leave our chairs by sliding sideways.

We scrunched into our seats at the closely packed table. I quickly coached Suzanne on survival skills in the deli. "You get two choices here, Suzanne, and only two choices. You can have authentic deli Kosher pastrami or authentic deli Kosher corned beef. I'm having the hot pastrami sandwich on Kosher rye bread, and recommend it highly. If you opt for the corned beef, you can just have it on rye or as a Reuben sandwich with cheese, sauerkraut, and Russian dressing."

I carefully closed our menus and stacked them to signal the waiter that we were ready to order. "In the old days all of the side dishes were on the table and you could just pig out on pickles and good stuff. Nowadays they serve controlled portions with your order, so you have to ask for what you want and pay extra for a la carte side dishes. The authentic experience includes cole slaw, a half-sour Kosher dill pickle, pickled green tomatoes, and even pickled red bell peppers that aren't spicy, just vinegary. The half-sour dill pickle is the key; that's the kind I like the best. Any real foodie will tell you the full sour pickles just aren't as good.

As I saw the waiter heading towards our table it seemed a good idea to give Suzanne a preview of coming attractions. I spoke quietly, directly to her. "And, let me give you a fair warning. The authentic New York City delicatessen experience consists of the food, which is unique and just doesn't taste as good anywhere else even if they pretend it's exactly the same food prepared in exactly the same way. But, it comes at a price. The waiters are incredibly rude. They don't give you time to think about what you're going to order. The waiter will expect you to order the second he gets here, he won't wait around while you decide, and they almost throw the plates at you. And we have to order the pastrami 'extra lean'. You get exactly the same stuff whether you order 'extra lean' or just plain pastrami, or even 'fat pastrami', but if you want to sound like an authentic New Yorker you have to insist on the 'extra lean'."

"Wadda ya want? I don't have all day." The waiter reminded us that his time was precious and we'd been given all our allotted time to decide what we wanted. We both ordered the hot pastrami sandwiches on rye bread and beer.

"Ya coitanly took yer time deciding," he chided us as he exited stage left to get our orders.

The meat actually took days to prepare, first being soaked in brine to remove excess fat, then slow cooked for hours. This part takes place out of sight of the customers. Three butchers were working full time to keep up with the demand slicing the meat to order behind a glass counter. The deli did a huge take-out trade as well as serving their standing-room only crowd waiting to be fed at the tables. Each huge sandwich had more than a half of a pound of the tender, juicy meat sliced ultra-thin and heaped on a slice of fresh rye bread. A second slice of bread to complete the sandwich rests several inches above the first slice. The huge sandwich is then carefully sliced in half and placed on its plate without dropping a shred of meat during the entire process from assembly to serving. Delicatessen mustard sits in jars brought to the table and you are expected to slather a bunch on the bread. The large dinner plate also contains a big dollop of cole slaw and the whole pickle you ordered, which you are expected to slice before eating. The green tomatoes come in a side dish and, like the pickles, have been marinating in a specially formulated brine recipe for days or weeks to develop each delicatessen's vision of the perfect flavor.

The gnome returned staggering under the weight of a tray balanced in his left hand containing our two sandwich plates, a jar of mustard, two bottles of beer, two glasses for the beer, and a dish of green tomatoes. He slammed the plates, bottles, and glasses on the table with his other hand as he ran by the table en route to who knows where. I told Suzanne she had to "paw her own".

Our resident restaurant critic, Suzanne, went through four napkins and had little to say until she had inhaled her first half sandwich. "That's yummy and you're right. It's totally better than the same deli sandwich in Los Angeles would taste. It must be fresher or something here since they sell so much. Or maybe it's the ambiance that makes the meal? Somehow it wouldn't be the same if a tuxedoed maître-de came by to ask if we were enjoying our dinner, which would be de rigueur in Beverly Hills."

Those two sandwiches, one for me and one for Suzanne, plus cole slaw, pickled green tomatoes, half-sour dill pickles, and two beers cost the gross domestic product of a small South American country, but worth every cent of it.   We went back to our hotel for some TV and quiet romantic time while we tried to get sleepy three hours earlier than usual.

Chapter4.The AKC

The next morning after a shower, shave, and room service breakfast charged to the AKC, I walked a few blocks over to the office building where I was to spend the day meeting my prospective new clients. Suzanne had to go across town, a half-hour ride on two buses, for her scheduled meeting with several scientists on the faculty of Rockefeller University. We walked together as far as her bus stop and said good-bye on the corner of Madison Avenue and 42nd Street, one of the wider streets that featured west to east bus service between the Hudson River and the East River along the width of midtown Manhattan.

I looked around me and was struck by the differences between a wide, heavily traveled avenue in New York City and its counterpart, where we lived, in the western part of Los Angeles. In New York, the high-rise buildings dominate, even on the broad avenues and cross-town streets. The impression everywhere was like being in an urban canyon with glass and concrete walls. Traffic is dog-eat-dog and parking is impossible. Not even worth bringing a car, it's a city for walkers and subway riders. In Westwood or L.A., a city where everyone drives everywhere, we have plenty of high-rise buildings but there is space between them. The wide streets and avenues become an urban river of vehicles of different shapes and sizes. I definitely prefer the California lifestyle.

The remainder of my walk along Madison Avenue to the AKC Building felt like I was participating in semi-organized chaos. Unlike Los Angeles, where we are all in our cars, here in The Big Apple it seemed like the entire city was on the sidewalk. Strolling and sight seeing was not for the faint of heart. The synchronized mob moved with focused purpose, not walking at a familiar pace, but more like a communal trot. If you didn't get out of the flow of people hurrying to work, or keep up with the frenetic pace of the mob, you risked drowning in the flood of people who would trample anybody moving too slowly who were blocking their way.

I arrived at my destination about five minutes early for my appointment and walked into an elegant broad lobby with granite tiles on the floor. A security arrangement dominated by an elaborate gate and turnstile arrangement running most of the width of the lobby corralled me just inside the entrance. Two security guards stood behind the only gap in the gate between where people entered the building through the Madison Avenue entrance and the bank of elevators in the center of the lobby.

Most of the people entering the building went through a gate with several turnstiles activated by the I.D. cards hanging from their necks containing the AKC corporate logo. An entrance without a turnstile at the north end was a gated area labeled "Visitors" beckoning to the common riff-raff like me. The two guards stood vigil just on the other side of this entrance, one on each side of the passageway.

"Do you have an appointment?" snarled one of the guards, hitching up his heavy belt containing a can of Mace and a wooden baton. I'd have been a lot more impressed with the security if he hadn't been about 5 foot two and 70-something years old, especially since he was the younger of the two guards. I'm 6'2" and 190 pounds, so he was even less physically impressive by comparison. I'm also 36 years old with blue eyes, but didn't have the Mace or the baton.

"Yes, I'm supposed to meet some people in the AKC offices."

Shorty continued his tough guy act. "I'll need to see your I.D."

I showed him my driver's license. He didn't need to know I was a private detective. He checked my I.D. against a list of names, checked off a name, and handed me back the license and a visitor's badge to attach to my jacket. "From California, eh? I guess that makes you a nut, a flake, or a fruit." He laughed at his butchered rendition of the old joke. "You'll have to wait right here a minute or two while we get someone downstairs to the lobby to escort you to the AKC offices"

He picked up a phone, dialed a number, and mumbled something into the mouthpiece.

He hung up the phone and snarled, "Someone will be here for you real quick."

And someone was. A beautiful 20-something woman in a business suit that did little to hide her qualifications for the escort job materialized next to me and introduced herself. "Mr. Bowman, I'm Candy. If you will please follow me."

She led me to the elevators, entered the nearest one, and punched the button for the 30th floor. We had the compartment to ourselves, so the trip was non-stop. The elevator ascended rapidly, while Candy briefed me on the essentials.

In a sultry voice she told me, "You'll be meeting several of our top executives, Mr. Bowman. The man in charge is Harold Carswell. He'll introduce you to the others. I have a copy of your itinerary for you to review when you get a chance. The initial meeting will be in the conference room just to the left of the elevator. If you need to take a break, the men's room is about three doors further down the corridor to the left. Your first appointment is with Mr. Carswell. He'll probably take you back to his office after you've met everyone you'll be seeing today. Do you have any questions?"

The timing was perfect. A bell dinged, the elevator stopped and the door opened. Candy led me to the conference room, which was exactly where she promised it would be, rapped on the door, opened it, and delivered me. She introduced me to the distinguished looking gentleman at the head of the large cherry wood conference table who stood up as we entered the room. He was tall, about 6 feet, and looked to be in good shape for a man in his 60s, neither fat nor thin. His most notable features were his full head of expensively barbered white hair and his eyes, a piercing shade of blue, deeply recessed beneath bushy brows. I shook hands with Harold Carswell while Candy exited. Carswell, in turn, introduced me to the rest of the people in the room, all men as I noticed immediately. They remained seated at the table so I assumed I was expected to skip the handshakes and attempt to memorize the names.

In rapid succession I was introduced clockwise around the table to Misters Forrest, Burnett-Smythe, Cabot, Rosswell, Lodge, and Stanley. Then I was invited to help myself to a cup of coffee, served in fine China, and the empty seat at the conference table. Carswell told us a little bit about the history of the AKC before he smoothly segued to the nature of the job at hand.

He stood up straighter, if that was possible, cleared his throat, and orated. "This is an old and respected organization," he intoned, "chartered here in New York City in 1884. The first offices in New York were rented in 1887, and the Stud Book, which became the register of pedigrees, came into being about then. The AKC Gazette began publishing two years later. Since then we've been here as an organization to foster pure bred dog health and breeding certification. We oversee the rules that govern the dog shows and the clubs that sponsor the shows, which currently feature a wide range of competitions including Field Trials, Hunting Tests, Conformation, Agility, Obedience, Tracking, Lure Coursing, Herding, Canine Good Citizen, Earthdog and Coonhound events."

He segued seamlessly and effortlessly into the pitch for the job. The job itself was simple as he described it: something (or things) was dreadfully wrong on the western conformation show circuit. The wrong dogs were winning too often. Several of the insiders could sense that things weren't right, although nobody could put their finger on exactly what bothered them, and profits were down because expenses were higher than had been budgeted. He assured us the track record of their computer models was excellent at predicting expenses and profits within a variance of a few percent. Yet the western shows were experiencing a large deviation from predicted values, which had never happened before. The AKC has its own investigative branch, staffed with retired FBI agents. Their best efforts to solve the mystery of what was wrong had come up with nothing thus far except data indicating the problem was real.

Carswell played briefly with a fountain pen before turning in my direction to talk directly to me. "And that brings us to what we are doing now. We're hoping an outsider will have some new and different ideas, and we're open to a proposal from you as to how we should proceed from here. This group has been empowered to hear your suggestions and make a decision whether to hire you to correct this situation." Six expensively barbered corporate heads nodded solemnly in agreement.

Carswell picked up the pen again and played with it for a moment while I digested his words, then continued. "If you look at your itinerary you'll see you are scheduled to be spending about half an hour with each of us in turn. We should be done by the end of the morning. Feel free to ask any of us anything you wish. This will give us all a chance to get to know you one-on-one. We'll meet back as a group for lunch and ask you to tell us your impressions and suggestions for approaching the task. After lunch this group will meet in executive session. You can take a well-earned break, while we decide whether you are the right man for the job. Assuming we decide to hire you, I'll spend as much time with you as we need for the remainder of the afternoon, working out the details of how you will proceed and how you will interact with us. Is that satisfactory to you?"

I didn't have a pen to play with. The best I could come up with was a nod of approval. "It sounds reasonable to me."

Carswell picked up the pen once again. "OK, there's no time like the present to begin. You and I will start in my office,

Mr. Bowman, and then you'll make the rounds of the other offices."

We walked a few miles up the corridor to his office at the northeast corner of the building. My first impression was Wow! There were large windows looking north and east. From 30 stories up we had an unblocked and spectacular view of midtown Manhattan and Central Park to the north, and the Borough of Queens beyond the East River to the east. The office was huge, thickly carpeted, and dominated by a huge oak desk strategically placed in front of the southern wall so the views from both windows were available at all times. The office smelled like money. Hanging on the walls were framed pictures of champion show dogs, usually with a smiling owner and serious looking handler receiving an opulent rosette ribbon or a silver trophy cup at a dog show.

Carswell sat down in a huge leather chair behind his desk. I was offered a comfortable leather chair alongside the desk facing him. "I assume Sherry Wyne filled you in on why you are here, at least as far as I discussed in the conference room."

I nodded again.

Some more playing with the pen preceded his, "Since our investigators weren't able to find out what's going on, we thought a stranger to the western dog show world might be able to learn more by slipping in under our perpetrator's radar. That could take a long time. You would need a solid excuse to hang around the dog shows getting to know the people and the atmosphere without posing a threat to anyone who might be leery of a detective. Did Sherry discuss that with you?"

When in doubt, tell the truth. Not necessarily the whole truth and nothing but the truth, but don't go with a complicated lie if it can be checked out easily. She might have already told him what we had discussed. "Yes, she did. She suggested I act the role of a well off, but inexperienced and none too bright sponsor. We'd need a dog to show and a handler who could show it for us as a cover identity."

Carswell mulled my answer over for a perceptible pause, fidgeted with the pen, and leaned toward me. "What did you think of that idea?"

I almost asked him to loan me a pen so I could kill a few seconds fidgeting with it while I formulated my answer, too. "It made a lot of sense to me. There's no other way to become one of the group quickly, and I'm sure the breeders and the handlers are close knit groups that don't open up to strangers they see as possible intruders."

Somehow, with little change in his posture or bearing, Carswell looked and sounded pompous. "Am I correct in assuming Sherry suggested she could sell you an expensive dog with show potential and handle it in the ring for you at AKC expense?"

I sensed that how I answered this rhetorical question would define what, if any, kind of relationship I'd have with Carswell, and by extension the entire AKC leadership staff if they decided to hire me, so I thought very carefully about the exact words I chose for my response.

"I don't know if you meant it to sound that way, but your question and how you phrased it implies a very cynical attitude on your part towards your staff and their motivation. You just suggested that Sherry was not necessarily acting in the best interests of the AKC when she approached me. I don't know either you or Sherry well enough to know whether your implication has any basis in truth, but if it does I shouldn't be hearing about it in this way. In my experience it's a bad idea to work for someone who doesn't trust his employees. You may demand as a condition of employment that the people you work with spend most of their time kissing your ass, rather than speaking the truth. If that's the case, I think I've heard enough to know I'm not interested in this job. And just for the record, no, your assumption of what Sherry suggested to me is not correct."

Surprisingly, Carswell sat back in his fancy chair behind his fancy desk, visibly relaxed, and even smiled. "Well, I guess I'd give you a grade of F as an ass-kisser, but I wasn't looking for one on this job. I do want to find someone who is their own person, gives me honest reports, and who I can trust. I am giving you a tentative score of A+ for honesty and speaking your mind. Whoever we hire would have to work pretty much on their own, with little or no direct supervision by the AKC staff. Obviously, if our best investigators weren't able to find anything, our perpetrators must know quite a bit about how the AKC works and who our investigators are. Whoever we hire would have to have little contact with us and be convincing in their undercover role. That means I need to be able to trust them to always be working for the AKC's best interests, without constantly looking over their shoulder. It sounds like you could be that person. Let's start over. What ideas for your cover story did you and Sherry come up with during and after your discussion?"

I let myself relax visibly, projecting honesty and sincerity. "Sherry offered to loan me her dog, Juliet, to live as our family pet for as long as it takes. We would appear as wealthy sponsors making intense campaigning possible for Juliet, which Sherry herself can't afford. Sherry suggested we show Juliet as a special towards her silver and gold awards. Whenever this job is finished we'd have to return Juliet to Sherry since she and her dog are very attached to each other. After speaking with Sherry, I discussed with my wife what might be reasonable for our family to do. We have a 9-month old son, Robert, and although we've wanted a dog we felt we weren't in a position to take on a young puppy. Suzanne felt that the offer of an adult, fully trained dog would work, but it would be very hard on Robert to return the dog when this job is finished if he became attached to Juliet, which we assume he will. One of the things Suzanne and I discussed on the plane ride out here was the type of arrangement I should request to reasonably match my need for a cover story on the dog show circuit with my family's need to be made whole after the job is completed."

I upped the honesty and sincerity quotient by leaning towards Carswell and looking even more earnest. "Suzanne came up with what I think is a win-win idea that should make Sherry and us happy. I hope it will work for you and the AKC as well. We propose to accept Sherry's offer and take Juliet on a long-term loan of indefinite length. Juliet would live in our house, be well loved, and be shown on the West Coast circuit in the Best of Breed competition through her Grand Championship to the highest level we can reach. She'll be entered in any show Sherry thinks is appropriate, up to one set of shows at a given location per week. Sherry will get her dog campaigned aggressively and vigorously as a by-product of this investigation, which seems to be a reasonable payment for giving up Juliet's company for quite a long time."

My earlier life as a lawyer came in handy here. That experience had taught me the basics of negotiation and manipulation. At this point, it was time for the counter-arguments so Carswell would believe all of this was his idea, not mine. "AKC would have to pay all of Juliet's entry fees in that scenario, so there would be some dog show-related costs for AKC to pay, but they should be predictable and reasonable. In addition, I'll have expenses that you'll need to reimburse for attending most, or all, of these shows, as well as my usual fees and expenses that I'll be billing to the AKC. Our nanny, Bruce, who also works for my agency part-time as a detective, would handle Juliet in the ring. He's fully qualified to do so based on his training in the military. You'll have to take care of whatever retroactive paper work is necessary for him to be licensed as a professional handler. I'll bill the AKC for his salary and expenses as one of my detectives on the case and he'll be our entry point into the handler world. There won't be any handling fees for AKC to have to pay Bruce for showing Juliet in that scenario."

Carswell actually smiled, a large genuine smile. "That sounds like a good deal for the AKC, Mr. Bowman. I like that idea. And I like the idea of having a second detective on the case. Four eyes are better than two."

As long as I'd made him happy, it seemed like a good time to ask for more. "We're going to need some additional expensive equipment that I don't have if we're going to pull this undercover assignment off and accomplish what you're hiring me for. Can I charge things that come up to expenses without having to clear them beforehand with you?"

He looked a bit more cautious. "What sorts of things did you have in mind, Mr. Bowman?"

I projected earnest and honest as hard as I could. "Where I live, finding an airline that takes dogs can be a problem. I plan to go to the dog shows just in California, and maybe in Arizona, until there's a reason to fly somewhere that's too far to drive. Over the long run a long-term lease on a comfortable minivan should be cheaper than flying to large airports and renting transportation each time we travel any distance with Juliet. I wanted authorization to lease a reasonably sized minivan that will hold three adults and an infant seat as well as a large dog crate for Juliet."

Carswell nodded. "Go ahead. I'll sign off on a 1-year lease for a new or used minivan when we get the bill, which I want you to charge directly to us. We get a substantial discount on things like this if you lease it through any major auto dealership. Personally, I'd recommend Honda for the minivan. Anything that has an obvious application to your assignment, like this, can be charged to expenses. For direct billing of major items to the AKC, just include an explanation of what it's for and why it's the best choice to facilitate your progress. We'll need receipts and detailed explanations for any requests for reimbursement from us, so use direct billing when you can. Is there anything else you think you'll need?"

This was a lot more than I expected. It was probably a good time to quit while I was ahead. "Not that I know of yet, but I'm sure things will come up as time goes by. I appreciate your flexibility and the implied trust in me.

"There's one more thing we should discuss now. Sherry wants Juliet returned to her when this case is over, to breed at some convenient time in the following year. Suzanne suggested that AKC buy one of Juliet's puppies for my family as a replacement when we return Juliet to Sherry. Since we have a toddler who will have gotten used to having a dog around, I believe we'll need a replacement. Bruce has already volunteered to cross-train the puppy for conformation shows and hunt tests. Sherry is planning on breeding Juliet in the next year or so, which should be about the right timing to make this work. I don't think this is asking too much from the AKC. Do you, sir?"

Carswell smiled benignly at me. "No, I don't. And I like the idea of your family ending up with a show dog and becoming part of the AKC family when this is all over."

It was my turn again. I leaned towards the big desk and decided to give Carswell a turn. "I assume you've checked me out thoroughly. Do you have any questions I can answer?"

We talked a little bit about the size of my detective agency, how I would arrange to juggle whatever other work we had with what would essentially be my half- to full-time commitment to AKC, and which other operatives I envisioned using on this case besides Bruce, and what their roles would be. Carswell was quite impressed with my background as a former homicide detective on the Los Angeles Police Department and as a practicing attorney before I became a P.I. I explained to him that over the last couple of years, much of my best detective work had been done in South America. He was perhaps even more impressed with the background that Bruce, a former navy SEAL, and Vincent Romero, a former CIA agent, brought to my agency and asked for additional details.

I explained a little bit more about Bruce and Vincent, who would be working with me on this case. "Bruce joined the navy fresh out of high school. As a Navy SEAL, he soon saw combat in both Iraq and Afghanistan. He was pretty young at the time and suddenly had a lot going on in his life. Needless to say, Bruce had to grow up fast. He reenlisted once, so he did two tours of duty in all, both in combat zones. As an obviously gay man with no college education, he realized he had hit a glass ceiling in his navy job, so he mustered out after his second hitch. Looking for a job back home in Wisconsin, Bruce unfortunately discovered a great deal of prejudice in the local police forces after he left the Marine Corps. After thinking long and hard about career prospects for gay policemen and how much he liked working with children he opted to go through Nanny School in Southern California instead. We are quite lucky to be his first full-time employers after his graduation. He's a superb Nanny and a man of many skills that come in handy as a part-time assistant in occasional cases of mine, especially as a bodyguard for clients. I had a chance to get to know him a lot better in Montevideo when we worked together on a complicated murder case, and I consider him to be a friend as well as an employee.

"Suzanne and I first met Vincent Romero during our pursuit of a serial killer through Peru and Chile. By coincidence, he was also born and raised in Wisconsin, but a generation earlier than Bruce. He was a professor of biochemistry at the University of Chile's branch campus in Iquique, a city in the far north of the country. He was also an undercover CIA agent down there for more than two decades. Vincent decided to retire from both the CIA and the University of Chile and move back to the United States. Shortly after we came home from Iquique, he moved to Los Angeles with his family. He works with me now as a bodyguard and a private detective."

We also discussed specifics about money and how much we'd be paid. There would be three of us, Bruce, Vincent, and I, getting fees and expenses for whatever time we spent on this case, plus a generous retainer fee for the agency to formalize the relationship, and an even more generous bonus if we solved the AKC's problems with the western dog show circuit. Now that we were best buddies, Carswell was offering to be quite generous with the AKC's money.

About 45 minutes later, we had covered everything practical that needed discussion at this preliminary stage. Carswell's body language and frequent glances at his wristwatch told me the interview was just about over. "For the rest of this morning, you'll be talking to my staff who you met when you arrived. Answer their questions as completely as you can with generalities, but don't get into the specifics we've discussed if you can avoid doing so. I would especially avoid any details about your plans once you've become a dog owner. I believe that everyone in the group is trustworthy, but better safe than sorry!

"After lunch you and I will talk some more about your plans as Juliet's sponsor, and what I think may be a good place for you to begin your investigations. You may assume that we'll formally offer you this job at lunch."

Chapter5.Making the Rounds

My next scheduled stop was at Nathan Forrest's office, just down the hall. I took a short detour en route, at a convenient urinal, to return the contents of a cup or two of coffee I had consumed then knocked on the closed door.

"Come in," answered a voice from inside the room.

I entered. Forrest sat in a large chair behind a large desk, both chair and desk considerably smaller than Carswell's, but still a big chair and a big desk. It was hard to tell as he sat in his elevator chair, but as I remembered from when he was walking out of the conference room, he was short, five foot five inches or so, pudgy, and soft. He was in his mid-50s, thoroughly unimpressive. His most noteworthy features were a hairline that had receded almost to infinity----he was almost completely bald----and the vanity that made him try to comb over what little graying hair he had left, in an attempt to make him look less bald than he was.

"Good morning Mr. Bowman." His accent was standard American without any strong regional inflection. He had the hint of a stammer in his speech, but it had been well corrected. It could only really be appreciated if you listened carefully as he spoke a few specific hard consonants of the alphabet. "C-can I get you a c-cup of c-coffee?"

"No, thank you. I'm just about fully loaded with coffee at this point."

That pretty much exhausted the pleasantries. Forrest asked me several questions about my usual business as a private detective, what I had done before I became a P.I., what kinds of dogs I liked, and whether I owned a dog. He seemed to be impressed that I had been a police detective, even more impressed when I told him I had been a homicide detective, and still more impressed when I told him I graduated from UCLA

Law School. I shared my liking of hunting dogs, especially German Shorthaired Pointers. He politely corrected me that in AKC-speak they were called Sporting Dogs. I made a mental note not to make that mistake again when I was claiming expertise on the dog show circuit. I kind of evaded the question about dog ownership for now.

Forrest apparently wanted to make a good impression on me, at least as much as vice was versa. He explained his job at the AKC. "I'm responsible for m-managing several IT functions here at the AKC, including a c-couple of very large databases. We have tens of thousands of past and present members registered and hundreds of thousands of dogs. We also m-maintain a DNA databank for specific c-canine identification. It is used for resolving disputes about ancestry that might arise, and for research purposes. Our databank has information on tens of thousands of dogs representing the 177 breeds currently recognized and registered by the AKC. That's a lot of doggy DNA and a lot of c-computer programmers to keep track of. F-fortunately we outsource m-most of the actual p-programming to India and Uruguay, so I d-don't get d-directly involved in any of that s-stuff."

Forrest leaned forward and asked me in hushed and confidential tones whether any of the AKC staff members had recommended me for this job. In my mind I translated this question as a discrete probe of how much juice I had with his boss, which would tell him whether he should be actively supporting me for this job if he wanted to stay in Carswell's good graces. This was an obvious opportunity to score a few points, so I did.

"It's my understanding that today's interviews are a chance for us all to get to know each other, but the decision to hire me was already made before the AKC offered to pay for my trip out here to meet you all. Isn't that what they told you?"

"Well, er, uh," he fidgeted and fussed while he thought of an answer. "Yes, that's exactly what Harold told m-me."

"Interesting," I thought to myself, "this guy's major goal in life is to keep Carswell happy. I wonder how many of the other board members are just here to give Carswell a majority vote for whatever he wants?"

We talked about California and New York (actually Connecticut and a long daily commute by train) as places to live, Los Angeles versus New York City as places to work and visit, and a whole lot of meaningless social chitchat to kill the rest of the time. Forrest was obviously impressed by the image of wealth, and he was quite surprised to hear that Suzanne and I lived in Beverly Hills in the famous 90210 ZIP code. Finally, our allotted time was up and I was sent off for my next meeting, with Eugene Burnett-Smythe.

All of the meetings subsequent to my time with Harold Carswell went along the same lines, with variants of the same topics being discussed. My brief first impressions of the majority of the Board of Directors (or whatever this group was) except for Carswell were pretty much what you'd expect. They seemed to be a mix of second and third generation of heirs to wealthy men and bottom of the barrel used car salesmen types, supplemented with two or three kids who grew up poor and made it to what was for them the top. The mix as a whole was a mediocre talent pool, in cushy and undemanding sinecure-type jobs, with a big income but with little stress or pressure to perform beyond keeping the boss happy.

Burnett-Smythe was another thoroughly unimpressive rich guy in his mid-50s, taller than Forrest at about 5 foot 9 inches, going to fat with a big belly, and had a pattern of red and broken veins on his bulbous nose that shouted "I drink far too much". Eugene was the AKC librarian and historian, whatever that meant. He spent pretty much the entire time we were together telling me about the man he considered to be the most interesting man in the world, himself. "I know just about everything there is to know about the AKC history, rules, and regulations. If you ever want to know which dog owner did what, I'm the man to come to."

Burnett-Smythe had strong opinions about just about everything. I heard a lot about the good old days when the dogs were better, the shows were better, and the whole AKC was better, too. He laid a finger beside his nose to indicate that I was about to hear some confidential secrets and told me in a voice just barely above a whisper, "If you need to know anything, anything at all, about dogs, dog shows, or the AKC, I'm the man to ask. And don't forget to take a look through the AKC museum while you're here today. I'm the curator of the museum's art collection, which is one of the best and most extensive collections of canine art work in the world."

Henry Cabot was a rail-thin man over 6 feet tall in his late 60s. He affected the academic image with a bow tie, a corduroy sports jacket with elbow patches, and a pipe he was constantly playing with. Judging from the lack of any tobacco aroma, he never smoked it. He compounded his pseudo-academic image by wearing a beret, which I assume was more to cover his bald spot than to stay warm in the overheated office complex. Henry was the liaison with the large subcontractors who actually handled the logistics and operations at thousands of events throughout the United States the AKC sponsored annually.

Cabot was another compulsive talker who went on and on about how complex and demanding his job was and how only he could do it. His only question for me was, "Wah on earth would y'all think y'all could be successful takin' on a job investigatin' dog shows with as little background as y'all have with dogs?"

He got the same sort of answer I'd given Carswell. "A lot of my work involves going undercover and playing a role, like an actor in a new play. It's not about being an expert about everything, it's about being able to create a believable character that can join the cast and fit in. I'll be playing the role of a first-time dog sponsor with plenty of time and money but who doesn't know much of anything about the whole dog show scene. I suspect that people will believe me in that role."

I didn't get the impression that he was hanging on every word of my answer, especially when his only reply was to check his watch, decide we had used up our allotted time, and with regional inflections of the deepest south in his voice bid me farewell. "It was real fine chatting with y'all, ya heah."

Robert Rosswell looked and acted like a used-car salesman. Medium sized, too quick and too firm with his insincere handshake, he made me want to check my pocket to make sure my wallet was still intact. His first words were, "Call me Rocket. I'm from Ballimer". I tuned out most of the rest of his blatantly overdone greeting. Needless to say, he was in sales. He explained to me that the AKC didn't actually do any hands-on supervision of dog shows.

"The two big contractors, Bradshaw and MBF, manage all of the larger shows with more than 500 dogs---venue rentals, dog enrollments, hiring judges, and keeping track of winners. There are more management companies to keep track of when you include the smaller shows. Supervision of the contractors is nominal since they've been doing this for over 75 years. Liaison with the two perpetual contractors is Cabot's responsibility, which is a good job for the dimmest bulb in our corporate chandelier. He's from an important family that over the years has made, and continues to make, big contributions to the AKC, to the museum, to our health and welfare funds, and to a lot of special fund raisers. I guess he's earned his job."

Rosswell picked up a shiny, fancy silver letter holder from his desk and fidgeted with it, as he continued. "The AKC makes a lot of its money selling things to its captive audience of members. Among the items we sell is record keeping software, paid access to all sorts of records and pedigrees, and DNA analysis for their dogs. They can also qualify for various levels of competitive awards, and buy impressive framed certificates to advertise their animals. There's also an AKC store that sells all kinds of merchandise provided by outside vendors. I'm responsible for all of those operations."

Rocket was yet another talker. Thus far, these interviews were easy----sit and listen, and try not to look too bored. Roswell was a self-important windbag who tried to convince me that without his sales of new awards and new tests to the members, the whole AKC organization would wither away and die from chronic money shortage. The only thing he said that really related to me or to the ostensible purpose of our meeting was to remind me to keep receipts for every expense I ever incurred on the job. "These bean counters here in the corporate office won't reimburse you for a lousy cup of coffee or tip for a taxi driver without a signed receipt. Make sure you get a receipt for everything, I mean everything, you buy on the job!"

My impression of Rocket was that he had the personality type who would always be trying to sell 100,000 T-shirts that he had been able to buy at a cheap price in Cambodia with another catchy logo like "My bite is worse than my bark!" but he'd never succeed.

For my next interview, Hunter Lodge was about 5 foot 10 inches, in pretty good shape at about 165 pounds, who looked and acted a lot more competent than most of his colleagues. He probably worked out in a gym, but was also outdoors enough to acquire a suntan. Lodge was the youngest of the group, still in his 40s. He was the corporate comptroller handling all things financial for the AKC, and was responsible for supervising a lot of employees in both New York City and Durham, North Carolina. His welcome betrayed a childhood spent in Boston, where the letter "r" has officially been banned from normal speech. "Glad to see you heah in the office. Manhattan is a whole lot like Bahston, only bigga".

He asked a lot of questions in his strong New England regional dialect about my detective agency's finances. I answered as honestly as I could when the information was easily corroborated from public records. However, when he tried to probe into my personal financial situation, I was a good deal less candid, knowing that these answers would be a lot harder for him to check out (very wealthy, thanks to Suzanne's inheritance and our combined incomes). In the last ten minutes of the interview Lodge turned human and asked me about hobbies and what I liked to do when I wasn't working.

This part was easy, since I could just tell the truth. "I work out pretty regularly and spend a fair amount of time practicing martial arts, especially Brazilian Jiu-Jitsu and karate. Suzanne used to work out with me, but it's become a lot harder for her to find the time since we had the baby. We have an infant son, Robert, who takes up a lot of our time outside of work. Fortunately, he travels well. Suzanne and I have done a fair amount of traveling around South America."

I learned that Lodge sailed, hunted, and played in several recreational team sports, especially squash and tennis where he preferred doubles. He seemed likeable enough based on this last ten minutes of the interview, and was almost certainly the most qualified of the board members I'd met so far that morning.

As I was preparing to leave, Lodge warned me in an offhand manner not to trust Carswell too much. According to Lodge, Carswell had a habit of always blaming the people around him for business problems that weren't being solved or mistakes he'd made himself. "Hmm," I thought to myself, as I made a mental note that there was an obvious rift in the AKC leadership.

Hunter Lodge was the only one of the interview group who was, more or less, from my generation. He seemed to be trying to nonverbally communicate to me that he could be a potential colleague, or at least a potential ally, within the group. He shook my hand warmly as he sent me to my final interview.

Finally, Stanley Morgan was the corporate counsel, a fancy label for the head attorney at the corporation. Morgan was a handsome 6 footer in his mid-50s, who was professionally groomed and dressed well. He appeared to have captured every nuance of the image of a successful attorney climbing the corporate ladder. Since I had been, once upon a time, a patent attorney, he was fascinated by my underused law degree and expressed mild disbelief that I might prefer the relatively underpaid life of the P.I. to the wealth that could be amassed practicing patent law. He spent the better part of five minutes advising me about the many available opportunities with firms specializing in intellectual property law in New York City.

"I've got friends at all of the big firms going back to my time in law school, which I attended here in New Yawk. They're always looking for new associates and they pay a ton of money if they want you in the firm. You should think about it."

The rest of the time we talked about my investigative plan, was I to be awarded this AKC contract. I described the overall proposal I had discussed with Carswell but gave as little detail as possible. He was a good listener and asked the right questions so time passed quickly. Surprisingly, Morgan was able to pull off my interrogation quite smoothly, without pissing me off in the process. This led me to believe that he was probably very good at his job, especially if it involved any litigation work. His speech pattern was well educated, with a trace of a New Yawk dialect underneath the long and well-parsed words. Of all of the people I'd met thus far from the AKC Board of Directors, other than Carswell, he seemed by far the most capable. He was also the one I'd assume was the most independent, therefore the most likely to stand up to the boss in public, not just rubber stamp any and all of Carswell's decisions.

I made another mental note that if there were any undertones of different factions among the AKC leadership, Morgan was the prime candidate to be the opposition leader. My guess was that if any organized opposition to Carswell's decisions ever arose, it would come from Morgan, with perhaps Lodge as an ally.

Eventually I completed my running of the gauntlet and it was time for lunch, served in the Executive Dining Room on the 31st floor of the building. We sat around a huge table, while multiple courses of soup, fish, salad (after the main course in the French tradition), and desert, were all served with wine by elegantly dressed wait staff. Discussion revolved around the problems with the west coast conformation show circuit and how to resolve them. I sat and listened, especially to a strong recommendation by Nathan Forrest that I be hired to solve these problems. Talk about casting one's bread upon the waters. For a change, I seemed to have become the recipient of something better than soggy bread crusts.

After lunch I was excused to take a break, but only a short break. I was expected to meet once again with Harold Carswell, in his office, in 15 minutes. At exactly the appointed time, I knocked on his open door and was invited in.

Carswell rose to greet me and shook my hand. He pointed to a couple of comfortable looking upholstered chairs off to the side by a coffee table with two fresh cups of coffee in front of the chairs. "Roger, you're now officially employed by the AKC to solve their problems with regard to the West Coast dog show circuit. Why don't we sit down together and discuss your plans in a little more detail? After today you'll be entirely on your own, at least on a day-to-day basis. We'll expect periodic reports from you to the New York office through Sherry Wyne. Will this fit into your usual operating style, Mr. Bowman?"

I decided to go with apparently frank answers, but to tell him what I knew he wanted to hear. "I'm used to working on my own. In fact, the biggest reason I quit the Los Angeles police force was because I'm not very patient with rigid policies and protocols, and prefer not to spend most of my time writing redundant reports. To move forward, in broad terms, my plans are to start going to dog shows in the role of a nouveau riche sponsor for Sherry's bitch Juliet, as we discussed earlier. I suspect we'll have to play it by ear after that. As far as the other owners are concerned, having leased Juliet from Sherry we'll be entering their world at the owner level, with a dog they already know and respect. According to Sherry, that should be our ticket to instant acceptance, either as real dog owners or as a naive sugar-daddy and sugar-mommy who just might be convinced to sponsor their dogs too. Suzanne and I will start by trying to get a feeling for what's going on from the owner-sponsor perspective. We'll try to get close to as many of the owners as possible to talk about what's going on. I suspect they'll have strong opinions about any judging irregularities that they might have seen or heard about. With Sherry's help and sponsorship I imagine we'll be accepted into their group and trusted to hear plenty of gossip pretty much immediately.

I picked up my coffee cup, which was made of fine China, and took a sip. "At the same time, Bruce will be in front of everybody at each show as Juliet's handler, and he'll try to build a similar relationship with the handlers that we're trying to do with the owners. He's a pretty good people person, and is excited to be working with dogs again. I'm sure he'll do very well playing that part."

I took another sip of the coffee, which was very good. "There'll be informal updates to Sherry, and she can report back to you. We plan to meet at the beginning and end of each show, when she can be seen as tutoring Bruce and me on the nuances of handling Juliet in the ring. As far as I'm concerned, that's all of the reporting you'll get from me until and unless we find out anything you need to know that I wouldn't want to share with Sherry. My office will send you monthly bills for hours and expenses. Is that satisfactory?"

Carswell stood up and shook hands. "That sounds perfect to me, except for one thing. You should probably plan on your involvement in this case stretching out for the entire season, which can be as long as 11 months, starting in January. I'm going to have to justify a large expense for your salaries and expenses to my Board of Directors, so quarterly reports from you would make my life a lot easier. You should plan accordingly."

"That sounds good to me," I replied insincerely. He'd get reports from me when I had something to report.

Carswell handed me his business card. "My personal cell phone number is on the back of the card. Please call me anytime, day or night, if you find out something I should know or you need anything that Sherry can't provide. In the meantime, think about all we've discussed for the rest of the afternoon. I don't expect any miracles, but the AKC will want to see steady progress from you. Spend as much as you have to so you'll have something substantial to tell me in each of those quarterly reports, even if it's just how many shows you've attended and how many people you've interviewed. If you think of anything else or have any more questions, we'll discuss it at dinner tonight at 7."

Chapter6.New York City nightlife

It was 3 P.M. I walked back to the hotel to relax and wait for Suzanne before we headed over to dinner with the AKC managers. Suzanne hadn't gotten back to our room yet, giving me plenty of time for a shower and shave. After that, I relaxed on the bed watching bad daytime TV for about half an hour before she opened the door, saw me lying there, and leaned over the bed to give me a kiss. It was very nice. Suzanne was completely back into shape after her pregnancy a year ago. At 5'8", with a lean athletic body and long blond hair, she was worthy of a long look or two.

After a long, lingering, sweet kiss Suzanne disengaged long enough to ask, "You're back to the hotel a lot earlier than you expected. How did your job interview go?"

I reached up to stroke her hair. "Smoothly. They offered me the job formally over lunch, and I accepted it. Basically, we have a free pass to every dog show on the west coast circuit and the loan of a top show bitch to take to those shows for a year, all paid for by the AKC. I got a huge retainer fee in the five figures to get started. As an additional incentive, I'll be paid all of my usual hourly fees and expenses for every dog show we attend, plus whatever additional time we spend on this case, and a huge bonus if we solve their problems while we're having fun showing Juliet. Bruce and Vincent will also get hourly fees and expenses for any of their time I can bill for, so over the next year the agency will make a ton of money from the AKC.

I gently played with a few of Suzanne's curls that dangled over my face. "What about your day, Suzanne? How did the visit to Rockefeller University go?"

She tousled my hair affectionately. "Scientifically quite well. Socially fine. And I found the perfect rug for our living room. Or at least one that looks just like it! Move over to make some room and I'll tell you all about it."

I scooted over on the bed while Suzanne kicked off her shoes and lay down next to me. She reached over to hold hands and fondle a few of my more sensitive spots while she talked. "The technology for DNA sequencing is improving so fast, it's hard to keep up with the field. The current commercially available machines are orders of magnitude faster and cheaper to use than the one I share in my lab group at UCLA. The ones I saw today are prototypes for the next generation of sequencers---better, faster, and cheaper. The slow step now is data handling. You produce so much data so quickly, the sequencers finish in hours what used to take a lot of humans working as fast as they could several weeks, or even months, to digest and analyze. The new machines have computers and software attached to analyze the data in a variety of ways, and to break through the data logjam, they use new Artificial Intelligence programs to interpret the data in real time. The next step will be on-line journals so the machines can publish the papers as soon as they crunch the data so all of this glut of information can be shared throughout the scientific community."

Suzanne spoke enthusiastically. She had obviously enjoyed her day. "I was able to set up a new collaboration with Joel Feinberg to get my DNA analyzed by deep sequencing. That way, we can compare a whole bunch of DNA from the same plants with each other, as well as comparing single plants from different species. It'll be nice to look at specific gene polymorphisms in the same plants and correlate the mutations we find with the yield and potency of the drug we've isolated from the individual plants. He's got a big lab with several post-docs who'll actually supervise the sequencing work. It'll get done much, much faster than my analyses get done now, and it will free up one of my graduate students for a new project we've been talking about her doing. It turns out that Joel manages his DNA sequencing as a core facility on a big Center grant and gets points with the NIH for showing collaborative use by other major research institutions. He's pretty happy that I chose his facility for this collaboration. While I still have to pay for the assays, it's a highly subsidized price that's actually a lot less than it's been costing me for slower and less complete sequence analyses on our own instrument back at UCLA. And I won't have to visit the post-docs here; everything will be done collaboratively through Joel. That's another plus for me."

She paused a bit before changing the subject. "One of those post-docs was pretty weird."

I looked more directly at her. "Weird how, Suzanne?"

She turned just a bit so she could look directly at my face. "Nothing that he actually said or did. It was more how he looked at me and how he made me feel when he looked at me. Like he was undressing me mentally and measuring me for something. He didn't say anything wrong, or try to touch me; he just gave me a creepy feeling when I was around him. He had a Russian or Polish name, something like Leninsky, but I don't remember it exactly. Anyway," she said with a shrug of her shoulders and a toss of her hair, "I won't be seeing him again so it's not worth worrying about."

It seemed to be a good time to change the subject. "I've never been to the upper east side of Manhattan where you visited today, Suzanne. What's Rockefeller University like?"

Suzanne shifted effortlessly into her teacher role. "As you know, Rockefeller University is uptown between 63rd and 68th streets east of York Avenue along the East River and is mainly for graduate student and postdoctoral fellow training in research. They gave me the grand tour of the university itself, which is very small and very elite. Less than 200 students go there, all graduate students working on Ph.D. or combined M.D.-Ph.D. degrees, plus about 360 postdoctoral trainees. It sits on a small campus, even by New York City standards of size, right across the street from a couple of big university hospitals. They have a huge auditorium for concerts and recitals, as well as meetings, called the Abby Aldrich Rockefeller Hall. The lobby area of the auditorium had a huge Oriental, I assume Persian, rug on the floor. It's spectacular and it's gorgeous. That's what I'd like to have for our living room at home. Someone told me that you could buy hand made rugs nowadays in China, India, and Pakistan big enough to work for our house. Some look like that rug, but would only cost a fraction of what that gorgeous antique rug probably costs. Did you have any plans on how you wanted to spend that juicy retainer fee you're getting for this case?" she asked with a mischievous grin.

Time passed quickly as it tends to do when we have privacy and no intrusions from family or work. There was just barely enough time for us to shower quickly, get dressed for dinner, then walk over to the restaurant. We arrived exactly on schedule, which made us the first ones there. I sat with Suzanne at the tiny bar and we drank some wine while we waited for the others to arrive. In honor of the restaurant being French and very elegant with a pianist providing soft mood music, I chose a wine I especially enjoy. We each had a glass of a nice Chateauneuf -du-Pape, a red wine from the Rhone Valley region near Avignon. The bartender approved of our choice. He also told us, "This restaurant specializes in French Provincial cooking, especially from rural southeast and south central France. I'd recommend that you stay away from the tourist favorites like entrecote or other types of steak. Instead, try the snails as an appetizer then the cassoulet for your main dish."

He mentioned a few other items on the menu we might also try if we had a spirit of adventure. Then he busied himself with another couple several stools away from us. About halfway through our wine Suzanne lowered her voice and spoke directly to me so nobody else could hear. "Do you have any feeling that someone might be watching us?"

"No, I hadn't noticed anyone looking at us or conspicuously paying attention to everything else but us. But I'll pay more attention, just in case. What was it that got your attention?"

"Nothing in particular. I just had the funny feeling you sometimes get when someone is watching you. Maybe it's just this place or jet lag or something else sending me false alarms."

Just then our group arrived and wandered into the restaurant in bits and pieces. Carswell spotted us and walked over to the bar. I stood up and spoke to Suzanne. "Or, you just spotted this crew on the street and saw them looking in the window. This is the AKC contingent coming in now."

I introduced Suzanne to Harold Carswell, who suggested that we bring our wine along as the maître d' arrived to lead us over to our table. Along the way Carswell managed to find time to take an appraising look at Suzanne, followed by a few sincere compliments. "I like your California approach to dressing for dinner quite a bit. The soft pants and tunic look is very flattering on you and looks more comfortable than the typical rigid and uptight New York fashion. It's perfect for this setting. And I'm even more impressed that you aren't caught up in the current shoe fetish that makes women look like they're walking on stilts."

Suzanne looked closely at Carswell and decided he was being sincere in his flattery. "Thank you for the complements, which I always like to hear. I'm tall enough without the stilt heels and really prefer wearing shoes I can walk in comfortably."

The maître d' led us through the dimly lit restaurant, taking a left turn as we neared the back, escorting our group to a quiet corner not visible from the entrance. We were seated around a large table that readily accommodated the nine of us, close enough together so we could all easily hear each other. The conversation, which was lubricated by several bottles of wine, swirled around us while Suzanne and I ordered our dinners and subsequently worked our way through courses of escargots with garlic butter, onion soup, an authentic cassoulet of white beans, lamb, duck, and pork sausage, various vegetables in interesting sauces served family style, salad, a chocolate and whipped cream-laced calorie bomb disguised as a dessert, and coffee.

Much of the dinner discussion was background about what the AKC actually did, as seen by the managers of the various functions. After having met all of these men one-on-one earlier in the day, I now got some general impressions of how they functioned with each other in a group social setting. Sitting directly on my right was Eugene Burnett-Smythe. He drank his wine quickly and thirstily. As his blood alcohol level increased, so did his participation in the discussion. He told several amusing stories about the history of dogs in the USA, especially the rise in social status of several of the sporting dog breeds. Initially bred in the southeastern and mid-western states to feed the poor who had to hunt for their meals, they are now the darlings of the show ring.

Burnett-Smyth made a big production of swirling his wine in the large goblet, sniffing it, and taking a big gulp. "The American Cocker Spaniel first came to the attention of the American dog loving public in the early 20th century as a compact field dog with a happy-go-lucky personality, small enough to live in an apartment if you lived in the city, but able to go out to the country for a full day's hunting. As the breed became popular with the show crowd, its lovely flowing coat became its star attraction. But there was a problem here. That coat got shredded in the field, and if you owned one of these dogs you had to make a choice. Either clip the coat down to go hunting, or keep it in all its full-coated glory for the show ring. Gradually, you no longer saw the same dogs in the field and in the ring, and people breeding for excellence in either venue bred for very different characteristics. A typical show cocker can't hunt to save its life, and a cocker bred for the field looks like a completely different breed in all aspects – size, coat, structure, even the shape of its head. There are few breeds that can still do justice to their heritage and work in the field as hunting or herding dogs like they were developed to do, yet also be highly competitive in the show ring. My hat's off to the current breeders of German Shorthaired Pointers, Kelpies, and Border Collies who are still producing blue collar working dogs that win conformation and performance titles in front of and after their dogs' names."

Immediately to his right was Rocket Rosswell, another serious drinker. He went through two martinis before his appetizer and a lot of wine during dinner. I couldn't tell if all the alcohol he consumed had any effect on him. Rosswell was still the excessive talker I had met earlier and told us quite a bit about how much money the AKC made because they were lucky enough to have him selling profitable items to an adoring public. The sponsoring clubs make the money from leasing space at dog shows to vendors and from sales of miscellaneous merchandise and dog-related crafts and equipment. However, as Rosswell proudly pointed out, one of those vendors could be the AKC itself, and they had a monopoly on AKC-branded merchandise. That was one of his areas of responsibility. The AKC also profits from DNA testing and record keeping for each registered dog and bitch.

Rocket chewed on an olive from one of his martinis while he let us in on a few more details. "Each dog can be entered in a single competitive breed class each day, and we call that an entry. Sometimes there will be additional competitions called non-regular classes like best brood bitch and puppy, best stud dog and puppy, best veteran dog, and so forth. Those would have their own entry fees. The contractors get most of the entry fees, but included in those entry fees are a $3.00 AKC Event Service fee per entry, plus a $0.50 AKC Recording fee for the first entry of each dog. Since the AKC's fixed costs per show are about the same whether it's a big show or a small one, the bigger the entry the better as far as our profit is concerned."

When I looked the other way, Suzanne sat immediately on my left. To her left was Stanley Morgan, who listened to everything, but didn't say much. When he did talk, it was relevant and to the point.

Next, going around clockwise was Nathan Forrest. He mainly talked shop, especially about how wonderful everything was at the AKC and what a great job all of them were doing. "It's all about teamwork and we're a team," seemed to be his oft-repeated mantra. Continuing around clockwise, directly across the table from Suzanne, was Harold Carswell. He played the role of the benevolent leader to the hilt---charming, gracious, had a good word for everybody. Coming back around the clock between Carswell and Rocket Rosswell were Hunter Lodge, sitting directly across from me, with Henry Cabot between us. Lodge was closer to our age than the others, and probably had more in common with us. He talked about the lifestyle in New York City and told us about several places we should visit during our next trip. Lodge was apparently into theater and the arts, so pointed out The Metropolitan Opera, The Lincoln Center, and the Theater District as must-see locations for evening entertainment. For daytime recreation, he suggested The Museum of Natural History, The Metropolitan Museum of Art, and several smaller specialty art collections downtown. Cabot was more shoptalk, especially with regard to his job as the liaison to the actual organizations that sponsored the shows. He had a fascinating problem herding cats to make this complicated system actually work, but he seemed to have developed an effective game plan.

We were asked about our background. Suzanne answered most of the questions about our family, especially Robert, her experience with dogs while growing up as an only child in Sacramento, California, and about her job at UCLA. It only took about 30 seconds of biochemistry to see the glazed eyeballs on all seven former liberal arts majors seated around our table. After she noticed this, Robert and dogs got the lion's share of Suzanne's discussion time. All of her recent reading of articles about dog breeds paid dividends. She sounded so much like an expert on the German Shorthaired Pointer, you could almost see and hear the collective sigh of relief around the table. We just might be convincing after all when we were introduced as dog owners.

After everybody had enough wine and liquor, the gentlemen from the AKC relaxed a bit and got away from shoptalk into small talk. We heard quite a bit about various families, and especially the recent accomplishments of some of the kids and grandchildren. My favorite line from the night came from Rocket Rosswell, who asked Suzanne in all seriousness, "I've got several thousand tee-shirts with the catch line 'Wag tails, not tongues' printed on them. Would you be willing to wear a few of them for me at the dog shows you go to?"

Stanley Morgan asked her, "Do you really think Roger being a private detective is a good idea, or do you feel like it's just a phase he'll outgrow and get back to being a practicing lawyer? Maybe when you discover some intellectual property in your laboratory that might be converted into a patentable invention would be a good time for him to consider making this switch."

Suzanne smiled sweetly and replied, "He can do both at the same time. As a matter of fact, he already has, Mr. Morgan. When UCLA decided not to pursue patenting one of the drugs I discovered in my research, Roger took care of everything for me."

Henry Cabot seemed especially interested in how Suzanne had spent her day today. He told us he had never heard of Rockefeller University before today and asked Suzanne exactly where it was and how she got there from our hotel. "Y'all know, I always thought about becomin' part of the academy like y'all have Suzanne, but there was never anyone heah who could take mah place if I left. Do y'all think Rockefeller University might be lookin' fer a perfesser with mah skills?"

Suzanne mumbled something non-committal.

Burnett-Smyth seemed reluctant to interrupt his drinking long enough to say much, but ask Suzanne whether she'd ever owned a dog before. "I grew up with one," she started to say, but stopped when he gulped his remaining wine and turned away to pour another glass.

Nathan Forrest asked Suzanne, "D-do you use C-c-computers in your ex-experiments, S-suzanne?"

"Yes, I do. Pretty much all of the time."

"D-do you d-do any of your own p-p-programming?"

"No, I use commercial software for data base management and statistical analysis of my results."

This conversation ground to a crunching halt.

Finally, Hunter Lodge who had been listening to this last exchange asked Suzanne "Do you have collaborators at UCLA who can do any computer programming you might need, or do you have to do everything with commercially available software?"

"Some of each," she replied. "I'm pretty much computer illiterate as far as programming is concerned, but there are plenty of experts on the campus who can point me in the right direction if I have a problem that needs solving. Most of what I do is mainstream DNA sequence analysis, and there's a lot of very good open source and commercial software readily available to meet most of my needs. The few times I've needed more I've found collaborators who had what I needed and were willing to share."

"You're very lucky," answered Lodge. "Here in industry it's a much more competitive environment and nobody ever helps a competitor. I'm used to either doing everything myself or hiring someone to solve whatever kind of problem needs solving for me."

Chapter7.Back to our hotel

After all of the food and wine we said our respective goodnights and goodbyes. The walk back to the hotel was most welcome. A block or so from the restaurant Suzanne touched my arm and asked softly, "Are you getting any vibes that someone is watching us? I feel that way now, a whole lot like I did at the bar in the restaurant."

"No. I'm not getting any vibes," I replied, looking around as discretely as I could without being conspicuous. "But that doesn't mean much in a crowded place like 41st Street in midtown Manhattan at nine o'clock at night. Did you feel like this while you went to or came back from Rockefeller University? Or did the bad vibes just start at our dinner?"

Suzanne thought a bit. "I'm not sure. As you know, buses and subways in New York City aren't my usual environment. I certainly wasn't feeling comfortable coming back to the hotel. But I don't know. The sense I'm getting now, and that I had at the restaurant, was more than just someone is watching. It's a prickly sensation up and down my spine--- like being in a horror movie---but this is the real thing. I don't remember feeling this way on the bus or subway. But it could have been the same."

Her normally lithe body was stiffer than usual and her expression was worried. "As you know, this feeling that something awful is about to happen isn't normal for me. I don't like feeling I'm under surveillance, and I don't like feeling worried. We both know I can take care of myself physically. This is different. It feels more like something truly evil is happening to me, and that I'm part of it."

I really hadn't seen Suzanne this up tight, literally and figuratively, before. When she first hired me as a detective to go with her to Salta to investigate her father's murder, she felt she was being followed and was concerned. But she hadn't been frightened. Thanks to her many years of training in karate and frequent workouts with Bruce and me, Suzanne had plenty of confidence in her ability to win a fight if attacked. This was the first time I had ever seen her frightened and I didn't like the image at all. Clearly this problem needed some serious investigation.

It was only three blocks south and half a block west from where we presently were, so we walked back to the hotel from the restaurant, which was on 41st Street between Park and Madison Avenues. To avoid the darker, and potentially more dangerous residential streets, we walked over to Park Avenue, which is wide and well lit for that neighborhood. Once on the Avenue, we moved at a reasonably brisk pace down toward our hotel, past restaurants, hotels, residential high-rise apartment buildings, and darkened high-rise office buildings. We continued walking without incidents as far as 39th Street on a seemingly deserted Park Avenue, deserted at least by pedestrians at this time of night. However, the steady flow of vehicular traffic, especially taxicabs, continued unabated. Suddenly, two 20-something young men in hoodies and baggy pants decided we were fresh meat from out of town, ripe and just right to take a bite out of, and jumped out of an alley between two darkened office buildings immediately in front of us.

Neither of the two men said a word. They just looked menacing as they slowly swaggered towards us. The first guy out of the alley was a skinny Hispanic, with long stringy hair, wearing baggy jeans and an "I Love New York" sweatshirt. He held a knife, which he kept switching from hand to hand trying to look like an experienced knife fighter and scare the heck out of what he expected to be two helpless tourists. He'd obviously watched too many bad TV shows and movies, but not enough marine combat training. The second punk was an equally skinny white guy, with his hair closely cropped on an almost shaven head, also wearing baggy jeans and a sweatshirt, this one with a team logo for The New York Yankees. He had another knife, which he held in front of him in his right hand and moved in big circles so he too could look like an experienced knife fighter and scare the heck out of us. He'd watched the same bad movies and TV shows as his buddy and equally obviously clearly didn't have the slightest clue of how to use a knife against an opponent skilled in martial arts. The second punk was about Suzanne's size so I figured she could easily take care of him. That left me with the taller of the two, about three inches and 20 pounds smaller than I am. Suzanne's knife artist broke the silence.

"Gimme yer watches, wallet, and purse or I'll cut both a ya real bad!"

I eased my way towards the street, to my left. The taller punk conveniently moved to his right to cut off my path to run away from him. That left us spread out exactly the way I wanted, as if we had choreographed this scene beforehand. Each of the hoodlums was directly in front of either Suzanne or me, and far enough apart that they wouldn't get in the way of either of us when the fight started. I looked quickly at Suzanne, who was poised and ready. I said something stupid like "Go", and went after my man. As he tossed the knife from his left to his right hand, the hard heel of my shoe connected at full speed with the front of his right knee. I heard a loud crack as the ligaments went, but by that time, I recovered my balance and launched a vicious kick to his groin area. Down he went, moaning piteously and grabbing his groin area with one hand. He still had the knife in his other hand. I stamped hard on his wrist where it lay on the concrete and heard more bones crack. At that point, figured he had enough to worry about, which would keep him from bothering us anymore.

Suzanne's opponent was still standing up, but just barely. He was doubled over and struggling to breathe as a result of Suzanne's kick to his solar plexus. He had dropped his knife, but that didn't stop Suzanne from following through with a roundhouse kick to his head that took him down and out. Fortunately, Suzanne at 5'8" tended to avoid wearing high heels in social outings with strangers, to avoid seeming taller than the men. She had learned this little trick in South America, where the male ego could sometimes be taller than the male. Her flat-heeled shoes were not only comfortable, but were functional for street karate. I kicked both knives into the gutter before suggesting we get back to our hotel before the police arrived to arrest us for a brutal assault on the two defenseless gangbangers.

"This is New York City where the local motto is 'Don't get involved'. There's a real good reason for this motto. If we let ourselves get involved, it could morph into an attack by two martial-arts trained hooligans on two locals who were just walking by and can't be held responsible for their actions because they come from poor socioeconomic backgrounds in the city's projects."

Suzanne looked at me, a bit shocked as she exclaimed, "We can't just leave them lying here, Roger."

I took her hand and gave her a slight tug towards our hotel. "It's OK. This is one of the busiest avenues in New York City, only a few blocks from Grand Central Station, with plenty of taxis and buses passing by. We just hit a minute of comparatively light traffic because of the cycle of traffic signals. Don't worry; someone will call 911 in the next couple of minutes. Let's move."

The two of us walked as quickly as we could the rest of the way to the corner. Before going into the hotel, we turned onto the cross street, just in case anyone was trying to watch where we went. We got back into the hotel with no additional noteworthy incidents. Suzanne had only one further concern to share as we stood in the functional lobby, waiting for one of the self-service elevators. "You realize that since I met you, Roger, this kind of nasty street fight has become so ordinary, all I can think about now is how I broke a fingernail during the fight, and that's a major annoyance. I think I'm being desensitized to the violence as I do more and more of this kind of fighting. But I have to admit, I not only feel OK about all of the fighting, but I love the feeling that I don't have to be afraid to walk around on a city street at night. And, it's hard for me to develop any empathy for those two muggers with the knives. They would have cut us for the sheer fun of it if they could have, and they got exactly what they deserved. But my broken fingernail still needs to be fixed as soon as we get back to the room."

As we rode up to our room in the elevator, surrounded by gilt mirrors and ornate brass work, I shared my thoughts about the street fight. They were a lot more analytical than Suzanne's. "It's possible those two clowns with the knives spotted us earlier and followed us to the restaurant, then back here. Do you think they could have been responsible for your feeling that you were being watched?"

Several Suzannes seen in sequence in the mirrors replied, "Anything's possible, Roger. But I'd say no. It's hard to describe exactly what I felt, but it had a much more personal feeling than I'd have gotten from two random muggers. I sensed that the watcher was truly evil, not two opportunists with knives they really don't know how to use. I felt like there was an intelligence behind whoever was watching me, not like a random street mugging. Does that make any sense?"

I squeezed her hand reassuringly, "Unfortunately, yes. I think we're both going to be very glad to get home tomorrow."

We made an early night of it and were in a taxi to the airport very early the next morning. This taxi had an honest driver and we got to the airport without any problems, except fighting traffic. The cab driver had us to the airport with plenty of time to be vetted by TSA and on board our flight home to LAX. The time difference got us home for an early lunch and an afternoon to catch up at work. Bruce took the news that he was now not only a nanny but also a dog handler, dog trainer, and detective with no particular show of emotion. However, there was an obvious small smile playing on his face when I left the house.

That afternoon, I spent some time with Vincent over a couple of cups of coffee to share what was discussed, what we decided, and the financial details of my new arrangement with the AKC. I sat at my desk in my regular chair with my feet on an open desk drawer, while Vincent sprawled comfortably on the client chair across the desk from me. Sunlight streamed in through the window, reminding us it was another beautiful day in Southern California. I didn't want to mar that fine old wood on the desktop, probably indicating that a little bit of the old yuppie lawyer was still left in me. The tone was casual, two friends discussing what was going to happen next. No matter what occurred at the dog shows, this case was sure to be a financial winner for both Vincent and me. I could envision a time in the not too distant future when I'd want to take advantage of Suzanne's and my financial independence. I'd cut back on my workload to spend more time with Suzanne, Robert, and another Bowman kid or two. If that was going to be a realistic dream, I had to start the process of making Vincent feel he was a real partner, not just a glorified office manager.

He had an interesting expression as he mouthed "WOW!"

Vincent looked a bit shocked as he continued, with just a nuance or two of sarcasm in his tone, "It seems like you're going to be spending most of your time on this new case starting almost immediately, Roger. It sounds like it could be a real tough job, too. You have to go to a bunch of dog shows with and without the family and pretend to be enjoying yourself, while you're being paid tons of money to play. What exactly do you see me doing while you're out playing?"

It was time to get a bit more serious. "The way I envision it, you'll be doing pretty much the same things you're already doing while I'm out playing, Vincent. The only obvious change in our modus operandi as a detective agency will be you moving up to become a partner and taking charge of the physical office in my place. I'll still do most of the agency work I've been doing from my laptop computer and you'd still take care of the bodyguard side of the business. With the AKC billings for my time, our agency income will just about triple, as long as we continue to bring in the same amount of work. As partners we'll share equally in the profits from all the agency work either of us do. That should increase your income dramatically in the coming year. And, if I play this right, we may have a permanent wealthy corporate client paying us an annual retainer fee, guaranteeing we'll be in the black every year before our first client walks in off the street. We might want to think about hiring another experienced detective to do a lot of the routine work, and maybe bring in some of their own clients too."

Vincent was a very happy partner after we ran the numbers. So was I; my routine workload would decrease by quite a bit and I'd be doing what I liked most, working undercover on a case.

Chapter8.Juliet joins the family

Thursday was another beautiful sunny day in Southern California. I called Sherry Wyne in Sacramento to tell her about my interview with the AKC, that I'd accepted their offer, and that we'd be working together. Now it was time to ask about making arrangements for Juliet moving to our house and becoming part of our family.

After a momentary pause Sherry replied, "I heard about the AKC hiring you. They called me the same day you were there. I also understand you followed my advice about asking them to underwrite your sponsorship of Juliet over this next season. Would the weekend be soon enough for you to get your hands on her?"

That was easy. "This weekend would be perfect. What did you have in mind?"

There was another short pause as she worked through the logistics in her mind. "I have to be at a dog show in the San Diego area over the weekend. Juliet is entered in two shows on Friday and Saturday. I could bring her to your house on my way back to Sacramento late Saturday afternoon or Saturday evening, depending on whether she wins the breed and we have to hang around for the group competition. I'll call you with a better estimate of the exact time after the breed competition on Saturday. Ring time is scheduled for about 10 AM. I should know before noon what time we could be on the road to L.A. Give me your street address, please, and I'll program it into my car's GPS system."

I told her where we lived and which exit to take from the 405 freeway. "What do we have to buy to be dog-ready between now and then?"

This time the answer came immediately. "Nothing. I'll bring Juliet's toys and her crate with me, as well as a couple of sacks of the food she eats these days. You shouldn't have to buy anything for at least a month or two, and you'll know exactly what she eats from the label on the bag of kibble. I'll also leave you the contact information for a UC Davis-trained veterinarian I trust, whose clinic is maybe a mile or two from your office. Just in case you need a Vet, Todd's not only a great veterinarian he's also a really nice guy. You and Suzanne should really like him. I'll see you guys some time Saturday and I'll leave enough time in my schedule to answer any questions either of you have. I suspect that Bruce is knowledgeable enough to handle anything else that might come up."

The two days passed quickly for me, but way too slowly for Suzanne. At about 11:30 Saturday, Sherry called to tell us she would be in Los Angeles in a few hours. At 2:30 she was ringing our doorbell. Suzanne opened the door to greet Sherry and Juliet, who demonstrated her very good manners as she stood in our front doorway waiting for an invitation to come into the house. Sherry gently tapped Juliet on the back of her head, which, as we learned in a few moments, was her release signal. Suddenly a 55-pound ball of energy exploded into the house, with an amused Sherry following close behind and Suzanne bringing up the rear of the small procession. Juliet headed directly for Robert and Bruce, who were playing together on the floor of the living room. Equally suddenly Bruce gave a sharp sit command, and order was restored. Juliet looked quizzically at Sherry as if to ask, "Do I have to sit when he tells me to?" She obviously was most curious about Robert, who was the only human around built to her scale, and wanted to get closer to him.

Sherry walked over to her dog and gently patted Juliet's head. Her body language was speaking directly to Juliet, answering the question with a loud yes. So was Sherry's low and calming voice, saying "Good girl, good Juliet." And so saying, she handed Juliet's leash to Bruce. Kneeling in front of the dog to say good-bye, Sherry was rewarded with a slurpy full-tongued kiss on her nose and a thorough face wash.

Sherry looked at us as she backed away from her dog. "Don't worry about Juliet wanting to follow me home. She's been left with handlers before, when they're taking her to a show. I can't always show her myself either because it's a conflict of interest when I'm the AKC representative for the same show, or if I want her in one show while I'm at another. For an experienced show dog like Juliet, home is where the crate and toys are."

Just that easily Juliet became Bruce's dog, looking to him for directions on what to do and how to behave. Bruce quietly and gently released Juliet with a soft tap on her head. We all watched to see what would happen next, as she focused her attention on Robert. She very slowly walked a few steps towards Robert, who squealed with delight and crawled toward the dog. Juliet lay down on the floor directly in front of Robert, careful not to allow her body weight to bang into him. He proceeded to grab her nose, poke her eye, yank her ears, and to pat her on her head, plus everywhere else he could reach. Juliet's expression clearly said, "Why not? It's attention." Robert climbed all over her and fell in love. Juliet looked very maternal, gently recognizing Robert's "puppyhood". Clearly dog and baby had bonded and their relationship was not destined to be a problem.

Suzanne hurried over, gently took Robert's hand, and guided him into giving Juliet gentle pat-pats. "We don't want to hurt Juliet, Robert. This is the right way to pat her."

Sherry applied a gentle correction of her own. "Don't worry, Suzanne. He can learn how to be gentle with her when the novelty wears off. Juliet's been around babies most of her life and knows they don't mean her any harm. Thanks for thinking of protecting her, but if he gets too rough she'll just get up and walk away."

Juliet voted with her feet. She leaned towards Robert, giving him free total access to her face, ears, and head, and got her body even lower on the floor. She clearly invited him to do whatever he wanted with her.

Bruce called Juliet in a calm voice. She extricated herself from Robert with great care not to step on him or flip him over, and walked across the room to sit by Bruce. Robert began to scoot over to his new friend as fast as he could crawl, but didn't get very far. Rather than pushing her luck with Juliet's benign acceptance of being mugged by Robert, Suzanne scooped the infant up and carried him over to her favorite wing chair. We all sat down in the living room and listened to the basics from Sherry, who had already found herself a comfortable chair.

Sherry began the complicated process of bringing us all up to speed as AKC show dog owners. "As you already know, a dog show is basically a single elimination format, starting with each individual breed competing among themselves for points based upon conformation, movement, and the intangibles of how they show. At this point, the dogs and bitches compete separately. There are several different categories to enter a dog or a bitch, including a whole bunch of different puppy classes by age group, and adult dogs 'Bred by Exhibitor', 'American Bred', or 'Open'. Sometimes there are other additional classes. The winners in each of these classes then compete for either 'Winners dog' or 'Winners bitch'. If your dog is one of these 'Winners', they earn points towards becoming champions.

"Next, these two 'Winners' will compete with all of the dogs in their breed that are already finished champions, to be named either the 'Best Opposite Sex' or the 'Best of Breed'. The 'Best of Breed' will go on to the Group competition and possibly the 'Best in Show' competition."

Sherry took a few moments to scratch Juliet behind her ears. "The number of points you get for winning depends on the number of competitors who were shown in your breed that day. You need a minimum of 15 points to become a champion, which will require several shows. If enough dogs come to a particular show and you beat them, you can win a 'major'. For the required 15 point total, two of the shows have to be 'majors', for your dog to qualify as a champion. In other words, you can't just compete in 15 small local shows, earning 1 point from each show, to finish a championship. The requirement for winning at least two majors maintains quality control in the overall process. It means that a finished champion has beaten a fair number of other competitors."

Sherry paused for another moment to catch her breath. "The last level of individual breed competition, where the finished champions compete with the day's winners for "Best of Breed", is where Juliet begins her day of competition. If she doesn't win "Best of Breed", the judge still has the option of giving her "select points" towards her Grand Championship. That's enough for now. When you go to your first dog show, an AKC representative will give you a presentation explaining all of this stuff. I strongly recommend you go to a few of these presentations. They'll really help you get oriented to the rules and the whole layout of a major dog show, plus you can meet a few of the different representatives. Is everything clear so far?"

Three human heads nodded. One canine also listened, but she looked bored and seemed to be struggling to keep her eyes open.

Sherry got up from her chair and walked over to Juliet, who had moved over to lie down beside Bruce. Sherry scratched behind her ears as she continued telling us what she thought we needed to know before our first dog show. "The dog shows used to be all over the place and people spent a lot of time travelling from show to show. After the oil embargo of the 1970s, the AKC developed "show circuits". They changed some rules to allow different clubs to co-sponsor shows in the same location. This encouraged larger numbers of people and dogs to participate in several key shows each year, creating a reasonable number of majors in key areas geographically. It also cut down the duplication of shows and the travel required to find majors.

"For the "Grand Champion" competitions that Juliet will be participating in, we prefer majors, to earn more points per show. You'll want to hit as many of the larger shows on the circuit as you can. Given the dates, you should be able to get to the shows in the Turkey Circuit in Stockton, just before Thanksgiving, and the shows in Woodland, near Sacramento, a couple of weeks later. These will be a good tune-up for Bruce. Then there's a break until the new season starts in late January, with the Golden Gate Kennel Club show at the Cow Palace in San Francisco."

Sherry made an obvious gesture of checking her watch and disengaged from scratching her dog's ears. "I'll be the AKC representative at these shows in Stockton and Woodland so I can handle all of the details about the required entries for you and Juliet even though it's already past the registration deadline. After that you'll be able to take care of your own scheduling."

Sherry refused our dinner invitation. She still had a 6-hour drive and wanted to get home to Sacramento at a reasonable hour. She and Bruce transferred a couple of loads of doggy essentials into our house. Giving Juliet a last hug, she left us as a new dog owning family.

Under Bruce's guidance, we organized two loads of doggy essentials for now and the foreseeable future. "Let's get to the basics first," suggested Bruce. "Juliet needs to know where she can find the things that are important to her, and what the rules are. There are some real advantages to adopting an older dog like Juliet rather than starting with an 8-week-old puppy. She's a very well trained, mature adult, who already has some established routines. Sherry ran me through her usual routines and left me her essential supplies. I also bought a few more necessities to set her up the way I think we'll all be happiest here. The more we stay with her familiar routines, the more secure she'll feel with us. The less we have to say "no", the better."

Bruce led Juliet and the Bowman family entourage to the back yard. With Juliet following us, we went out through the kitchen door to a stucco- and shrub-walled area. Suzanne explained to Robert and our new dog what awaited them on the other side of the door.

"This is Beverly Hills, so you'll see some hills back here, but nothing too steep. According to our local laws, the swimming pool is fenced off to keep you both safe. You'll have plenty of chances to play in the pool when it's warmer outside. The little house by the pool is for dressing, changing, and keeping pool toys and equipment. At night we like to sit by the table on the patio and look at the stars in the sky, but that's too late for you to stay up, Robert. From now on I think we should keep a supply of tennis balls out here to play with."

Juliet gave Suzanne a look that said very clearly, "I have my own way of figuring this stuff out". She ran happily from one end of the yard to the other three or four times at high speed, then started exploring with her nose at a slower pace, stopping at each tree and bush to sniff for interesting scents. She found a few bushes on a mound near the back corner of the yard that she bounded over several times just for the sheer joy of flying through the air. The local trees included nut, fruit, and avocado, offering a variety of smells to sample. There were still a few nuts lying on the ground under the towering walnut tree. Juliet helped herself, broke and chewed the nuts, swallowed, and barked happily.

The ground was thick, tough grass. Juliet tested the grass by running back and forth on it and declared it ideal. Suddenly, her hunter instincts kicked in and she locked on a rock solid point position at one of the trees. Bruce lined himself up tail to nose and pointed to a gray squirrel standing on a branch about 20 feet above the pointing dog. He tapped her head once to release her from the point and she happily barked at the squirrel till he ran off through the trees. Robert gurgled with delight as Juliet continued exploring the yard and running around in it.

Bruce watched Juliet playing with a very pleased expression on his face. He was clearly in his element here. "The German Shorthaired Pointer is a terrific athlete. They need lots of regular exercise to be happy and stay in shape. If you think she looked fast running around back here, she has a couple of higher gears she can shift into in the field. Based on sheer speed she can outrun most other dog breeds. Even more impressive is the GSP's endurance. A GSP in excellent condition, like Juliet, can run 20 or 30 miles pretty much continuously at a fast trot and probably wouldn't even be breathing hard at the end of the run. She can jump over a 5-6 foot fence anytime she wants, but she'll stay here in the yard here once she learns it is her home. One of us will have to stay back here with her for the first week or two while she gets used to her new space. After that we can let her out a few times a day to empty on her own. I can train her to use one corner of the yard for that purpose."

Juliet slowed down for a few seconds and trotted over to us for praise and pats of approval. Now that she wasn't a blur of motion, I could take a closer look at her. She was white, with dark brown ticks all over. Her head and much of her face were brown, as was a big spot near the base of her tail and her ears. I was soon to learn that GSP owners called her darker color "liver", rather than brown. All three of us human adults kneeled down to pet and scratch her, telling her what a good dog she was. Robert just poked and pat-patted her with all the vigor an infant could summon to the task. Juliet rewarded each of us with a few sloppy doggy kisses, each kiss featuring lots of tongue with indiscriminate aim. Then she went back to work, looking for squirrels and whatever else was waiting to be found in this strange and wonderful place. Suzanne and I looked at each other and burst out laughing. My dark blue velour vest was covered with white dog hairs, while Suzanne's cream-colored sweater appeared to be covered with liver-colored hairs shed by Juliet. Bruce congratulated us both on our new GSP look. When your dog is a full-body contact people lover like Juliet, being perpetually covered in dog hair was one more thing we had to get used to in our new life. On the other hand, Juliet got brown-nose points ("liver-nose" points?) with all of us for combining her shedding with kissing.

We all returned to the house. I walked directly through the high ceilinged family room to the elaborate wine cellar off the dining room to retrieve a bottle of our favorite Chardonnay to celebrate Juliet's arrival. Colorful oriental carpets protected the polished hardwood floors in the dining and living rooms. However, Juliet's toenails made a loud clicking noise on the hardwood surface of the family room floor. "I'm going to have to keep those nails pretty short or we're not going to be happy with what she does to the floor," Bruce observed.

The rest of the house included our huge master bedroom, a formal dining room, enough additional bedrooms for a family of five and a few visitors, enough bathrooms for a mid-sized family with chronic dysentery, and a recently modernized kitchen with high-end major appliances and lots of additional small appliance toys. We spent most of our time in the modern and informal family room and a less formal dining area just off the kitchen. Juliet would have about 7,500 square feet to wander through and explore, including seven bedrooms, six full, and two half bathrooms.

Suzanne had already decided that "Juliet's room" would be the large family room, where Bruce and Sherry had piled Juliet's stuff before Sherry left. The first thing that came out of the pile was a large dog crate, already fully assembled, with a soft pad on its floor. Bruce put the crate into the far corner of the room saying, "We've talked about dog crates before. This isn't a doggy jail. It's a Juliet-cave, where good things like meals and sleep happen. She already knows the command 'k-e-n-n-e-l'. I spelled it out so Juliet wouldn't respond to me, but to you, this time. Try the command, Suzanne."

Suzanne walked to the front of the crate and said, "kennel" in a firm tone, at normal volume. Juliet walked into the crate, turned around twice, and lay down on her soft bedding. Bruce removed a large dog biscuit from his pocket and handed it to Suzanne. "Give her one of these as a reward whenever she goes into the crate and you'll never have a problem with her wanting to disobey the 'kennel' command."

Suzanne handed the biscuit through a slot in the grillwork of the front door to Juliet lying in the crate. The dog took it carefully in her mouth and lay there happily, chewing, as Bruce demonstrated to Suzanne and me how to latch the crate closed. Bruce arranged a basket of Juliet's favorite dog toys near the crate. Then he put a large bowl of dog biscuits on a shelf conveniently accessible to humans taller than Robert, but high enough to be safely out of the dog and infant's reach.

Chapter 9. Suzanne gets a gift

Just then the front doorbell rang. I got there first and opened the door to greet a teenager delivering a paper-wrapped bundle of flowers from a florist's truck parked at the curb in front of our house.

A bored teenager looked up from the papers he was carrying. "Does Suzanne Bowman live here?"

Who'd be sending Suzanne flowers, I wondered. Did I miss her birthday or our anniversary? No, both were months away. "Yes, she does."

"Sign here, Mister."

I signed and was handed the flowers, wrapped in green paper. The delivery guy stood there, clearly expecting a tip. I gave him one, got a mumble of thanks, and off he went. I took the flowers inside and handed the conical-shaped arrangement to Suzanne.

She was clearly surprised, not expecting a floral bouquet. "What's this for?"

"I don't know. Why don't you open them and see if there's a card?"

Suzanne carefully unwrapped the package to find a dozen long-stemmed red roses. A card dropped to the floor. She bent over, picked it up, and read it aloud.

"To my dear Suzanne:
Roses are red and violets are blue,
Because of your beauty I share these with you.

Your loving admirer."

Suzanne looked directly at me. Her expression was not a happy one. "Is this your idea of romantic, Roger?"

Suddenly I was on the defensive. "No, I have no idea who sent these. I'm guessing some kind of whack job. A dozen roses delivered aren't cheap, so they're definitely meant to send you some kind of message. Have you gotten anyone pissed off at work lately?"

Suzanne shivered slightly and looked worried. "No, I haven't. But do you remember that feeling I had when we were in New York that someone was watching me? I wonder if it's possible I picked up a stalker while we were there? But if the stalker came from our trip back east, how would they have found my home address? Can I assume you only gave your office address to the AKC folks and our hotel?"

"Nowadays, if they know how to use a computer, I'm afraid all of that type of personal information is available somewhere."

I picked up the card and wrapping and found the name and phone number of the florist. It took only a few seconds to dial the number. It rang three times and a deep male voice said "Hello."

"Hello. We just got a delivery to our house from your store of a dozen roses for Suzanne Bowman. Can you tell us who sent them?"

"Just a sec!" I heard the sound of his phone being dropped on the counter and some noises in the background. About a minute later he was back on the phone. "It was an Internet order paid for by cash through a third party site. I have no way of knowing the name of the person who paid or who placed the order. I can't even tell you whether the order originated locally."

I thanked him for his help, hung up, and turned to Suzanne. "Did you get any bad vibes at Rockefeller University or while we were at the hotel, or was it only while we were at the restaurant?"

She thought deeply for a moment before looking up at me. "Just at the restaurant. And I think I see where you're going logically. If we don't believe in the random chance someone we passed on the street fell in love and somehow found my name and address, my stalker is most likely to be one of the AKC staff we had dinner with, right?"

"Right. I'll have Vincent run some background checks on all of them tomorrow and we'll see if anyone has done anything like this before and gotten caught at it."

Suzanne carefully put the roses in a vase of water. "Anyway, the flowers are pretty, and they'll look nice on the dinner table."

She put the vase of roses on the dining room table, took a long look at it, shivered, walked over, and hugged me. "As you know, I can take care of myself very well. But this really, really creeps me out." On that note she turned around to pick up the vase and move the flowers onto a table in the front hall, as far away as possible from where the family tends to hang out and still be in the house.

I hugged her back and gave her a kiss. "I don't think you have to worry too much about your personal safety, unless this creep escalates what he's doing. Flowers or chocolates are pretty impersonal. If he shifts to underwear or personal stuff, we should take some serious precautions. In the meantime, I'll have Vincent try again via the florist and the Internet site to see if he can find out where the order originated. Let's also tell Bruce about this at dinner. He can keep half an eye on you and Robert at a slightly higher stage of alert than usual."

The next day Vincent tried his computer magic, which didn't tell us a thing.

I explained Vincent's efforts to Suzanne that evening. "I asked Vincent to do a little bit of his computer hacking magic on the florist's computer, to try to find the IP address of the person who ordered your roses. He couldn't. Whoever ordered those flowers covered their tracks pretty thoroughly. They used a computer program similar to one called Tor, which conceals your identity. Anyone can just download it free from the Internet. It's a fancy program that makes the sender's computer address anonymous by running the message through a bunch of encrypted relay points along the Internet. It works the same way as if you take a twisty-turny route from here to there, to throw anyone following you off your trail. Your secret admirer either has some really impressive computer savvy, either on their own or has access to some pretty good corporate-type Information Technology people who taught him or her this trick."

Suzanne frowned as she leaned towards me, put down the scientific journal she'd been reading, and looked up from her chair. "So, what now, Roger? Should we call the police or is it better not to do anything and hope he goes away when he gets bored with this stupid game?"

We really didn't have a whole lot of choices at this point. "I think we should watch and wait for now. He'll either back off or escalate. If he escalates he'll make a mistake."

Chapter10.Starting the dog show circuit.

Bruce, Juliet, and I packed our shiny new minivan, compliments of the AKC, and started our long drive to Stockton. We drove a few miles west on Sunset Boulevard to the entrance for The San Diego Freeway going north, then on I-405 to its merger with I-5, then north on I-5. Bruce had rigged a tight fitting wooden frame in the back of the minivan, allowing him to bolt Juliet's crate to the frame. With this contraption she could ride safely and comfortably in her dog crate with her favorite bedding and a few selected toys wherever we went. She also took up a lot less space in the car than if she was loose to climb around, and could easily fall asleep when she was bored.

Travelling with an intact bitch in season was like I imagined travelling with an elderly grandfather who had prostate gland problems would be. When in season, a dog is biologically ready to have puppies. She may have some minor bleeding and definitely needs to relieve herself more often than usual. I-5 turned out to be convenient for this task. It has rest stops about every 50 miles with well-marked areas for dog walking. We stopped a couple of times to take Juliet for a short walk to empty her bladder. The rest stops at least broke up the boredom of this long, straight interstate highway that traveled endlessly through California's flat agricultural heartland. The posted speed limit of 70 miles per hour apparently translated to 79 mph and faster speeds, which experienced drivers cruised at all the way from Bakersfield to Stockton. Ominous signs alongside the road warned us of airplanes enforcing the speed limits. We never saw or heard one, but the other drivers must have believed the signs as most drivers adhered to the unofficial 79 mph limit. The only change in the endless vista of farms, fences, and sandy soil lying fallow were clusters of tired looking oil wells pumping slowly with little enthusiasm. Occasionally a crude sign posted on a fence alongside the highway identified the crop being grown behind the fence. Notable crops included cotton, alfalfa, various fruits and nuts, and just about every variety of vegetable imaginable.

Bruce had included a 26-foot long Flexi-lead type leash that retracted or locked into a plastic housing at the touch of a button in our collection of supplies. This device gave Juliet plenty of room to roam at the end of the leash while still being controlled enough that she couldn't dart into freeway traffic or in front of cars entering the rest stop. Juliet had travelled up and down I-5 dozens of times in her show career. She was an old hand at this and knew where to go and what to do when she got there. The only thing slowing us down was her need to smell every spot previously used in the dog area to find just the right one to choose. Thus, 30 seconds of peeing required at least 5-10 minutes. Responsible dog owners were expected to pick up behind their dogs, but that was obviously wishful thinking. You really have to watch your step in these areas. Even so, Bruce had also included a box of plastic poop bags to use for this purpose. CalTrans supplied covered, 50-gallon barrels by the dog walking areas at these rest stops for the used bags, more wishful thinking on their part.

As we stood around feeling out of place waiting for Juliet to find the exactly right spot to empty her bladder yet again, I turned to Bruce and asked him what he was thinking about.

"Life's funny," he answered. "A year ago I had no idea what I wanted to do with my life and decided to give Nanny school a try. Now I'm looking after Robert pretty much full time, training and showing a dog I just met for the first time, and even getting to play private detective and bodyguard every now and then. I'm living in Los Angeles, which is like heaven after Iraq and Afghanistan, and making more money than I ever dreamed of earning. I'd say I'm having a lot of fun and really enjoying not knowing what to expect next. Not bad for a small town kid from rural Wisconsin.

Bruce gave a gentle tug on the Flexi-lead and turned back towards the parked minivan. "I think Juliet's good to go, so let's get going. I'd just as soon get settled into the motel before it gets dark."

Five hours or so northwest of Los Angeles on Interstate 5 is Stockton, a large industrial city in the San Joaquin Valley about an hour or so south of Sacramento. It has a big deep-water port connected to San Francisco Bay by the deep-water channel of the San Joaquin River. Constant dredging of the river allows large cargo ships to reach the inland port city, a major facility for shipping agricultural products from the San Joaquin Valley via the Pacific Ocean. Despite the busy port, Stockton has serious financial issues and one of the highest homicide rates in the United States.

Stockton annually hosts a large dog show the fourth weekend in November, which is usually after Thanksgiving. We had driven up to Stockton on Friday for the Saturday and Sunday shows, which were held at the San Joaquin County Fairgrounds. The large venue has plenty of space for a thousand dogs and their associated owners and handlers, as well as thousands more spectators who came to watch the dogs and the competition. Sherry had arranged rooms for us at a local dog-friendly motel. It would be Bruce's first and second chances to show Juliet.

The motel manager recommended a restaurant half a mile or so from the motel for dinner. It was part of a chain of places called "The Feedlot's Finest", celebrating the local beef cattle industry. The steaks and roasts were especially recommended, and by L.A. standards a real bargain. For about $25 each we had a very, very good steak dinner with all the trimmings and a couple of beers. Our discussion was unusually personal, which was not our usual way of interacting. Bruce kicked things off by reminding me of our day of fun and games together in Montevideo a few months ago.

"Do you think things are likely to get physical during this case, Roger, like they did the last time? I wouldn't mind a little physical action again."

Bruce was reminding me of our visits to several drug dealers while we were solving the case we called The Matador Murders. "Not at this stage of things, Bruce. I think you're about to learn that the life of the Private Detective doing undercover work is mostly just kind of boring. As far as I can tell, we're just looking at shadows and suspicions now. If we succeed in this investigation, we'll most likely find some white-collar crime at worst. But what makes this kind of life fun is you never know for sure, and it's a real good idea to stay alert if you want to live into old age."

"You never told me how you got into this line of work, Roger. I've just picked up bits and pieces, like you used to be a cop. What's your story?"

I speared a piece of steak onto my fork and chewed my T-bone. Then I drank a little bit of the beer. "My dad was military police in the Navy, then civilian police in San Diego. I grew up in San Diego with everyone in the family assuming I'd follow in his footsteps and become a cop, but I wasn't ready for that when I graduated from college where I majored in chemistry. So for my next step I went to law school at UCLA. The law degree and my B.S. in chemistry got me into patent law, where I made a ton of money and was bored stiff with my job. By that time I was ready to follow in my Dad's footsteps. At the time the Los Angeles police department was hiring and I was qualified for the police academy, so that's where my police career started. I was good at it and had the law degree so moved up to homicide detective pretty quickly. With real good case clearance rate, I was fast tracked for success by the time I realized it was the wrong job for me. Too much political B.S. and too many rules for someone like me who needs to be his own boss. I had some money saved up and a bunch of nice office furniture from the former law practice that belonged to me, which along with my police experience was all I needed to get a P.I. license and here we are."

Some more steak with a forkful of mushrooms got chewed and swallowed, followed by another drink from my glass of beer. "Nothing much happened for the first six months or so after I opened my P.I. office. Then I lucked out and had a bunch of business come to me all at once, mostly stuff I could do anywhere I had access to a computer. One of my first big cases was a client who walked in off the street and asked me to go with her to Salta, Argentina to investigate who murdered her father. That's how I first met Suzanne and that's how we both got interested in South America. I fell in love with her less than 30 seconds after she walked into my office, and we clicked as a couple. Her father left her a ton of money, plus the house in Beverly Hills free and clear, so we can afford a full-time Nanny and the occasional trip to interesting places. Neither of us would know what to do with ourselves if we weren't working, along with our quality family time and the occasional murders in Montevideo. And that's how we got to this point in our lives."

I slathered a generous amount of butter on a slice of some superb warm sourdough bread and took a bite. "How about you, Bruce? Have you figured out where you want to be in 5 years?"

Bruce pondered how he should reply for a moment, then looked directly at me and smiled as he answered my question. "I'm not sure what I want to be in 5 months, much less 5 years from now, Roger. I'm just taking life as it comes these days. Right now life is good with you guys and I love Robert. I'm kind of hoping he'll get a little sister in a year or two so I can hang around a while and maybe become their Uncle Bruce, but that's kind of up to you guys. I don't see a college degree in my future because I don't like school and tests, which puts some limits on what I can be and do, but that doesn't bother me too much. I'm enjoying the whole private detective thing, when you give me a chance to help out. Lately, I've really enjoyed the chance to train Juliet. For now, the dog shows thing sounds like a lot of fun"

Bruce glanced at his watch. "We have an early call tomorrow morning and it's getting late. We still have to walk Juliet. Are you ready to head back to the motel yet?"

The next morning we had an early breakfast at one of a well-known chain of restaurants near our motel famous for their big breakfasts and headed to the Fairgrounds.

Bruce and I went through the orientation, which was run by Sherry. We learned not only the rules for the dogs and handlers inside and outside the ring, but also such essentials as where the food and bathrooms were in relation to the show rings, and the location of ring #7, where Juliet was scheduled to compete on Saturday. We were given a quick tour of the fairgrounds as part of our being oriented to find our way around this huge show venue. The county fairgrounds was a sprawling area of grass, dirt and gravel roads, paved parking areas, and buildings to support the county fair, an annual event to showcase the agricultural productivity of California's vast Central Valley. The dog show used a small fraction of the total space, with parking for RVs, trucks, and cars radiating outward from the core area where the show rings were set up.

We learned the RV parking areas were very expensive to rent space in, but included convenient hook-ups for electricity and water. There was plenty of unused space on the fairgrounds for walking and exercising dogs and to empty them. These areas were not fenced and dogs were expected to be on leashes at all times. Just about all of the regulars who camped in their RVs at the fairgrounds had exercise pens in their vehicles for the dogs to use while waiting to be shown. These collapsible metal devices were open wire mesh enclosures that set up securely on grass or dirt. They gave the dogs plenty of space to move around or to lie down and spread out, relax, and occasionally socialize with other dogs through the openings. Larger exercise pens could accommodate several dogs in a single structure.

Sherry and I stood together out of Juliet's line of sight watching Bruce's inaugural appearance on Saturday. Sherry maintained a running commentary, initially for my benefit but later on to vent her frustrations about what was happening, while we watched. Bruce did a pretty good job of stacking Juliet for her detailed examination by the judge. Juliet's tail and head were held high and her ears were eagerly perked forward as she looked for treats that were not forthcoming. "Give her the liver now, Bruce," Sherry implored under her breath. "You're supposed to be baiting the dog when she's stacked the way you want her to look."

However, disaster loomed when Bruce was asked to gait her across the ring and back. In this maneuver the judge can see whether the dog's movement is consistent with what they would predict from her structure when stacked. Halfway to the other side of the ring, Bruce gave a quick jerk on the leash to adjust Juliet's position. Juliet's tail and ears drooped and she dropped into a "heel" position, moving slowly beside him. I heard Sherry saying "No, no, Bruce. This isn't obedience training. You want her out in front of you looking eager and perky. Bait her with some liver to get her head up and get her moving! Oh no, Bruce, don't correct her. Encourage her. Play with her."

When Bruce tried to speed her up with another quick jerk on the lead, her nose dropped to the ground and her strides became even shorter. By this time they reached the end of the ring and turned back. Juliet was completely confused as to what Bruce wanted her to do, so she ducked under his arm behind him to get back to the judge by the most direct route possible rather than going around Bruce as half of a dynamic pair. "He needs a lot of work with her," Sherry mumbled. "He's got it all wrong, but it should be easy to fix."

The next maneuver, a big circle around the ring, didn't go any better. Juliet trotted slowly and dispiritedly around, showing none of her ability to fly when moving. She looked very ordinary, not like a dog shouting to the judge and spectators "look at me. Look at me." Every time Bruce tugged at the lead to lift her head up and quicken her pace, she responded by dropping her nose to the ground and slowing down. You could almost see and hear her asking Bruce, "What do you really want me to do here?"

Bruce is a quick study. He didn't win any points with Juliet that weekend in Stockton, but he quickly transitioned from looking like he wasn't sure what he was doing on Saturday to just another professional handler in serious competition with some of the best German Shorthaired Pointers in the United States. Saturday afternoon, after the competition, Sherry had taken Bruce aside to show him the different responses Juliet had, depending on how she was handled. A strong man with perhaps too firm a hand appeared to Juliet as a dominant male, so she responded with submissive behaviors. By contrast, Sherry, who she trusted, guided her using positive reinforcement, praise, and a happy upbeat attitude. Juliet responded with exactly the correct mix of sassy self-confidence and showmanship in the ring. Juliet was actually being seriously looked over and considered for the points by the judge on Sunday. As Bruce's confidence and understanding of the human-dog dynamic increased, he guided Juliet with a much lighter touch and positive rewards. Juliet went from looking confused and having her tail tucked under her butt on Saturday, to having fun in the ring on Sunday and clearly telling everybody to look at her as she trotted around the ring with her head and tail in the air.

This time Sherry's comments while Bruce showed Juliet sounded a lot better to me. "That's the way to bait her. Good job! Very gentle hands, don't tug on the lead. Look at her. She's actually having fun in there. Great job of moving her out!" The transformation in Bruce clearly pleased Juliet, who put her front paws on Bruce's shoulders after the competition and planted a great big slurpy kiss on his face to encourage his new behaviors.

When I wasn't watching Bruce and Juliet in the show ring, I spent my time just walking around, listening, and absorbing the vibes at the show. I had several impressions from what I was seeing and hearing. Just about every dog or bitch had a rooting section among the audience: owners, family, and fans. Many of the handlers were professionals, leaving the dog's owners as part of the audience. When an owner handled their own dog in the ring, they usually had pertinent others or family and friends in the audience to cheer them on and perhaps help to favorably influence the judge's opinion. There was a lot of excitement during the judging, with smatterings of applause and cheers for individual dogs as they came under the judge's watchful eye. After the judge's decisions were made, there seemed to be a lot of second-guessing and bitching by the fans and owners of the losing dogs who weren't selected.

After each of Juliet's ring appearances, Bruce and Sherry got together for her to critique in great detail his handling in the show ring and to discuss what had occurred. I sat in on these talks and learned a lot.

"There's no shame in being on a learning curve, Bruce," Sherry told him. "We've all been in that situation when we started out. I'm amazed at how fast you're picking this stuff up. The judge yesterday would never have picked Juliet as a winner, no matter how well you showed her. He's looking for a tall, long legged bitch who pushes the breed standard for height. Juliet is 22.5 inches at the shoulder, 0.5 inch less than the breed standard and 1.5 inches shorter than the maximum allowable height. Part of what I love aboot her conformation is how compact and muscular she looks and how fast and effortlessly she can run. Today's judge tends to pick Juliet's type more often than yesterday's judge, but he wasn't ready to pick her at this level of competition with a less than perfect job of handling. He gave her a good looking over, though, which is encouraging. You must have done a good job of handling her in the judge's eye to get her noticed.

"During my next break, let's go over a few tricks you can do with Juliet to make her show better, and in the next two weeks before the Woodland shows, let's have a practice session with her. Juliet knows what she's supposed to do in the ring. A lot of how she actually performs relates to her level of comfort with her handler. The more you two can practice together and get used to each other, the better. You'll get her best effort if you can make the entire show experience into a big game for Juliet to have fun. I think we can get you up to competitive speed by the next show or two if you keep practicing with her between the shows.

Sherry turned directly towards me. "Both judges picked excellent dogs to get the regular points and the grand Champion select points, Roger. I didn't see anything particularly hinky going on concerning which dogs were picked. The judging for this breed seemed to be fair and honest, and well within the range of differences between what each judge likes and is looking for."

This seemed to be a good time to clarify something, so I asked Sherry a question I'd been wondering about for the last couple of days. "I've heard a lot of complaining about the judging results. A lot of owners are saying they're ready to quit the whole thing and stop spending tons of money just to lose because the judges are so wrong about who they pick as winners. If dog owners are dropping out of competition, it could account for the decreased revenues and higher costs the AKC thinks it's seeing this year."

Sherry looked thoughtful for a moment or two before answering me. "People, especially owners, have been complaining about the judging for as long as there have been dog shows. Judging a dog show is pretty subjective. The old saying aboot beauty being in the eye of the beholder means that you, me, and the judge could pick three different dogs as the winner and we'd all be right. Two owners would complain and one would approve. I don't think there's any more or less complaining about the judging this year than I expect to hear, and I expect a lot."

She paused for dramatic effect or to gather her thoughts. "California, and most of the rest of the country, is just beginning to recover from a major recession. A lot of people can't afford the gasoline to drive around to dog shows, the entry fees, and all the other costs of this very expensive hobby. I suspect that's the reason for lower revenues. You have to remember the overpaid New York City executives like the AKC bunch aren't in touch with the real world economy. I just don't think they understand how real people live when they suggest that fluctuations in income and expenses aren't just a reflection of what's going on in the broader economy."

Obviously, just listening to chatter in the stands wasn't going to get this job done. I decided Bruce and I should play our undercover roles cool, allowing the veteran owners and handlers to come to us. It might take a while before they were convinced we'd be regulars on the circuit, but it seemed to be the best strategy if we wanted to be convincing in our roles. It was OK for us to be perceived of as close to Sherry, since all of the regulars, and anyone who read the program, would know that Juliet was her dog, which she had bred and shown. It was natural for her to introduce us into this world as her new sponsors.

We returned to Los Angeles late Sunday night. Suzanne was in the living room sitting in a large wingback chair with all of the lights in the room turned on, reading a biochemical journal. She looked up at us with a little concern in her expression.

As she reached out to absentmindedly pet Juliet, Suzanne let out a big sigh and looked right at me. "Everything was OK here except I missed you a lot, Roger. I missed you too, Bruce. I also got a weird telephone call. At first I thought it was just a wrong number, but the more I think about it, the less sure I am. I answered the phone and there was somebody on the other end who didn't say anything. He just breathed into the phone for half a minute or so before hanging up.   It could have been a wrong number, but it just didn't feel right."

It wasn't like Suzanne to be bothered by what could have been just a wrong number. "Could you tell whether the caller was a man or a woman?"

She continued scratching Juliet's head absentmindedly. "No, not really. It felt more like a man, but I'm not sure."

I decided we had to treat this episode like a real threat, just in case it was. "I'm sorry you had to have this happen, especially with me not here to help. If there's a next time, why don't you try talking to the caller to try to maybe get an idea of whether it's a man or woman on the other end of the line. In the meantime, do you want me to report this to the police?"

"No. I really haven't any reason to think a crime has been committed. But I do appreciate you taking me seriously rather than just blowing off my concerns, Roger." Which earned me a hug and a kiss.

Chapter11.The next dog shows

Two weeks later Bruce and I were at the Yolo County Fairgrounds in Woodland, CA, about fifteen miles north of Sacramento on Interstate 5. It was another sprawling venue of several hundred acres, at the south end of the small city with more than 50,000 residents. We were here with Juliet to compete in the next two shows on the Circuit, which would be sponsored by the Santa Clara Kennel Club on Saturday and the Camelia Capital Kennel Club on Sunday.

Sherry had invited us to stay with her over the weekend. Her house was on a 1-acre lot in an old neighborhood in a Sacramento suburb called Carmichael. The area was still zoned for horse owners to be able to keep their animals on the property. In the backyard, several shorthairs romped on a not so well kept lawn on top of dirt. A few large mature trees, accompanied by some native shrubs that should have been low maintenance, provided a bit of shade for the dog pack. Pride of place among the larger old trees was a huge American walnut standing about 60 feet high and perhaps 40 feet across at the widest part of the canopy. Dog runs with cyclone fencing and concrete pads backed up to the house, with dog doors opening into a large doggy rumpus room inside the house.

The house itself was old, about 1600 square feet of living area in a ranch style, one story building painted light green with dark green shutters on the windows. There were three bedrooms and two bathrooms, plenty of space for guests like us to stay. Everything the dogs had access to, or could get into, needed a little repair and maintenance, as might be expected for a single woman like Sherry who had to travel a lot for her job.

Juliet was in high spirits after visiting with several canine buddies, including her mother and grandmother, at Sherry's house. The dogs were all shorthairs, and all of the girls looked a lot like Juliet as far as size and shape. Paint jobs differed between them, so you could tell them apart.

Bruce had spent a fair amount of time practicing stacking and moving with Juliet. He had some questions for Sherry about the specifics of how best to present her to the judge. He, Juliet, and Sherry spent some time together in the back yard Friday evening before dinner, working out some nuances of handling, with me watching as a spectator. There was a small fenced off area with the typical dimensions of a small show ring, where most of the green grass still remaining in the yard grew. They worked in this ring, mostly on Bruce's handling interactions with Juliet, with Sherry playing the role of the judge.

"We discussed all of this in general terms at the Stockton show. Forgive me if I repeat myself here, but you're ready for the details now. It's all about making it fun for Juliet so she sparkles. You're a little too much into the obedience part for a bitch like her. One of her prettiest features is her free stack. You want her to stack herself for the judge. When you bring her into position in front of the judge, grab her attention with a dog treat, slowing her down a few steps before you reach the judge. Then trust her to do the right thing. She already knows how to step into a perfect stack, but if she arrives off balance give her a "step" command and shift your weight to encourage her to take another step and readjust herself. Hold your bait at her nose height to keep her head in the right position. Just tempt her with it; you don't have to give it to her yet. After the judge looks at her you can reward her with the bait and your praise. When you move her, it's important to keep her attitude up. Moving is fun and a reward in itself. Don't make it into a discipline."

Sherry explained the rationale, "As you know, Bruce, no dog is perfect, even Juliet. Much of the handler's skill in the show ring comes in being able to emphasize her best features while hiding or minimizing the flaws. That's especially true when you stack her for the judge's inspection, which you do very well. But it's also true at all times in the show ring when the judge isn't looking at her. You have a tendency to let her relax while the other dogs are being examined. A good handler assumes the judge may look up at any time to check her while they're examining another dog. You need to always keep her stacked to show her best features, just in case.

"Juliet has a great front end----chest, shoulders, keel, and head---that's what you want the judge to notice if he looks over toward her casually. Keep track of where the judge is and make sure he will always see her from the perspective you want him to. This means continually changing the angle of how she is standing, in subtle ways, as the judge moves along the line of bitches in front of her.

"When the judge has you move her around the ring you can choose your speed and the length of your stride. Juliet moves beautifully if you can get her up to a quicker speed. You might want to try taking longer strides yourself and going a bit faster when you're running her around the perimeter of the ring. Then just let her flow. The more you make her reach out with her front legs to keep up with you, the better she'll look. When you're moving out and back, the same principles are in play, but try keeping her a little closer to you by shortening the lead a bit. That will make her look better going out and exaggerate her reach coming back."

We went through a second orientation at the fairgrounds with Sherry the next morning. Sherry pointed out the early Christmas mood. The ringside area reserved for taking photos of the winning dogs, their handlers, and owners contained a photo backdrop of Santa driving a facsimile of his sleigh. Bruce and I were both welcomed by our respective peer groups, handlers and owners, noticeably more enthusiastically than at the previous shows in Stockton. It was a good sign we were making some progress with selling ourselves in our undercover identities. Even better, Juliet and Bruce picked up three select points, even though she wasn't chosen as "Best of Breed". Obviously Bruce was incorporating some of the subtler handling tricks Sherry had taught him to best present this specific breed and this specific bitch in the show ring.

Several of the owners we had seen previously in Stockton made it a point to come over and congratulate Bruce and me on Juliet's earning three points. One couple, the Breeds, who owned that day's "Best of Breed" Winner Bitch, invited us to join them for a drink after the Best in Show competition was over. "Meet us over at the RV parking area when you've watched enough of the show to be happy," invited Steven Breed.

Lunch was an excuse to see a bit of what Woodland was like. We drove north on East Street to a Mexican restaurant someone suggested, which was supposed to be famous for its chiles rellenos. The ambiance was blah, the stuffed chiles very, very good, and the cold Dos Equis beer was a good pairing for Pasilla peppers stuffed with cheese. Traditional beans, tortillas, rice, chips and salsa rounded out the lunch. The whole meal cost less than half of what the same lunch would have cost at home in Century City or Westwood, where the ambiance would have been fancier.

We watched other handlers with other breeds in the afternoon. After the last event Sherry came over to congratulate Bruce. "You handled her very nicely today. She looked like she was gliding around the ring when you moved her out. Even more importantly, she looked like she was having fun out there. It was like she was shouting, albeit discretely, "Look at me, look at me!" I loved watching both of you in the ring."

Chapter12.Meeting the owners

The other handlers' congratulations that Bruce received after he showed Juliet seemed sincere. Several of the owners in addition to the Breeds offered to buy me a drink. The post-show party seemed to be a good place to begin my real job, so after the show I walked back to the parking area where Helen and Steven Breed were waiting for me. They led me to a huge and expensive RV parked in a cluster of recreational vehicles of all shapes and sizes. I was welcomed inside, shown a well-stocked bar, and asked what my usual drink of preference was.

A quick look at the bar told me the right answer included only booze or liquor. "Scotch if you have it."

"Blended or single malt?"

The Breeds seemed to be affluent, as did many of the dog owners we had met thus far. I assumed the RV cost more than $250,000, all tricked out as it was. "Single malt, please."

So there I was sipping on some excellent and well-aged Glenlivet, making small talk with the Breeds. Since Sherry had warned me that gossip was the major activity among the owners and breeders after the dog shows, I was careful with my answers. Whatever I said now would be the cover story we'd have to live with for the rest of this case. Mostly I explained that Juliet was now our dog for the foreseeable future and would be living in Los Angeles with me and my family, that we had our own handler, and that our goal was to show her to a Grand Champion title or beyond, campaigning her aggressively throughout the west coast circuit. We had a short visit, but a productive one. I was able to plant some of the seeds that over time would blossom into our image among the owners.

Two RVs over were the Schlecks, another GSP family. Their champion male Max was sitting in an exercise pen alongside their RV, like a lighthouse beacon beckoning me to my next Port of Call. It turned out to be easy. Max offered his head and ears for scratching as I passed by. Less than half a minute later, we were best friends. A middle-aged woman, stylishly dressed like a handler, opened the RV door, took a single step down onto the second stair, and said hello to me in a booming voice. We introduced ourselves to each other, then Ingrid introduced me formally to Max, while hollering into the RV for her husband Howard to join us. Howard, who was dressed more casually than Ingrid, shook my hand while introducing himself, and asked which dog was mine. When I told him we now had Sherry Wyne's Juliet, I was welcomed effusively into the club with the offer of another drink, which I refused on grounds of already reaching my capacity two RVs back.

Howard leaned towards me and continued talking. "You know that our Max and your Juliet used to take turns going 'Best of Winners' until they both finished their championships. These days the Grand Champion points seem to be hard to come by for both of them. Who'll be handling Juliet now that you're backing her? Will it still be Sherry or will the new handler we saw today be showing her now?"

I told him the answer as if it was top secret, being shared only with him, assuming that would most encourage everyone in Yolo County knowing this information in the shortest time possible. "No, we'll use our own handler, a gentleman named Bruce. We hope he'll be able to break Juliet's slump even though he's new to this circuit. He's new to showing GSPs too, but has a lot of experience with some of the other sporting breeds."

Howard answered quite naturally, "Ingrid has been showing Max since he was a puppy. We think showing him ourselves is the most fun part of competing in one of these shows. But I'll admit it's a lot easier to get those points with a professional handler; a lot of the judges give the wins to the wrong end of the leash if you ask me. It's supposed to be about which is the best dog in the ring, not which handler is the most popular or most winning."

We both looked over towards Ingrid, who spoke to me directly. "A bunch of us were planning to barbecue dinner on my gas grill tonight between a couple of the RVs. Would you like to join us and meet the rest of the Shorthair owners who are staying on the grounds? You're welcome to bring a pertinent other or friend along if you'd like."

This was going more easily than I had anticipated. There wasn't anything wrong with that! "Sure, I'd love to. What can I bring?"

Ingrid looked over at Howard and some kind of nonverbal signal passed between them. "If you'd like to bring a couple of bottles of red wine to share, we'll supply everything else. I've got all sorts of steaks and sausages to barbecue and the other guests will be bringing side dishes and desserts. Why don't you come by around 5 or 5:30, when it's starting to get dark around here?"

It wasn't clear to me how much of a class structure might exist between owners and professional handlers, but I thought "To heck with it," and brought Bruce. I had also bought three bottles of a nice Cabernet Sauvignon wine from the Napa Valley at the local wine and liquor store a few blocks walk on East Street from the fairgrounds to bring with us to the barbeque. There were several people there already, including the Breeds and the Schlecks who I already knew. I introduced Bruce to both couples and left the wine with my hosts, who thanked me and opened one of the bottles to pour glasses for us.

"You're spoiling us," joked Howard Schleck. "That's the first cork I've seen on a wine bottle since the show circuit began. We usually see cardboard cartons and screw caps around here."

Bruce and I wandered around and met the other owners. There were three married couples and one couple who were bonded by their mutual love of dogs rather than to each other. They were all regulars on the circuit, part of the RV crowd who stayed on the show grounds. Melanie and Irwin Todd were from Southern California, near Riverside, where they had retired several years previously. Both of them were in their 60s, owned and showed Labrador retrievers, and had done well today in the show ring. They were friendly, but with different breeds and different life styles we really had little in common and used up the pleasantries in a few minutes.

We approached the next couple, another pair in their 60s that had picked up a couple of plastic cups of the wine we had brought and complimented us on our taste in Cabs. "I'm Albert Schaefer and this purty little thang is my wife Sadie. We're dove hunters from West Texas and are regulars with our Brittanies on this little circuit every year. What kind of dogs do you folks have?"

We chatted a while about Shorthairs versus Brittanies, with Bruce dominating our half of the conversation. He continued to amaze me with his depth and breadth of knowledge about all things dog. Bruce is not large, at 5 foot 9 inches and about 170 pounds, but with lightning-quick fast twitch muscles he moves as fast and gracefully as a German Shorthair. He can be noticed in a group or blend into it, as he prefers, by adjusting his sometimes dramatically flamboyant personality.

Albert sipped some wine and turned to Bruce. "There's more than a few gay owners and handlers on this dog show circuit, including some of our best. Out here in California you should be comfortable wherever you go. I think you might still need to keep a low profile in West Texas, though. There's a lot less toleration in the Bible Belt."

The gossip mill worked remarkably well around here. My cover story had gotten from the Breeds through the party in record time. Bruce was the center of most of the attention. "What's your story? How did you become a handler? And are you really a Nanny for Roger's kid, too?"

"I grew up as a cheesehead, in a small town in rural Wisconsin, which I couldn't wait to leave. Fort Atkinson was a pretty conservative town and by then I pretty much knew my gender orientation. I decided to join the Navy and see the world. Nobody in the Navy seemed to be worried about my sexual orientation. My job description included training our guard dogs and keeping them in good physical condition as needed for our squad. I did my job well, so my squad all liked me, and vice-versa. I was also able to show dogs on the European circuit for some of the officers. But between being pretty obviously gay and lacking a college degree, I knew I wouldn't get much beyond the rank I held. After a while, I'd spent enough time and seen enough killing in deserts and jungles that I was ready for something else."

Bruce took several sips of his wine before he continued. "After my second hitch ended, I went home to Fort Atkinson and applied for a job as a cop. Nobody ever said anything about my sexual preferences, but the local police force and the state patrol kept hiring the other applicants for the positions available. I spent a couple of months living off my mustering out pay from the Navy and reconnecting with my extended family. I started to notice the social awkwardness whenever we went anywhere together. I finally got the message and thought some more about my career choices.

He finished the rest of the wine left in his cup. "I like kids and dogs. So I thought about jobs, lifestyle, kids, and what I was actually qualified to do. Being a Nanny in a big city like Los Angeles, which has a lot of tolerance for diversity, seemed to fit perfectly with my personality, at least for now. I spent most of the rest of my savings on an intensive, 3-month icourse at a Nanny school in West Hollywood, where I received my credentials as a certified Nanny. Roger's family is my first full-time, live-in Nanny experience. I really enjoy the job and the family. The pay is great, and now that we have Juliet the travel is a bonus."

We talked a bit longer with the Schaefers, about their life on the dog show circuit, and what it was like to live in an RV for several months with a lot of dogs. Like the Schlecks, they were also owner-breeders who didn't use a professional handler. Sadie summed up how the RV had been customized with people and dog space. "As much as we love our dogs, we need our own space and the RV is purty tiny after a while. We also need to keep the dogs safe when we're outa here or drivin' 70 miles per hour. So we had this here mobile home customized. We took out a section of seatin' and bolted a pile of dog crates to the walls and floor, so they don't slide around. The dogs like this set-up, except the old girl who puts up a fuss unless she gets to ride on the dashboard and help steer."

Albert looked up and added, "Sometimes, when we have time between dog shows, we like to hang out at the RV parks. The dogs are real popular there especially with some of the good old boys. That's got us a lot of good invites to go hunting."

Sadie told us they had the best dog in the ring, but it didn't place because of bad judging. "We hit one of them thar handler's judges, who only look at dogs being handled by professionals. He completely ignored my puppy because I was showing him. That's been happenin' a lot too often around here, if you ask me. Well, things should even out since tomorrow's judge has liked our dogs in other shows."

Another couple overheard that last part and walked over. "By now you folks should know dog shows are just like Lake Woebegone on the radio. All of the dogs are above average. They should all win each time. The only problem is the judges always get it wrong, except when they pick my dog. Hi there. I'm Pete and this is Jewel Harris. We own one of the GSP bitches you beat today, plus about six other dogs and bitches. You'll get used to seeing us as you campaign Juliet out here. You have a lovely young lady in Juliet, and we think the judge got it right today."

The group grew a bit more as the last couple we hadn't met joined us at the party. Pete introduced us to Elbert Hearst and Sarah Cord. Elbert was a former co-pilot with a local regional airline, in his 50s and an obviously gay, while Sarah was in her late 60s. The couple was a living legend in the German Shorthaired Pointer world. They lived together, sharing ownership of a dozen or so dogs they bred on a small ranch owned by Sarah in rural Northern California, about an hour's drive east of Sacramento. They showed the dogs quite successfully. Elbert, who handled the dogs in the show ring, nodded to Bruce as if to say, "I've been hearing about you."

I was starting to get the hang of this. We were a generation or so younger than most of them. The well-dressed owners like Ingrid also handled their dogs in the show ring. The casually dressed ones like Howard were the pertinent others, usually a spouse. If both members of a couple were dressed casually either they had a much earlier ring time, or they used a professional handler. Bruce was most welcome, especially by the owners who also handled their own dogs. This was not a stratified society in the social sense, at least not among the sporting dog owners. Handlers and owners were equals here. Everyone bragged as much about how well the dogs hunted and "worked" as they did about how well they performed in the beauty contests of the show ring. Many of the owner-handlers had been middle-middle class, blue-collar workers while they made their money, with several former military, electricians, and plumbers in the group. Others were married to white-collar types, who were indulging the spouse's passion for dogs, often as half of a retired couple.

We chatted a while about where both Bruce and I came from, my family, and our level of experience with show dogs. They were quite interested in Bruce, who they all seemed to want to size up. A new professional handler on the circuit was a rarity and they wanted to hear all about where he worked previously and which dogs he had shown. Elbert seemed especially curious about Bruce's history in the dog show world.

Bruce indicated he'd handled dogs in European shows while he was in the army, making sure to be vague about the specifics of where and when. I made a mental note to ask Sherry about the best way to discuss Bruce's background in the future, while inventing answers like "I don't know" for the time being.

The increased camaraderie from both groups carried over to Sunday when we arrived at the show ring. Bruce and Juliet celebrated by picking up three additional select points, even though the Breed's dog, Butch took "Best of Breed" again. Sherry's debriefing at the end of the GSP judging was short and to the point. "Good job, Bruce. I couldn't have done any better myself. The best dog won. Butch is at least as good as Juliet, and all else being equal, a good shorthaired dog will do better than a comparable bitch at the group competition level. Size matters."

After Juliet and the other GSPs had finished, we settled into what had become our usual routine for the rest of the dog show. Bruce and I became spectators and watched some of the other breeds compete, especially the judging. At random, we picked a ring or two to observe the judging while we got to know the other handlers faces and styles. We began to recognize that certain handlers tended to show specific breeds, and noted the styles of dog particular judges seemed to favor. Bruce and I bought catalogues and made notes of what we saw, discussing what we were seeing as the judging took place. Bruce was strong on the technical parts, focusing on what flaws he saw in the dogs, especially when they were stacked or moving, and what mistakes he saw the handlers make. I focused on how the spectators reacted, especially whether the judge made popular choices of winners or if the crowd complained about which dogs were being selected. As we watched and learned, our ongoing discussions became more sophisticated. I was starting to learn how to watch the competition and what to look for in the ring.

Our ultimate reality check occurred at the end of each day, when we got Sherry's debriefing. The judging at this particular show had been completely on the up and up as far as she was concerned. "Roger, the judges picked the right dogs. I didn't see anything here yesterday or today to make me question the integrity of the judging. If something suspicious were going to happen, I'd bet it would be in the Golden Gate Show. The stakes will be higher because it's a bigger and more prestigious show."

Once we got away from Sherry, Bruce had some interesting observations to share. "The handlers do a lot of gambling among themselves, like golf caddies betting on their golfer at a tournament. But there's more to it than just loyalty or chauvinism. The handlers know their dogs very well and can take into account which dogs are in the right mood to show at their best. They also know most of the judges and their preferences very well too. They know who likes big dogs versus small ones, light colored versus dark, dogs that move well versus dogs that look better stacked, and a whole bunch of other idiosyncratic behaviors that help to explain why a judge picks a specific dog to win on that day. There's a lot of money riding on each event for the individual handlers, in addition to the handling fees they earn. There's also the money they bet on themselves, and the under the table money some of the owners pay as bonuses for big wins. Needless to say, not all of this income gets reported to the IRS.

Bruce walked a little bit faster, as if to make doubly sure Sherry couldn't hear him. I had to lengthen my strides to keep up. "After I didn't do much in the first two shows in Stockton, they all assumed I wasn't going to be competitive and nobody was betting on me here in Woodland. The odds were pretty good, so I bet on myself. When I walked off with over a thousand dollars in winnings for the last two days, there was a lot of mumbling that I had dogged it in Stockton to set higher odds against me here. Strangely enough, they admired me all the more for suckering them and setting myself up for a big payoff at the next show. The best news is, nobody is going to ask why a professional handler like me started out so badly in Stockton and got so much better the next week in Woodland."

I looked closely at Bruce. "Obviously there are some possibilities for corruption of the impartiality of the show ring here. Do you think the AKC needs to know about this?"

He stared right back at me, looking me directly in the eye. "I'm pretty sure the AKC already does. It has probably been a tradition for decades. I haven't seen anything yet that makes me think any of the handlers would ever bet against themselves or deliberately lose by messing up in the show ring. The damage to their reputation would be too big of a risk. On the other hand, if a handler and a judge colluded there'd be easy money to be made in these betting pools. That might be something we should be looking out for in subsequent shows."

Chapter13.A short break between shows at home

After an uneventful eight-hour plus ride, we were home. Our hands were full of our bags and we had an eager Juliet, who knew where she was and what was waiting for her inside the house, on a leash. Bruce rang the doorbell. The door opened and Suzanne planted a big kiss on my lips. "How was the dog show?"

We walked in and deposited our junk on the floor. Bruce took the leash off Juliet and let her loose to explore her house. "Fun," I answered. Bruce got some rosettes and some points on Juliet this time around and I got to schmooze with some of the owners. You're going to have to set up a rosette and trophy area in the family room. How about your weekend with us gone? Did everything go smoothly without your favorite Nanny?"

Suzanne paused perceptibly before answering. "I really enjoyed the quality time by myself with Robert. He's easy to take care of and play with. But I had another deep breather and hang-up telephone call. It was almost as if the caller was checking up on whether I was here or with you in Woodland, and was afraid I might recognize their voice if they said anything. I think we have a real weirdo on the other end of the telephone."

I didn't like the sound of this at all. Suzanne could take care of herself, but it was impossible to predict what a weirdo like this might do. And now there was Robert to worry about, especially with Bruce not being there to protect him for large blocks of time. "That's what people have caller ID for. What number did the call come from?"

Suzanne looked as frustrated as I felt. "I don't know. The caller ID was blocked."

Maybe there was a better way? This couldn't just go on or we'd both start climbing the walls. "I'll have Vincent set up a tap on our home phone line tomorrow. We can get past caller I.D. blocking the next time they call, if there is a next time."

There weren't any majors scheduled for next weekend so we finally had some non-working time at home without a dog show we had to go to. It was time for Suzanne and me to learn more about the daily life of a dog owner.

Having a dog is like having a kid, except it grows faster than a human and can't talk back. The terrible twos for a human, when every other word is "NO", is replaced by the 12 week old puppy who needs to see how far it can stretch the leash at every opportunity to get into trouble. Bruce reminded us frequently during these early days as Juliet's humans that responsible dog ownership requires the human to think of the pet's needs at least as often as they think of their own.

Bruce looked over to Juliet, who lay contentedly at his feet waiting to see what new adventure awaited her next. "If you're going to keep a happy and well-adjusted German Shorthaired Pointer as your pet, you have to remember how much the breed needs plenty of exercise. That means just about every day, not just on weekends. Short walks with Robert won't be enough exercise for Juliet. They're more like a warm-up. She needs to get a chance to run a bunch of miles regularly. Otherwise she'll get bored and restless. That's when things get chewed on and broken. Always remember that idle paws are the devil's playthings! Someday you'll need to think about getting her another dog to play with. Then she could get some of that exercise in the back yard, but in the long term you and she will have a lot more fun if you can use her exercise as quality time for the three of you."

Juliet barked once to let Bruce and us know she was listening to all of this advice and agreeing with it. "With a mature adult dog like Juliet, there's no such thing as too much exercise or too much running. Her body is designed to keep going and going, just like the Energizer Bunny. For future reference you need to be careful not to run puppies the same way. Until the growth plates in the legs are closed, their bones are still too soft for constant impact. You can't take puppies on multi-mile runs without risking serious orthopedic issues. Once the growth plates seal and the bones harden, somewhere around 18 months of age for this breed, they're ready to become your running mate. You guys are joggers. Figure that Juliet can get some of the exercise she needs by running with you, especially once you're confident she'll obey you enough to let her run around without a leash."

Bruce leaned over to scratch Juliet's ears. She licked his hand and purred contentedly. "When you get a dog from a serious breeder like Sherry, who shows her dogs in conformation competitions, you should be able to assume that a lot of money was already invested in your pet. It would start with health screening on their sire and dam before she bred them. This would include X-rays of the hips and elbows for the Orthopedic Foundation for Animals to certify that their puppies will likely be structurally sound. I checked Juliet's paperwork and both of her parents passed that particular test, as did Juliet herself. Juliet and her parents also had cardiac, thyroid, and eye exams done by specialists, as well as genetic tests for specific skin and eye diseases. It cost a lot of money to run those tests, but that's what you have to do if you want to breed dogs that reliably throw sound and healthy puppies. After all that investment, you can bet that Sherry raised Juliet with the same amount of concern for her physical and mental well-being, including getting lots of exercise."

Since Bruce was on hand to watch Robert, Suzanne and I took advantage of the freedom to get back into our own former, pre-Robert, exercise routine of jogging. We had promised each other to get back into our regular exercise routines together. This was the right time to do it. But now it was the three of us. Our new dog came fully trained and physically ready to go jogging. We planned our runs to include Juliet in our exercise routine whenever possible. The trick was to find places where she could be off lead to run with us. There was no way she could get her needs filled on a leash trotting at our speed and distance. Most of the time we took her to the nearby hills and canyons where we could run on a well maintained trail, while she could run around to her heart's content in the surrounding fenced off area of woods and grassy meadows.

I loved watching her bound over fallen logs and stretch herself out as she quite literally flew through the meadows and leaped over fallen branches. It looked as if her feet never actually made contact with the ground and she might soar after the birds during her endless pursuit of anything that flew. The basic equation seemed to be she covered 3-4 times the distances we did on these runs at 3-4 times the speed. If we ran a mile, she ran four miles. It didn't matter how fast we tried to run. She had no trouble lapping us, even if she bounded off exploring wherever the whim took her.

Perhaps because she was so well exercised, Juliet didn't have a "hyper" personality. It was more like she had an on-off switch. In the field she loved nothing more than to run as fast as she could, as far as she could. We could see pure joy in her bounding gait and flat out speed. The occasional opportunity to chase down a squirrel until it climbed a tree brought bliss to our beautiful bitch. At home, she was a totally different dog. If someone came to the door she'd bark an alert. The rest of the time she would lie curled up on one of the two couches designated as our 'shared' space. Juliet was most content when her body was planted firmly in contact with Suzanne, Bruce, or me. Part of her regular ritual was to crawl into Suzanne's lap at night in front of the TV, when Suzanne was reading papers in journals or grading exams. She would curl up into a compact ball and lay in Suzanne's lap gently snoring or just hanging out there, until it was time for bed. At night, she slept in her crate, which was kept in Bruce's room as per his request. That way he could let her out in the mornings without waking up Robert.

Juliet was first and foremost Bruce's dog. She looked to him for training, guidance, breakfast, and dinner. But she loved Suzanne, who was her personal human, in a very special way. She also loved Robert, who she would protect to the death, as she would have loved her own puppy. I was a trusted friend to play with or hang out with, but clearly not on the list of those she was responsible to protect. To Juliet, if you were a human, any human, you deserved a kiss or three. She was most generous with her doggy kisses, a lick of the nose or face with her tongue. If you were a human, you deserved a kiss or three. It took her about a second or two to size up a visitor or someone we'd meet on the street. Most were offered kisses. But she had an almost perfect sense of who was not a dog lover or was afraid of dogs, and these folks got more restrained greetings.

One Sunday morning, the three of us were more than ready to go for a run where we could see some new scenery, preferably grass and trees in their less formally gardened state. Suzanne and I changed into running gear and Suzanne drove east on Santa Monica Boulevard to North Highland Avenue to Franklin Avenue to Canyon Drive to Lake Hollywood Park. We hit practically all the traffic lights, so it only took us about twenty minutes to drive the eight miles from our house to the lake.

We got out of the car with Juliet. "I don't remember having been here before. Where are we?" I asked.

Suzanne lapsed briefly into professor mode. "You've been here with me once before, a long time ago, just about when we moved in together. But we drove here a different way this time, so I'm sure everything looks new. This lake and park is a fenced-off reservoir maintained by the City of Los Angeles. There's a nice path running along the fence, about a four-mile run around the perimeter of the lake. It's far enough off the usual roads, even people who live in the same zip code don't know about it," she replied.

I hadn't ever seen Juliet turned loose in such a large area before. "Do you think it's safe to let Juliet run off lead in a place this big? Until now we've been letting her run in a large overgrown dog park where her boundaries were defined by the fences, but here she can get pretty far out of our sight. Will she come back when we call her?"

Suzanne smiled proudly. "Bruce and I have been working on her off-leash recall, Roger. Apparently Sherry had her well trained to come back to her if she called Juliet when she wasn't on a leash. We've managed to transfer that behavior to Bruce and me. She might even respond if you call her. We'll have to experiment a little bit today and see whether she'll come back to your call, or whether she'll be more comfortable responding just to me."

Suzanne and I ran side by side, comfortable maintaining the same relaxed pace for most of the time, about ten minute miles. Our four-mile run took only a little longer than the total time we needed to drive here and back to home. Meanwhile, Juliet covered about 15 miles, running ahead of us, alongside of us, and into and out of the woods on either side of us. She chased a few squirrels, pointed a few birds then chased them, and even pointed a tree or two she mistook for something more interesting. For the humans, much of the time we were running there was a spectacular view of the famous Hollywood sign on top of the hill. For Juliet there were the sights and smells of nature. She pointed and chased the birds that flew by or stood still long enough to find and point, she dug for rodents, and the occasional dogs we passed by each became another opportunity to race or play "catch me" with. Plus, for the record, she came back to me when I called her name as comfortably as she responded to Suzanne, thanks to Bruce's superb training.

We had come to recognize that German Shorthaired Pointers are vastly underrated athletes. Even though they are mid-sized dogs made of solid bone and muscle, they are incredibly fast runners, especially the ones that are structurally well put together, like the successful show dogs. Juliet weighed about 55 pounds when in good condition, and she had to be in excellent physical condition to win in the show ring. The breed has an enormous amount of chest for the size of the dog, which translates to an incredible level of cardiovascular endurance, allowing them to run long distances. Inside those relatively huge chests are big lungs and a big heart, to get oxygen to muscles efficiently by matching ventilation to perfusion. When Juliet finished running 15 miles at an average pace of roughly 15 miles per hour she wasn't even breathing hard. She would sleep well that night, but she would happily run 15 more miles if we let her.

Today, she managed to surprise us again. As we jogged back towards our car near the end of our run, we met another couple running in the same direction accompanied by a neutered male greyhound they had rescued from a local animal shelter. They told us that six months ago he had been a racing animal at a nearby dog track in Orange County. The two dogs sniffed one another for a bit and started up a game of chase-me. Over an improvised race course of several hundred yards of straightaway Juliet was able to keep up with the former racing dog. This was the first time we had ever seen her stretching out into a full gallop, with all four legs off the ground at some point in each stride. She could quite literally fly. In flight her ears flapped out like a jackrabbit's. It wasn't clear whether they acted as stabilizers or steering devices, but they must have been doing something. It was an amazing sight, one well worth seeing. The greyhound set up an alternative racecourse with multiple curves in the pattern. He was a little bit bigger than Juliet, about 65-70 pounds and taller, but was built differently. With his arched loin and exaggerated rear angulation he was built to corner at high speeds and could take the curves faster, so he easily won the race over the curved track. They seemed to be happy chasing each other and played some more without competition until the other couple had to go.

After a short walk to cool off, enjoy the park scenery, and to allow Juliet to calm down a bit we drove home with a much more relaxed dog and two much more relaxed humans. We spent most of the afternoon catching up on our Robert time and checking off the list of chores around the house. Shortly after dinner the phone rang.

Bruce picked up the phone in the middle of its third ring. "Bowman residence. Who would you like to speak to?"

A few seconds later he gestured in my direction that the call was for me as he replied, "He'll be right with you, sir." Bruce handed me the phone as he told me it was Stanley Morgan on the other end of the line.

"Hello, Mr. Morgan. What can I do for you this evening?"

"I'm in town for a meeting that finished earlier than I expected and suddenly have a couple of hours free in my schedule. I'll be flying back to New York first thing tomorrow morning. Are you free to meet me for a drink in the next hour or so?"

I tried not to let the surprise show in my voice. "Sure. Where are you staying?"

"I'm at the Beverly Hilton Hotel. That shouldn't be too far from your house."

Actually, it was about a 5-minute drive away. "I'll meet you there in 15 minutes if that fits your schedule."

"Perfect," he replied. "I'll meet you in the Lobby Bar."

I drove over, parked, and walked into the lobby of the most famous hotel in Los Angeles. Morgan waved to me from a table in the bar area. Less than a minute later we were sitting at the table ordering drinks---a martini for Morgan and an Indian Pale Ale from a well-known Northern Californian microbrewery for me.

While we waited for our drinks Morgan made small talk about some of the celebrities and near-celebrities sitting at tables around us. The conversation halted as the waiter arrived with our drinks and served them. With our privacy restored, the discussion resumed. "I'm sorry to take you away from your family with no warning like this, but it seemed to be a good chance for us to get to know each other a little better and I didn't want to pass up the opportunity. I think there's a good possibility we can help each other out a little bit."

I sipped my ale and waited expectantly. Morgan drank a bit of his martini before continuing, "As I'm sure you figured out during your visit to New York, the AKC board doesn't always run by consensus. Harold Carswell has a majority to support him on any issue, because a majority of the group owes their jobs to him and is beholden to him. Those board members tend to rubber stamp any proposal he makes. So far, this seems to have worked out pretty well for all of us and for the AKC, so nobody is complaining too much about the status quo. But I have to admit I find myself disagreeing with his decisions every now and then. Of course I think his decision to hire you was exactly right for the AKC."

He sipped a bit of martini before continuing. "I got the feeling when I talked to you in New York City there's a lot more to you, both intellectually and ethically, than the others realize. Most of the gossip among the board members after you left seemed to be intimating you seemed harmless enough, not too bright, and therefore not likely to succeed. You obviously left an impression that didn't seem to threaten anyone. Maybe I'm prejudiced because you graduated from an excellent law school, but I think you and I want many of the same things. I suspect we could become friends, as well as colleagues, if we didn't live 3,000 miles across the country from each other. Anyway, I'd like to suggest if things seem not to go right in your relationship with the AKC, feel free to contact me directly and let me try to help."

He stopped and looked at me expectantly while he sipped his martini. It was obviously my turn to say something.

If there was anything I learned in law school and my short career as a patent attorney, it was to beware of lawyers bearing gifts and instead, assume everything they say isn't the truth, the whole truth, and nothing but the truth. I let my brain race over what I'd just heard, asking myself what angle Stanley Morgan might be playing here and stalled by pouring the remaining ale from bottle to glass. I finally settled for a safe and noncommittal answer to see where we were going with all of this. "There's no such thing as too many friends. Did you have anything in particular in mind that might happen for me to think about calling you?"

I obviously gave him the wrong answer as he visibly pulled back and said, "No, nothing in particular. Just keep this offer in mind as things play out, and feel free to call me anytime."

We chatted a while longer, but the mood had changed and nothing much was said. Finally, I stood to go. We shook hands and said our good-byes, and I drove home even more confused than I had felt driving to the hotel. The trip was spent mentally scratching my head, as I tried to figure out what this meeting had really been about. Obviously, Morgan had an agenda and equally obviously, he wanted something from me. What? I didn't have a clue. He could be a powerful ally if I needed one and trusted him, but at the moment I didn't need an ally and I certainly didn't trust him. I made a mental note to add the $10 ransom on my car for parking at the hotel to my expenses, and left it at that.

Chapter14.Our first family dog show

We left Los Angeles on Friday for the about 400-mile drive to San Francisco. Suzanne, Robert, Bruce and I fit quite comfortably up front, with Juliet in her crate in the back of the minivan. We stayed in two rooms at a local hotel in reasonable comfort and close proximity to the competition venue, a huge indoor dog show at the Cow Palace, on the peninsula just south of San Francisco overlooking the Bay. The Cow Palace had its origins in a highly successful livestock exposition at the 1915 Pan-Pacific International Exposition in The City. It fell into disrepair, but after The Great Depression fundraising efforts helped build the magnificent venue as a WPA project in the late 1930s. It finally reopened in 1941, just in time to see military service throughout World War II. Finally, in 1946 the venue was used as planned when it housed the Grand National Rodeo and the Grand National Livestock Show, both resounding successes. The following year it became a major sports arena and is still going strong hosting college basketball, minor league hockey, roller derby, The Ringling Bros. Barnum & Bailey Circus, rock concerts, rodeos, other popular events, and of course the annual dog show we were attending.

The huge building is laid out with seating for well over 15,000 spectators around a rectangular arena containing multiple show rings. Two attached buildings called North and South halls provide additional space for the benched part of the show. Six large halls to the east of the arena are filled with vendors selling all things doggy. A box office complex on the west end of the building controls access to the facility from its 4,000-car parking lot.

Everybody was in a competitive mood. I reminded Bruce and Suzanne about the most important reason why we were here, to act as if we were dog owners. We would watch Bruce handle Juliet in the competition as a "special" and cheer her on. Like the other owners and many dog show enthusiasts gathered for this event, we would be just another couple of owners here to support their favorite dog.

"Don't forget we're here under cover and are actors playing roles. The goal is to make it appear we're newbies who've been sucked into this ever-expanding money pit just like everyone else here. We're new to the scene and don't know much, but we've got plenty of money to back a dog at this level. All you understand, Suzanne, is that you're here to root for her to win as a "select" bitch today so she finishes her first level of Grand Championship and qualifies for the Eukanuba Invitational Show. If she does, we'll get to go to the second largest dog show in the USA later this year. And the more confused you are about everything else that's going on, the better. OK?"

"Sure," she nodded. "And I'm not sure I'm going to have to act a whole lot to seem confused!"

The San Francisco show was the first time the entire family would be there to watch Juliet in the show ring and Suzanne was appropriately excited. For Bruce and I, it was a most welcome change in our routine after leaving Suzanne and Robert in Los Angeles during the Stockton and Woodland shows. This family experience would help solidify my cover as a wealthy dog owner who could afford the pay to play world of Grand Champion dog show competition. Robert was a very, very accomplished babe magnet, especially if you think of grandmas as babes. His presence would likely catalyze some growth in our circle of dog show friends. It was also Juliet's (and Bruce's) first-ever benched show.

We were chatting with Sherry Wyne at a benching area in North Hall amid total, but organized, chaos as hundreds of dogs were receiving their final primping and preparation to be beautiful in the show ring. At this particular dog show, Sherry could celebrate her freedom from the responsibility of being the AKC representative. Today she was showing a class bitch of her own who just happened to be a Juliet half-sister, and was hoping her bitch could finish her regular championship.

Sherry was trimming the whiskers on her Shorthair and generally primping her dog. Doulla was really a lovely animal according to Bruce who, as befitted his new identity as a professional handler, already thoroughly understood canine conformation and the whole dog show scene. Sherry spoke loudly to enable anyone who might be listening to get the idea we were newbies to the show ring who only knew Sherry by virtue of leasing our show dog from her.

"You folks are new to dog shows and didn't know today's scheduled judge, Orval Shultz. He was the classic 'handler's judge', which means the winning dogs he picked were always the ones being shown in the ring by the most popular of the professional handlers. It didn't matter which dog was best when you showed under Orval, it just mattered who the handler was at the other end of the leash. That's where he got his nickname, 'Awful', and believe me, he deserved it."

Note that Sherry was using the past tense to refer to old "Awful". If there were such a thing as an appropriate end for a handler's judge, Orval ("Awful") Shultz achieved it at this now most memorable show at The Cow Palace. He was found lying on his back early that morning when the venue opened, with a show lead wound tightly around his neck, very dead. It was an ultrathin show lead typically used by handlers while showing a dog in the ring. The body was left on a bench in the area set aside for the Sporting Group, the dogs he was assigned to judge today. By the time we arrived at the show Orval's fate was the only topic of discussion. Yet, among the participants, the show was expected to go on. Dogs were groomed, trimmed, and primped while owners and handlers hastily removed, relocated, and rearranged all the dogs' equipment they had so carefully set up the night before, and waited for the rest of the crowd to arrive and the judging to proceed.

Total chaos reigned before the first dog could even step into a ring! There were a whole lot of early arrivals among the owners and handlers, many of whom had been parked overnight in their large RVs at the show venue's hook up space.

Suzanne played her role as a wealthy and somewhat confused new owner. "Does anybody have any idea who killed Mr. Shultz?" Suzanne asked Sherry.

Sherry continued trimming Doulla's whiskers with a barber's scissors while talking to us. "No, they don't. At least I haven't heard anything about it if they do. But whoever actually did it would win the big rosette and trophy as today's "Best in Show" if all of the breeders and dog owners got a vote. I gather they found another judge who was able to get here quickly enough for the Sporting Group competition to start on time, and the Shorthairs are scheduled to be the second breed up. We should all be heading over to the ring pretty soon."

Suzanne, Robert, and I walked over to the ring where Juliet was due to be shown. As Bruce had suggested, we stayed well back from the ring behind a few rows of spectators where Juliet wouldn't be distracted by seeing her new family. She had rapidly adopted us as her pack over the last two months, and would respond to seeing Suzanne or Robert at a dog show if she noticed them while she was in the ring. She was used to seeing Sherry and Bruce in the ring while being shown. They weren't a distraction any more, but I always watched from a distance.

Suzanne picked Robert up and set him on my shoulders so he could see over the people standing in front of us. Even though he was too young to understand what was going on, Suzanne believed in treating Robert like a small adult, so explained things to him while they were happening. "Oh, look, Robert. The judge is checking Juliet's teeth now. Do you think Bruce brushes them every morning?" This was followed a moment or two later by, "Can you see Bruce running with Juliet? She looks like she's having a lot of fun."

During the formal competition, a lot of things were happening in the show ring that didn't directly involve the dogs we knew. Suzanne and I took the opportunity to listen in on some ongoing conversations between owners, handlers, and spectators gathered nearby. OK, so we eavesdropped, but that didn't make the conversations any less funny to listen to. Most of the discussions revolved around the dogs in the ring and the judging. We watched separate classes for male and female puppies 6-9 months old and 9-12 months of age; 12-18 months old; amateur owner-handler class; Bred by exhibitor; American-bred; and open classes. Other than the open classes, which any dog could be entered into, some of the more arcane classes had only 1 or 2 entries and the judging moved quite rapidly. The 9-12 month puppy and open classes had larger entries and took longer. The judge looked carefully at every puppy and dog shown in every class, both stacked and moving, so the entire process took quite a while. Winners Dog and Winners Bitch then joined all of the specials for the Best of Breed competition.

Neither of the dogs we were most interested in was competing during the earlier stages of the formal competition. Suzanne overheard a conversation she urged me with a sharp poke of her elbow to listen to as well. A couple of owners had their dogs entered in the 9-12 month puppy class, which had ten males competing. The judge had made her preliminary decisions and moved the dogs around, putting her first four picks at the front of the group, to lead them in a large moving circle around the ring. Apparently, neither of the women next to us owned one of the favored four dogs. The two women were discussing what was wrong with the four in front and why the judge was clearly blind as to what was important for proper sporting dog conformation. One of the top picks lacked proper hind-end angulation, according to our local experts, while another didn't have enough "chest". The leading, soon to be winning, dog in this class had a "bitchy head". And the fourth dog didn't have enough reach with his front legs while trotting.

Suzanne listened to the diatribes with mild amazement and strong irritation. "This is worse than a couple of mothers at a beauty contest making excuses for why their children are losing. It's never the DNA, always the judge's fault. The winners can't just be better. They have be torn down so it's somebody else's fault when their baby loses.

"I thought when we came here this was supposed to be a dog show. Now I'm listening to a couple of catty people making catty remarks about everybody else's winning dogs. If this is the norm, I understand a whole lot better why the AKC is giving you a lot of their money to make sure that all of the losers' bitching about 'we was robbed' by the judge doesn't have any basis in fact."

As the day progressed, the pattern became clear. All of the cattiness and complaining was not just in this ring at this time, but was typical of many of the owners' and handlers' discussions during and after the show. One of the many lessons we learned this day was that we were truly in Lake Woebegone, where in the eyes of much of the audience all of the dogs and bitches were above average and all of the judges weren't.

Finally we got to the important part of the GSP competition, at least important from our point of view. From his perch well above the crowd Robert watched as Sherry's young bitch Doulla came out of the "open" class as the winner. She would go on to Best of Winners in the breed competition to compete with Juliet and an excellent Specials class. Thanks to Bruce's skilled handling and her own innate quality and exuberant personality Juliet won Best of Breed, which also earned her 5 more points towards her "Grand Champion" title. That meant we not only had to stay around for the benched part of the show, but we'd also get to see Juliet compete later in the day against all of the other winners from the various breeds that make up the Sporting Group to determine which dog would finally compete for the coveted Best in Show title. As a shorthaired rather than heavily coated breed, Juliet had a less than excellent chance to win at the next level, but it was an honor to get that far in the competition, especially in a show as large as this one.

After the breed competition in the ring was completed, we stayed around to congratulate Sherry on going Best of Winners with Doulla and getting the number of points needed for her to now officially become Champion California Vintage Wyne. We watched the professional photographer take the stock photo of the winning bitch, her owner-handler, and the judge for the competition. Bruce and Juliet also got their picture taken with the same judge to commemorate this important win for Juliet.

Sherry told us she hadn't expected to finish today under Orval Krause, and this was a most pleasant surprise for her. That seemingly casual comment earned a raised eyebrow from Suzanne. I made a mental note about Sherry having the homicide detective's holy trinity of motive, means, and opportunity. After the photo session, Suzanne, Robert, and I headed back to the benching area for the rest of the ritual at a benched dog show. Bruce and Juliet had already returned to Juliet's designated bench area and were waiting for us there.

Bruce, who was very far out of the closet and made absolutely no attempt to hide his sexual proclivities, was surrounded by a half-dozen subtly stated to flamboyantly gay males of various ages. Thanks to the Cow Palace's proximity to San Francisco, Bruce was discovered today by a pod of potential groupies, just like a rock star. As they wandered through the benched area, they were probably drawn as much to the handler as to the dog at this particular show.

Suzanne talked directly to Robert, who gurgled a response to show he was listening. "A benched show is just like a regular dog show as far as the judging part in the ring. The benched part is an additional requirement. The dogs are kept on or around a specific bench position they've been assigned from

10 AM till 4 PM except for the hour or so of scheduled ring time. Anyone at the show can come around, look at the dog a lot more closely, and ask questions of the breeder, handler, or owner, who's expected to be here all of that time. It's a good way for the spectators to see a lot of different breeds close up and decide which is the right breed for them. Now it's your job, Robert, to let everyone see how wonderful Juliet is with babies."

Like most smart, successful, and experienced show dogs, Juliet could pretty much stack herself. Sherry, and now Bruce, had trained her well. She stacked herself when people came by the benched area to look more closely at her than they could when she was in the ring or to ask Bruce questions about her conformation, temperament, and breeding. Some of these people asking all of the questions were trying to decide what kind of dog they wanted to buy for their own families, so Bruce had to field questions like: "How long do they live?" "Are there health issues with this breed?" "How are they with kids?" "Can show dogs also be used to hunt?"

As the noon hour approached, all of the activity in the rings came to a halt as the judges took lunch breaks between their various breed assignments. At the same time, some very official looking gentlemen and ladies, accompanied by a hovering entourage, came by our benching area. Someone asked if anybody could point out an owner named Roger Bowman. I stepped forward and introduced myself to the distinguished looking man wearing an expensive suit in the front of the entourage with an oversized belly spilling over his belt. It was significant, perhaps, that he was also wearing suspenders. He in turn introduced himself as Colonel Kenneth Carstairs, President of the Golden Gate Kennel Club sponsoring this show. He introduced several of his companions in the entourage, whose names I promptly forgot. They were the officers of the same local dog club that Col. Carstairs presided over and all looked and acted more or less alike.

Somehow the Colonel was able to act and sound pompous even while asking for my help. "We have a huge problem here today. As a dog owner, we know you will be happy to help us out. You must have heard by now we had an unfortunate incident occur at this event. The police are asking everybody questions. I'm personally asking each of the dog owners here to cooperate with the police investigation however they ask you to do so. Will you please do so?"

I looked over to Suzanne. "What do you think about this, Suzanne? Should we cooperate here? This could give help us with that other matter we're interested in."

Suzanne nodded affirmatively, I said yes, and Carstairs nodded at both of us, offering a limp handshake. Then, he and the entourage wandered off to do whatever else dog club officers do at a large dog show featuring a dead judge.

I took Bruce aside. "Hey Bruce, I assume the professional handlers gossip among themselves. For the rest of today, when you don't have to be handling Juliet I'd like you to mingle with the other handlers and listen to what they say about this murder. Do they suspect any of the handlers or the owners? Talk with as many of them as you can."

Bruce smiled and looked like he was going to have a lot more fun as a detective than he was standing beside his beloved Juliet answering lots of bizarre questions. "They certainly do gossip. I'll see what I can find out."

I turned back to my wife. "Suzanne, I have a hunch that this killing is somehow closely tied in with my job with the AKC. We need to spend some time investigating it. I'd like you to schmooze with the dog owners. Take Robert with you to break the ice. See what they have to say about the killing and whether they have any favorite suspects. I'll chat with the show judges and club members. Let's reconnect in an hour or two here at Juliet's bench and compare notes. And Suzanne, can you and

Robert handle Juliet without Bruce's help? That would give him a free hour without doggy care between now and the Group competition to gossip with the handlers."

Suzanne nodded her agreement. She had always enjoyed being an active participant in our detective team and I could see her perking up. "Sure. Can I tell Sherry what we're trying to do? She knows all of the owners in the sporting dog breeds and can make talking to a lot of strangers a whole lot easier for me. The original benching area for sporting breeds has a large chunk roped off as a crime scene. Now we're pretty scattered as a breed into two different buildings and can use all of the help we can get with the sporting dog fanciers coming by here, as well as all the ghouls and lookie-loos who want to see where the body was found. Maybe Sherry can ask the other Shorthair owners benched near Juliet to keep an eye on her while we wander around and mix with the other owners."

I thought this question over for a bit. Sherry was an ally who was supposed to be here to help our investigation. But, technically at least, she was also a suspect in a murder case. I decided to trust my gut on this one, at least for now. "Getting Sherry's help is probably a good idea, but ask her not to tell any of the others what you're doing and don't tell her any more than you have to about our plans."

Chapter15.Detecting at a dog show

We broke up to go our separate ways. I went back to the roped-off crime scene in the former benching area to introduce myself to the cop in charge ---good etiquette in this situation. It's also required by the licensure regulations if you are a private detective from a different part of the state who might be getting involved in a police case. The detective in charge was pointed out to me as Inspector Callahan (Steven not Dirty Harry). The Inspector looked clean, so his not being named Harry seemed appropriate. He was about my age, experienced enough to know what to do at a crime scene, and seemed to have the situation under control. I introduced myself and explained how the AKC had hired me for an undercover job that might overlap his murder investigation.

Inspector Callahan, who was about my size, straightened to his full height and assuming his most intimidating manner, introduced himself by flashing his badge and I.D., and ignoring my outstretched hand. His first question was, "Do you think you can stay out of our way? If you can't, I can have your license revoked."

This was, unfortunately, a typical and all-too familiar attitude among regular police officers towards private detectives, and obviously called for a response. "I was a homicide cop in L.A. once upon a time. Before that I went to law school at UCLA and got my degree before I ever became a cop and a P.I. We can co-operate here or I can do my own thing. That's your choice. If you want to invent laws to justify being a jerk, be my guest. I'm not impressed and you can't intimidate me. If you want me to share whatever I find with you, let's start over. I'm Roger Bowman. I'm a P.I. from Los Angeles. The American Kennel Club, which charters the local dog club and sponsors shows like this one, hired me to conduct an undercover investigation to try to find out whether anything illegal or unethical is going on with the dog shows this season. I am voluntarily sharing that information with you because it's my responsibility to do so and because I think we have the same goals here with respect to solving this murder."

This time he offered his hand for a shake. I could hear the faint remains of a regional accent from back east, probably New York, in his speech. "I'm Steven Callahan, Roger, and I'm glad to meet you. Sorry for acting like a jerk. It's been a long morning already. I can use all the help I can get on this case. Go ahead and do your thing; I assume you know the dos and don'ts as far as staying out of our way while we do our thing here at the crime scene. I'd appreciate hearing anything you find out about this case as soon as you get the information. Just call me at either of the numbers on my card," he said, handing me his business card with his cell and office phone numbers on it.

We shook hands again and I wandered off to find Col. Carstairs. I wanted access to the judges and needed somebody in authority to arrange for me to ask them some questions. I also wanted to get their take on the murder. I found the Colonel and his entourage in a VIP suite where the police had parked them pending their interviews. The VIP suite was a large partitioned-off meeting room on the first floor on the west side of the arena, set up with comfortable chairs, a wet bar, and a table of bread, salads, and cold cuts to make into do-it-yourself lunches or snacks as desired. The walls were bare and the room had an aura of temporariness about it. Now came the tricky part; I needed an excuse to get local club sponsorship to introduce me to the judges while I continued to be just another dog owner to maintain my cover story. That meant I couldn't use my P.I. license to open those doors. I decided to try playing a different card.

"Hello again, Colonel Carstairs. I wonder if you could help me here." I greeted him.

He stood up and offered a weak smile. "Mr. Bowman. I didn't expect to see you so soon again. I'm always glad to help a dog owner," he replied insincerely. "What can I do to be of assistance to you?"

"I'd like you to take me to wherever the judges are being kept and instruct them to talk to me."

He looked like he had just tasted something bitter. "Why would I want to do that?"

I smiled and tried to look dishonest. "Because I'm a lawyer and the Club might appreciate the results if any of the surviving judges who decide to lawyer up retain a friend of the dog show circuit."

He thought this through for the better part of a minute before he could make a decision. "Hmmm, that makes sense to me. OK, I'll take you there." Carstairs led me to another, smaller, VIP suite upstairs above the arena where the judges were sequestered between events, protected from inappropriate contact with the spectators and owners. Things were pretty complicated, because the police were also interviewing the judges one-by-one. Judges were coming and going as their assignments to rings were called or as the police called their names for interviews. Meanwhile, the between-event and between-interrogation judges were sequestered in this crummy VIP suite to keep them away from spectators, owners, dogs, would-be killers, and other dog show riff-raff.

Carstairs knocked firmly on the door, which was opened by a tall middle-aged lady, wearing a grey business suit, with glasses and gray hair pulled back in a bun. She looked like, and almost certainly was, one of the judges. The small judges' VIP suite was a much less comfortable room than the club officials had been given in the large show venue. There weren't any luxuries there, either. This VIP room had less comfortable chairs, no bar, and a much more modest table of deli-lunch ingredients for the hungry do-it-yourselfer. Bare walls, no rugs on the floor, and a sense of being temporary gave this room a very low score for ambiance.

She looked at me, then at the Colonel. "What can we do for you now, Colonel Carstairs?"

The colonel hemmed and hawed a bit, then came out with an intriguing mixture of truth, fiction, and self-serving baloney. "This is one of our newer owner-breeders, Roger Bowman, Mrs. McGyver. He's also an attorney retained by the club during the police investigation, to make sure all of our interests are being protected. The club feels an obligation to our judges, so Mr. Bowman can offer any or all of you free legal advice at our expense, if you think you may need it. In return for this, we hoped you could answer his questions regarding the events that occurred before he arrived here for today's show."

Marlene McGyver looked at me for a moment before replying to Carstairs. "He's certainly cute enough to be worth my time. You can leave him here while we chat." The other judges nodded their assent as Carstairs left us to return downstairs and continue being important.

"OK, Roger," she continued. "We all know that pompous blowhard has only one person's interests in mind, and that person is himself. But you really are kind of cute. Can I assume that you really are a lawyer? What would you like to ask us?"

I tried as hard as I could to look sincere. "Yes, I really am a lawyer. I'd like to know two things----first, did any of you see or hear anything out of the ordinary today? And second, I'd like to know how the whole judging selection process works for these dog shows. Is there a core group of regular judges at most of the shows, or do you all get your assignments at random? That is, would anyone have known that Orval Shultz was judging today's sporting group dogs here before the programs came out? How far in advance of this show did they publish the names of the judges? Were any substitutions made after the program was published?"

"That's more than two things," began Marlene as she settled her tall frame into an uncomfortable looking metal folding chair, "but we'll try to answer your questions. I for one didn't see or hear anything unusual. That was the first question the police asked me after my name and address. How about everyone else?"

One by one they nodded no. That added up to a dozen nods agreeing with Mrs. McGyver. I asked everyone where they were from---five from California, one from Woodland, but that meant Woodland, Washington, and the rest were from New York, Florida, Kansas, Nevada, Oregon, and South Carolina.

Mrs. McGyver continued, "There's no core group; any of us can only judge shows in the same area once every few months, to prevent any judge from getting too close to the clubs or the owners. The judges are selected many months in advance. Some of the all-breed judges actually sign contracts the better part of a year in advance. The programs are published before the entries close, so owners can choose to enter a show based on whether or not they think the judge will like their dog. Many of the judges work in this area a few times a year. After a couple of years, most owners think they know what almost all of the different judges are looking for in the show ring. Are all of you the original selections or were there any substitutions?"

Two hands went up. A middle-aged woman from nearby Santa Rosa, about an hour north of San Francisco, spoke up. "I'm a breeder and only judge infrequently at dog shows. I was called in to judge working breeds a couple of weeks ago. They told me the original judge was from Guadalajara, Mexico and couldn't make it at the last minute because he had visa problems."

A second middle-aged woman from Milpitas, southeast of San Francisco in the bay area, also chimed in. "I'm a breeder too, and also judge pretty infrequently. I only accept assignments a short distance away from my family. They called me a couple of weeks ago to judge some of the hounds and miscellaneous breeds. They gave me almost exactly the same story they told my colleague," pointing to the woman from Santa Rosa, "that the original judge was from Mazatlan, Mexico and couldn't make it at the last minute because he had visa problems."

"Does anyone else have anything to add?" asked Mrs. McGyver. Nobody replied.

"I think that's it then, Mr. Bowman. I hope this was helpful to you even though I don't see how it could have been."

I thanked Marlene and the other judges and walked back to Juliet's designated bench area.

Suzanne and Bruce were already there, waiting for me. Robert was taking a nap peacefully in his baby carriage. Several people stopped as they walked by to ask whether he was "benched" or not in that configuration. Juliet was on display on her bench, drawing attention from quite a few passers-by, which in turn kept Bruce pretty busy.

We compared notes from our various groups. Bruce had spent enough time with the handlers to come away with the impression there weren't any new facts to share, although there were a lot of opinions and gossip. The general consensus among the handlers was a pissed-off owner with a losing dog from a previous show had evened the score with old "Awful". A few of the handlers that "Awful" favored would miss him, but the handler group as a whole didn't seem to care too much about his sudden demise. However, it was making the entire show a lot more interesting for them.

Suzanne had liked the owners she'd met, mainly from the sporting group, whose dogs were benched near Juliet's assigned spot. Several had wandered over to meet Juliet's new owners.

Some of them had already met Bruce and me at the Woodland show and greeted Suzanne and Robert as if they were old friends. Suzanne was mostly struck by how they all seemed to be warm and generous people, trying hard to make her, a newcomer, feel at home in the dog show world. Unless they also owned German Shorthaired Pointers, in which case they were competitive, critical, and generally catty and cantankerous. One older woman with a GSP, who was a good eight inches shorter than Suzanne, actually elbowed her out of the way as she walked by.

The consensus of opinion among the small set of owners Suzanne had talked to was that "Awful" had died in a random act of violence. A popular theory was it might have been a crazed drug addict committing a robbery to feed their habit. Generally, the owners assured Suzanne the murder was totally unrelated to the victim's status as a judge in a prestigious dog show.

I repeated what I had learned from the judges and told Suzanne and Bruce we were now on the good side of the local law enforcement agency.

The rest of the day was more of the same both in terms of showing our new dog to the local fans who walked by and gossiping with our various cohorts of dog show personnel. I spent some time walking Robert around in his carriage. He was quite a babe magnet, but all of the babes were the age of my mother or grandmother. Still, it was fun and something I didn't do enough when I was home and busy. Juliet eventually returned to the ring to compete in the Sporting dog group. The judge took a long look at her, which Bruce later explained meant that he liked her. She made the cut into the top eight in the group, which the judge selected by pointing to the individual dogs, who were lined up separately in the center of the ring while the other dogs stepped back out of the way. Sherry was getting very excited by this time, but Juliet didn't place and her day in the show ring was over.

The police detective in charge of the murder case, Stephen Callahan, came by the ring to congratulate Juliet and ask if I had learned any more about the murder during the day. I told him everything Bruce, Suzanne, and I had learned that could be useful to him, which didn't take long.

He handed me a folded sheaf of papers. "I checked you out with a friend of mine on the LAPD. He told me I really lucked out if I can get to work with you on this case. Here's a little light reading for you when you get a chance. It's some background material on the murder victim and the preliminary forensics I can share. Look it over and keep talking to people. Something may ring a bell with you. Here's another copy of my card. Call me anytime you see or hear anything that might be useful. Quite frankly, we haven't a clue who did it and I have a bad feeling about whether this one is going to be solved."

We said our good-byes while I put the pages in my pocket for future study when things quieted down.

Sunday was more of the same, except no new dead bodies. Juliet was awarded 3 points as a Select Bitch, but "Best of Breed" went to Ingrid Schleck's dog Max and "Best Opposite Sex" went to one of the other specials competing. Sherry's bitch Doulla didn't win anything, but she looked good in the ring to us. We chatted some more with owners and handlers, as well as with people who stopped by our bench area. Many of these people had just come to the show for the day. Often they knew little about dogs and were here trying to figure out which breed they wanted to buy for themselves as a pet. We got lots of questions about temperament and how the GSP was around little children (excellent) or babies (perfect). Only one event marred the day.

Just after lunch we were all standing in Juliet's benched area trying to decide when we could leave. A 20-something year old man wearing a gray Tee-shirt labeled Clarkson Florists on the front and "Our Business is Blooming" on the back, delivered a bunch of flowers (red roses and blue violets) to Suzanne. It was a replay of the first flower delivery in Beverly Hills. I grabbed him, slipped him a $10 tip, and asked who had sent the flowers. The order had been made over the Internet and the delivery guy had no idea who the person that had sent them was, or even where the order had originated. He had little to add except the florist had been given detailed instructions about how to find Suzanne in the chaos of this huge venue---the benching area where Juliet would be. Obviously, we were dealing with a stalker who understood the dog show scene. It was yet another piece of evidence that Suzanne had picked him up during our dinner with the AKC executives.

There was a card embedded in the floral arrangement with a verse clearly written with fancy calligraphy software on a laser printer. The poem read:

Roses are red
Violets are blue
There's a cold dark place
Just waiting for you

From your biggest fan,
Suzanne.

Nasty stuff, however you interpreted it. I called Vincent on his cell phone at home to get him started trying to trace the flower order, but wasn't too hopeful.

Suzanne was less upset and much angrier than I expected. "This is starting to very seriously piss me off," was her comment. "I think it's time we did something about my twisted admirer. We can discuss what, and who, during our drive back."

Shortly after this episode everyone said their good-byes and started home. We touched base with Sherry just before we left. While she didn't agree with the judge's picks in GSPs at this show, nothing looked or felt terribly wrong with the dogs the judges did pick during the two-day show. Consistent with the prevailing opinion of the other owners, Sherry ascribed the murder to a random act of violence and didn't think it was related to our job with the AKC judging issues.

We were home in Los Angeles before midnight, all agreeing that something had to be done about Suzanne's flower sender. Unfortunately, nobody had any good ideas what or to whom.

My bedtime reading consisted of the papers Detective Callahan gave me at the show. There were a couple of pages written in police jargon confirming the cause of Orval Krause's death as strangulation with a thin show lead and he'd died before eating breakfast. He'd been in reasonably good heath except for mild hardening of the arteries and recently treated gonorrhea. Several additional pages contained miscellaneous background material on the victim, obviously supplied by various law enforcement sources, which I read carefully.

Orval was born 60-odd years ago in the small town of Cloaca, Arkansas. When he was 5 years old, his family moved to a small border town on the Rio Grande River in West Texas named San Francisco, where he lived until he graduated from high school. He then moved to El Paso and remained there for the rest of his life, becoming a used car salesman shortly after arriving in El Paso and turning out to be very good at selling junk cars. Orval made a lot of money and progressed to owning several new and used car dealerships. The excess income led him into breeding and showing dogs as a hobby. His breed of choice in the heat of West Texas was the Doberman Pinscher, a short-haired breed. He had never been arrested or convicted of a crime, but there were several interesting paragraphs of gossip, innuendo, and "intelligence" regarding Orval's sources of wealth.

In dry, jargon littered "cop-ese", the report told me "Orval made too much money for the demographics of his car dealerships," "he travelled extensively in connection with his duties as an AKC judge," and "he is alleged to have had a lucrative market for his guard-dog bred Dobermans among drug cartel members and associates on both sides of the border." These entries were in the "hard data" part of the background material. There was also a section labeled "Speculations and Conclusions". The major assumption was Orval was dirty and involved in the drug business, either peripherally as a supplier of guard dogs to bad people or directly in some manner yet unknown.

I poked Suzanne in the ribs, provoking a grunt of acknowledgment. "You know what? Old Orval Krause was probably an awful person as well as an awful dog show judge."

The response was a mumbled "Go to sleep!"

Chapter16.Tempus fugit and we fidget: The second wave of dog shows

The next three months went by in a blur of travel and dog shows. Bruce and I hit six show weekends on the circuit over a span of twelve weeks. After a bit they seemed pretty much all the same---a long trip by car, a boring motel, the local county fairgrounds or a similar venue of comparable size. Most of the shows were larger events, with many more dogs entered, which would allow the winning dogs to score more points. Because of the AKC's concerns, we deliberately went to a couple of smaller shows as well. We rapidly discovered that most of the shows we would attend were in Northern California, a long way from Los Angeles,. The venues for the dog shows had to accommodate thousands of dogs and people so the county fairgrounds in California's Central Valley, the agricultural part of the state, were a relatively inexpensive place to hold these events. Quite simply, the rural areas of Fresno, Stockton, Woodland, Vallejo, and Sacramento not only had larger venues for the events, but also affordable food and lodging. The much higher population density in urbanized Southern California had pretty much used up its convenient space for large outdoor events. Except for the old-fashioned, even anachronistic, indoor facilities like the Cow Palace, the San Francisco Bay area also had too many people in too little space for hosting large dog shows.

Our first show after the Golden Gate in San Francisco was the Sun Maid Kennel Club of Fresno's All Breed competition, a smaller event hosted two weeks later. It was held at the Fresno County Fairgrounds, located on the aptly named South Chance Avenue in Fresno. As we would get used to, we drove north on Interstate 5 ("the 5" to Southern Californians, with its long, straight, exceedingly boring, well-maintained highway, 70 mph speed limit, de jure, and 80 mph speed limit, de facto) until the proper exit, and with gentle guidance by our GPS unit's calm voice were soon at the fairgrounds.

Fresno is the center of the raisin industry in the United States, so a "Sun Maid" Kennel Club sponsoring the show made a certain amount of sense. Several of the dog show circuit regulars who we had first met in Woodland had already parked their RVs and welcomed us warmly upon our arrival. We said our hellos to the Breeds, Schlecks, Todds, and the others. I assured Howard Breed that we had brought a few bottles of wine that actually had corks in them to share later this evening. Bruce picked up a couple of wins with Juliet, who went Best of Breed both days against a slightly less competitive cohort of bitches and dogs than we had seen at the Golden Gate Kennel Club show. We also had an interesting episode take place on Sunday.

After the breed judging was completed, Bruce led Juliet to the photo station set up by the club to get a photo taken of them with the Judge and the new rosette ribbon she had just won. As Bruce walked towards the platform, with its floral backdrop featuring the club's logo, a fat 40-something owner of one of the bitches Juliet had just beaten walked in front of Bruce and Juliet, deliberately inserting himself into Bruce's space. He looked like a high school lineman gone to seed. At about six feet tall he towered over Bruce and looked to be twice as wide. His nose had the broken capillaries of a serious drinker. There had probably been a lot of muscle on his arms and body in his youth but too many beers and not enough exercise had taken its toll. In a shrill but clearly pugnacious tone dripping with accents from the south and full of malice he challenged Bruce.

"Mah name is Billy-Bob, you little California fairy. Y'all don't belong here. If y'all don't want to regret today for the rest of youah lahf, y'all'd best go home and play with all the other little fairies."

Bruce tried to ignore the hateful behavior but the guy was drunk and wasn't going away without a fight. Bruce knew a fight on the grounds would get both of them expelled from the show and he'd be suspended from handling Juliet.

Juliet was less tolerant of drunks and fools than Bruce was. She moved closer to Bruce's side, making sure her flank was in full contact with his leg, bared her teeth with her head low and body rigid, and growled at the drunk. Her body language was saying loud and clear, "Get away from my human's space or I'll protect him, and attack you if I have to."

Bruce gave Juliet a correction in a soft voice. "Stand down Juliet. I appreciate your help but I don't need it. This isn't your fight."

Juliet looked lovingly at Bruce and crouched down by his side with her tail up and quivering. Her hind legs were tucked under her, ready to spring and obviously on the alert. Her body language was now saying, "I'll do whatever you want me to do. I'm here if you need my help."

Bruce's lack of a direct response to the bully and his calming influence on Juliet just made the fat drunk bolder, foolishly bolder. Billy-Bob took another step, even closer to Bruce. "What's the matter Twinkletoes? Ah y'all scared?"

He finally got a response from Bruce, who spoke in a well-modulated tone, but loud enough to be heard by all of the spectators gathered around the show ring. By now there were a lot of them. "In all fairness I should probably tell you I was a Navy SEAL and served two tours of duty in Iraq and Afghanistan. I don't want to fight you, but if I have to, I will. You won't be at all happy with the result. So, in the immortal words of my favorite actor Clint Eastwood in my favorite movie Dirty Harry, 'Do you feel lucky today? Go ahead, make my day!' But whatever you plan to do, please do it right now."

Apparently a modicum of sobriety remained and reason finally prevailed. Billy-Bob, deciding that discretion was the better part of valor, ungraciously muttered "some other time, Twinkletoes," and stalked away.

Several of the professional handlers and a few of the dog owners around the ring broke into spontaneous applause and gave Bruce a classic standing ovation. The professional photographer and the judge, who were waiting for Bruce and Juliet, joined in the applause.

The following weekend we had a break. It was a typical evening. We were all sharing the Family Room, just hanging out and relaxing. Suzanne and Robert were playing a lively game of construction and destruction with Robert's blocks. Suzanne built small houses and interesting piles. She worked as fast as she could, but couldn't keep up with his rapid demolition of whatever she built. Loud giggles and squeals punctuated Robert's ongoing orgy of destruction. I was watching TV, while Bruce was trying to fix a dysfunctional electric shaver and Juliet was napping on the floor alongside Bruce's chair. Amidst the chaos, relative peace and quiet reigned supreme. All of a sudden, with no warning of any sort, Juliet ran at full speed to one of the front windows and started barking loudly. She continued barking and jumped up on a chair to see outside.

Not only was the continuous barking extremely irritating, but I couldn't hear the TV over all the noise. "What's going on, Bruce? I thought you had her better trained than that!"

"I do. She's alerting us. That's exactly what she's supposed to do. Nobody's going to be able to sneak up on you, Robert, or Suzanne ever again. Wait a moment or two longer and you'll see."

On cue, the doorbell rang.

Suzanne received yet another floral gift, this time a plant with lots of pretty buds and flowers and another bit of poetry.

Violets are blue
Roses are red
It won't be long

until you're dead.

"He definitely doesn't seem to like me anymore," declared Suzanne. "We really have to do something about him."

"I'll take care of it," I promised. But I got sidetracked by the next round of dog shows and allowed it to slip from my mind.

The following weekend we were entered in one of the larger and more prestigious dog shows, sponsored by the Santa Clara Valley Kennel Club in San Jose, at the southern end of San Francisco Bay. Techies know the area as Silicon Valley, the center of the universe for computer makers, computer programmers, and American technological innovation. The show's conformation events are held inside big cavernous buildings, occurring simultaneously with obedience competitions on the grounds outside these buildings. It's a very busy venue during the time that the competitions are being held. The Sporting Dog breeds, including us, were competing in Pavilion Hall in the middle of the grounds. Toy Breeds were in Expo Hall to our east while the obedience competition was using all of the available space between the indoor venues. There was a big crowd with a lot of local spectators. The indoor rings were noisy enough to make some of the younger and less experienced dogs noticeably nervous. The veteran animals were used to the noise and crowding. It was just another day at the office for them. Juliet did well, earning a few more points and another rosette, while we learned a bit more about dog shows.

For the first time since we had started the circuit, Bruce was invited by potential clients to handle dogs in other breeds. He was beginning to be noticed as he continued to collect wins with Juliet week after week. "What should I do when someone asks me to handle their dog, Roger?"

That took only a few seconds to think through. "Take the commission and keep the extra money you make. The more people see you as an all-breed handler, the more it will help your cover story to be credible. We want to get to know as many of the regulars at these dog shows as we can. Getting a perspective from some of the other breed people about whether they think there are problems with the judging would be helpful."

Over the next few weekends Bruce built up his clientele and found himself busy all day with the four or five breeds he was now expected to show. He started working for over a dozen owners and became a popular participant in tailgate barbeques with several different groups of owners and handlers. He won a fair share of competitions and seemed to be well liked by everybody. I tagged along for a few of his parties, but tended to maximize my interactions with the sporting breed owners. Bruce got to know owners in the working, herding, toy, and hound groups. Everyone complained about the judging, which made sense if everyone's dog was so good it should always be the one selected as the best of breed, which seemed to be the prevailing theme in every group. Everybody wanted to win badly enough that it seemed they would do whatever it took to beat the other dogs, as long as it was fair and within the rules. For some, however, it seemed that the only limitation on what they'd do to win was that they wouldn't be caught if they cheated.

For a change we drove home from San Jose on State Highway 101, a high-speed older road that runs north and south along the valleys between the western coastal range and the Pacific Ocean parallel with I-5. The different scenery and occasional stretches along the ocean were a welcome variation in our routine. Bruce was snacking on some beef jerky and drinking a cup of coffee while he discussed his impressions of dog show life as seen by a professional handler.

He sipped some of his coffee before continuing. "There's a lot of excitement and all kinds of cash bonuses from some of the owners and sponsors when you win, but it's always your fault when you don't. I've watched owners giving thick envelopes to winning handlers on one day and cussing them out the next. Two of the owners hinted I could make a lot more money than you pay me by handling their dogs if I was available, and another one asked me flat out what it would take to make me work for her rather than you. The amateur handlers and the semi-professional owner-handlers who only show their own dogs are competitive at the class level, but the judges far too often tend to pick the dogs handled by professionals in the breed and group competitions."

Bruce bit off a chunk of the beef jerky, chewed it carefully, and swallowed. "The professionals all know each other very well since the same handlers see each other at every show. They make a living by handling a lot of dogs, the more the better. That means they have to be able to show a lot of different breeds if they want to make a good living doing this. Most of them are supportive of one another when they need help. I've watched handlers competing all out with one breed and talking trash at one another, then handling the other person's dog as well as they can when the first handler has to be in two places at once. You'd be surprised how often that happens if you have a lot of dogs to handle and more than one of them wins at the class level. But the pro handlers never seem to tank it; it's an unwritten rule that if you stand in for another handler, you do your best on his or her behalf."

He stopped to sip some more of his coffee. "It can get pretty boring spending your weekends in a bunch of small towns, with a dozen crated dogs for company, parked in an RV in a lot attached to the local county fairgrounds a few miles from downtown. There's a lot of drinking and RV sex going on in the evenings, mostly among the handlers and including some of the owners. There's also a surprisingly large supply of excellent street drugs and coke available all over the place. Somebody's making a lot of money from the recreational drug franchise at these shows."

I asked Bruce the obvious question. "If I wanted a snort or two of coke next week, who would I have to see to buy it?"

There was another pause to sip coffee while he thought about the correct answer. "I don't know yet. It's there, it's pervasive, but nobody's approached me. I may be too new for them to trust or I still may not be a full member of the club."

For the third weekend out of four, we had a dog show to go to. It would be almost a month before Juliet's next scheduled outing, a break we were all looking forward to. This show was sponsored by the Silver Bay Kennel Club of San Diego and held in Del Mar near the racetrack on the Pacific Ocean, just north of La Jolla. It was the second, and last, smaller dog show we entered. There would not be enough dogs or bitches to make it a major in the class entries for German Shorthaired Pointers, GSPs or Shorthairs as I was now calling them. But Sherry had explained to me, if your show dog was good enough to win Best of Breed and thereby compete with the other Sporting Dog Best of Breeds, there were more points possible to earn for placing high in the Group competition. This show was less than a two-hour drive from our house so I could commute both days. Bruce opted to stay overnight so he could explore San Diego with Juliet and a couple of friends he had made among the handlers. Because it was so close to home, Suzanne was planning to join us with Robert for one of the two days. She was becoming sophisticated enough to check the ring times for GSPs on her computer. For this weekend, it was later in the morning on Saturday, which meant she could sleep in before we had to start driving south.

The setting was beautiful---blue sky, the deep blue Pacific Ocean just to the west, and the best of California's coast as we drove south accompanied by moderate weekend traffic through Orange and San Diego Counties on I-405 and I-5. The GSP competition on Saturday left something to be desired. Best of winners went to a 10-month old puppy whose greatest distinction we could figure out was that he was owned by the local Club president. The same puppy went on to win best of Breed, which was outrageous when he was compared with Juliet. We could speculate that the judge, a Mexican National specially imported to judge this weekend's shows, had been wined and dined by the club and was returning the favor. Perhaps the wine was exactly the right vintage. This was our first experience of an egregiously unfair decision by a judge. It went into the notebook for my report to the AKC, but everyone knew this kind of reciprocal backscratching happened on occasion between invited judges who made a good bit of money from these dog show gigs and the local club leadership who decided which judges got the invitations. It certainly wasn't part of some major conspiracy to fix multiple major dog shows like we were looking for, but probably explained today's small entry in GSPs.

To Suzanne's credit, there weren't any catty remarks about the puppy, and to Bruce's credit, he just said, "There are good days and not so good days. Juliet did her best and showed well. That's all we can ask of her."

"I've got an idea," I said to Suzanne. "Let's get out of here and skip the Group competition. The winner might be a three-legged Chihuahua with the right connections and that would piss me off a whole lot more. Somebody told me about a place in Carlsbad that raises flowers all year round and has beautiful displays open to the public."

So we visited The Flower Fields at Carlsbad Ranch, where 50 acres of brilliant colors from multiple species of flowers, including Ranunculus and Freesia, bloom on a large hillside overlooking the Pacific Ocean. Robert was entranced by the explosion of color and pointed at one group of flowers after another. It turned out to be a nice day after all. It also turned out to be an interesting day in yet another unexpected way.

As we walked around with Robert we did a bit of people watching to complement our flower appreciation. Most of the visitors were locals, mainly retirees from San Diego and the local communities near Del Mar. But there was also a smattering of tourists like us, and even a few faces we recognized from the dog show. We were walking past a huge hill covered with red and yellow flowers in full bloom when Suzanne grabbed my arm and yanked me next to her.

In a quiet voice, so as not to be overheard, she said, "Look over there, by the trash cans at the top of the hill! Do you see the tall woman in the blue sweater and the tall Mexican gentleman dressed like a pimp?"

It was a succinct and excellent description. The tall man was looking totally out of place for Southern California in a three-piece suit and tie with polished shoes. I recognized the judge who had just dumped Juliet in favor of a 10-month old puppy in the earlier competition that day. Suzanne very quietly informed me, "The woman in the sweater is the President of the local dog club sponsoring the show, who owns the puppy that beat Juliet. That's an odd couple to be out looking at flowers this afternoon, wouldn't you say? But this place is well off the beaten track and the odds of anyone from the dog show world recognizing them here together must have been pretty high against. "

I pushed Robert's stroller back and forth to keep him happy and looked at Suzanne. "Do you know if there are any AKC rules about showing dogs if you're the sponsor of the show? There probably ought to be."

As usual, Suzanne surprised me with her depth of trivia knowledge. "Yes, I do know the answer to that. I looked it up on the Internet for some reason when we first got into this whole dog show scene. There isn't any particular AKC rule about this, and it's pretty common for the smaller clubs and the smaller shows to encourage turnout of the local dogs to get as many entries as possible into the competition. Several of the clubs, especially the larger ones, prohibit their members from showing their dogs at any specific show they are sponsoring, but it's OK to show the next day if another club is the sponsor. Hey, look at what they're doing now!"

The woman was handing the judge a thick envelope of about the right size and thickness to contain a substantial sum of money. It disappeared quickly into an inside breast pocket of the judge's suit.

I couldn't keep from smiling. "You know what? I think we just became real dog show owners. We're not only complaining about the judging but we're accusing the judge of taking a bribe and being a crook. Welcome to the answer to what's feeling wrong about the judging at this particular dog show."

The next day was another early afternoon ring time for the GSPs. One of the other handlers who lived in the area told Bruce about a local dog beach where Juliet could play with a bunch of local dogs and get some real exercise. We drove down to the Fairgrounds fairly early in the morning, at Bruce's request, to pick him and Juliet up for the short ride south on I-5 along the Pacific Coast. Between Del Mar and La Jolla we turned off at a bridge spanning a small creek bed and parked on the edge of the road near a railroad trestle. It was a short walk to a large sandy beach, long and quite wide at low tide, which was the case now. Despite the size of the beach it was pretty crowded near the parking area. There must have been more than fifty dogs and their families running around on the sandy beach and in the shallow water of the ocean itself, chasing balls, each other, and the myriad birds flying by. The birds got into the game, teasing the dogs by flying just out of reach and detouring over the deep water if a dog got too close.

Juliet joined the scrum of dogs chasing birds and one another. She ran as fast as she could in broad sweeps of about 500 meters in either direction from where we were, occasionally checking back with us to make sure Robert was OK. This was doggy heaven---plenty of birds to chase, other dogs to play catch me if you can, seawater to wade in and taste, plus the occasional dead and decomposing sea creature on the beach or sand dunes to roll around on to really share the smells. Her favorite game was to run into the water until it was about knee deep chasing a low-flying bird, then to run parallel to the beach staying in the knee-deep water until the bird swerved back to the shore. She was totally fearless when the occasional large wave nailed her. With webbed feet and GSP instincts, she was designed to be a strong swimmer and was confident in her abilities in the water. Robert discovered sand for the first time. He and Suzanne built all sorts of castles and sculptures for Juliet to knock down on her short visits back to us. The seawater is still pretty cold around this area, especially in the spring, so the sandy beach was as close to the ocean as we allowed Robert to play.

All good things come to an end and Juliet was spending more time with us and less running around when Bruce announced it was time to get back to work. As we drove back to the Fairgrounds with two sandy and dirty little children, one human and one canine, Suzanne asked whether Juliet could be cleaned up enough to be shown in less than an hour or two.

Bruce laughed. "One of the biggest benefits of a short-haired dog is you only need a hose and a little bit of elbow grease to be all set for competition. Coat care is not a big part of the preparation for the show ring with this breed. You can hunt her in the morning and show her in the afternoon. That's one of the reasons GSPs are so popular among owners who are looking for an all-purpose dog. It'll take me less than 20 minutes to bathe, dry, and primp her for the show, and you'll see that she cleans up real well. The real tricks in Shorthair coat care are the right nutrition and keeping her coat brushed out ahead of time, especially when she's shedding."

Sunday, a clean and sweet smelling Juliet again finished behind the puppy in the Best of Breed competition. While the judge was different, we presumed he enjoyed the same fine wine and gourmet dinner hosted by the local club, plus the fringe benefit package exchanged at some off-site tourist attraction. I learned a valuable lesson from this weekend. Nothing is certain, and bottom feeding in the small shows is not necessarily the road to easy points on the dog show circuit. Now I understood why most of the regulars chose to skip some of these smaller shows, unless they were already in the area for another event.

Chapter17.Suzanne's stalker

During our break after Fresno, San Jose, and Del Mar, we had a chance to take stock of what we'd learned during what I thought of as our intense orgy of dog shows. Juliet enjoyed the whole travel and dog show experience as long as we remembered to bring her favorite toys and bedding for her crate. She won points at several different shows, while at others she didn't even place among the top animals. Same bitch, same handler, usually the same dogs as opponents. The only difference was the judges. But, as we settled into the routine, I became much more sensitive to small deviations from the norm. We saw more deviations than we might have expected due to pure chance or flaky judges. In two of the three shows where judge's decisions in the GSP class seemed off to me, Sherry expressed concern with the results of the judging from a broader perspective of multiple breeds.

I was slowly but surely developing a theory to explain the deviations from normal that the AKC had hired me to investigate, which might also point towards the identity of the murderer who had killed Orval Krause. Officially, the police had kept the investigation open, but it was clear that they weren't going to solve "Awful's" murder in San Francisco. There weren't any clues and no witnesses had come forward over the two months since the killing at the Cow Palace.

The same lack of progress haunted us in our attempts to identify Suzanne's secret admirer. She received another delivery, this time more clandestine and considerably creepier. It was a spiny cactus left in front of our house in the middle of the night, making it completely untraceable. The card said:

Suzanne, you're the one I admire
You're the one to whom I aspire
Like the spiny plant herein enclosed
Like the portrait for which you've posed
It's important that you see

You're the only one for me.

Suzanne studied the note and the cactus plant carefully. "Is it just me, or has my secret admirer's verse taken a decided turn towards the dark side? This time I feel like he's threatening and stalking me in a way the other gifts only hinted at."

It was my turn. I sensed, given Suzanne's present mood, that it was important for me to convey the right words in the right way. "I'm sorry to say I have to agree with you. He's escalating. The choice of a cactus plant, with lots of needles to stab you and no beautiful flower to offset the danger, is definitely less romantic than roses and violets. I think we've run out of time to just ignore this stalker. It's time to do a little strategizing. How we can flush him out and stop his fun and games before someone who matters to me gets hurt? What can we guess about him?"

Suzanne thought for a moment before making up her mind and turning towards me. "I think we should go with the probabilities on this one and assume he's one of the AKC staff we met for dinner in New York. That was where I had my first real sense of being followed. If, and when, we clear all the AKC types, plan B will be checking out the Rockefeller laboratory people as a backup. Didn't you have Vincent run background checks on all of them last month?"

I blushed becomingly. "Yes I did, but I haven't done anything about it. With all of the dog shows and travel to and from them, I've only had two and three days a week to get any real work done. I can get started reading Vincent's reports later this morning, and triage them for the most likely suspects. I'll bring them home tonight for you to get up to speed on our new suspects."

Suzanne looked energized and satisfied. "That sounds like a plan. We can talk more about strategy over dinner tonight."

I was true to my word this time and dug out Vincent's reports first thing after getting to the office. They made voluminous, but interesting, reading. He had done his usual thorough job on each of the names on the list. I read each biographical sketch with care looking for some hint of deviance, no matter how minor, in the records. My old law school and cop training kicked in and I made extensive notes as I went along.

The pile of reports started at the top with Harold Carswell. My guess of his age at mid-60s was exactly right. He was born in New York City in 1947, just the right age for Vietnam when he graduated from college (Duke, 1968, business and management) and served two years in the army as an officer (2nd Lieutenant, infantry). No record of combat. For his entire period of army service, he was stationed either at Fort Dix, N.J. or Fort Hood in Killeen, Texas. I assumed political connections kept him out of the killing fields of Vietnam, but in Texas he would have been training combat units for Vietnam. Honorably discharged, he then went to work for a large publishing company in New York City and climbed the corporate ladder for 15 years, before joining the AKC. He became their head honcho 10 years ago. No arrests, no criminal record, not even a parking ticket. Married for 40 years to the same wife, three children, six grandchildren; he seemed to be an exemplary member of the community where he lived in New Jersey.

I thought about Carswell for a bit, while I put down my pen and stretched my arms to loosen up. He graduated from one of the top universities in the USA, had a good military record as an officer, and climbed the corporate ladder just about to the top. He was a good family man with a stable marriage and strong ties to his community. He was pretty much the type of CEO I'd expect to be leading a wealthy and prestigious corporate organization like the AKC. His record said that he was one of the good guys---I put his packet down, starting a pile I marked mentally as Very Unlikely to be Suzanne's Stalker (VUS).

I stood up and stretched, then walked over to pour myself a cup of coffee and drink a few sips. The mostly full cup was set down carefully on a coaster on my desk as I started into the next report. Nathan Forrest had the first biography to go into the other pile, Possible Stalker (PS). No military service. Born in Missoula, Montana in 1956. Graduated from The University of Minnesota in 1977 (math major). Worked for an insurance company in Minneapolis for five years, then moved to his first Information Technology job in Chicago. He bounced through two other corporate IT positions before landing at the AKC in Durham, NC in 1998, and transferred to his current New York City post in 2007. No criminal record, several parking tickets, a couple of speeding tickets. Married in 1977 for five years and divorced just before leaving Minneapolis. No children. Married a second time in Durham in 1999, he's still married to his second wife, living on Long Island, and has two children. Forrest, like Carswell, graduated from a good university and climbed the corporate ladder systematically and successfully. He made it to the PS pile only because of his obvious computer expertise.

This was slow, boring work. Each report was 10-20 pages of densely packed information, all of which I had to read carefully. I refilled my coffee cup and dove into the next file. Gene Burnett-Smythe's was the second biography to go into the PS pile. Born in Dayton, Ohio in 1957, too late for Vietnam, he did not have any military service. He graduated from Kent State University (1980, history major). Went to work for a manufacturing company in Cleveland, where he stayed for six years. Moved to New York City in 1987 to become the librarian at the AKC, remaining there in that capacity until now. His childhood, however, wasn't so mundane. He was orphaned by a car accident at age six and was in and out of foster homes until his 18th birthday. There was a missing year in his early life, which accounted for his age at college graduation being 23. I assumed a sealed juvenile court criminal record could account for this. He had two DUI arrests on his adult record and apparently gave up his car after the second DUI conviction. He was single, had never married, lived in an apartment in

Manhattan near his job, and there was no record of his ever having children. There were the sort of red flags I was looking for to add someone to the PS pile, an unsettled childhood, not happily married, a missing juvenile year, and a known adult criminal record.

I got up to refill my coffee cup once again and to think about Gene Burnett-Smythe a bit more. He had graduated from college, but not a particularly good one. He didn't do anything to distinguish himself before snagging the librarian job at the AKC, and he stayed at the same job level for more than 20 years. No family, no obvious ties to a community, a history of drinking too much, and criminal convictions for driving under the influence. What was a mediocrity like him doing on the Board of Directors of an important organization like this one? I wondered what he knew and who he knew it about to explain his movement so high up the corporate ladder for no apparent reason. My notes included the question "What's he doing here??????" I stood by the window admiring the view of the mountains for a couple of minutes while I asked myself these questions. I didn't have any answers, at least not yet.

My inseparable coffee cup and I sat down at the desk. I yawned, scratched my head, and picked up a freshly sharpened pencil. It was time to move onward to the next report. Hunter Cabot was born in 1944 in Charleston, SC. Graduated in 1966 from a small Christian college in his home state with a degree in "General Studies", whatever that meant. After working for a year at his father's drugstore, he was drafted into the army for two years in 1968. Cabot served in a combat infantry unit in Vietnam for 1.5 of those two years where he must have seen some serious action at a young age. He returned home with a couple of medals and, I assume, a lot more sophistication and probably a lot less religion. He moved to Raleigh, NC where he found a new job having nothing to do with drugstores, selling furniture at a retail store. He moved from sales job to salesman job every 4-5 years until he ended up at the AKC offices in Durham, transferring to the New York office three years ago. He was married in 1974 to his present wife. They have five children and fifteen grandchildren. No criminal record, living in Queens. Cabot had a good military record as a decorated combat veteran and a stable marriage. Professionally he had a mediocre career and had graduated from a mediocre college. Like Burnett-Smythe he had seemingly grossly overachieved to become an executive in a large corporation like this one. I added another "What's he doing here??????" to my notes, followed by another notation "Something strange seems to be going on here!!!!" He nonetheless earned a place in the VUS pile.

I took another short break to clear my brain. This time I went for a 10 minute walk outside the building before starting to read the next file. Now it was Rosswell's turn. Rocket Rosswell was born in 1955 in Baltimore, MD. I was tempted to put him in the PS pile on general principles. He was a typical salesman, everybody's buddy, with a personality type I tended to dislike. However, I forced myself to read his dossier. He was raised in a series of foster homes and a church-sponsored facility for troubled youth. Graduated from Our Lady of the Sacred Heart High School in 1973. He completed two years of junior college with an Associate something or other degree. No military service. Worked as a used car salesman in Baltimore for seven years. Arrested and convicted for vehicular manslaughter in 1980, served 8 years of a 5-10 year term in the Maryland State Prison system. The accident, which was his fault, occurred when he was drunk (blood alcohol level of 0.18) and killed a family of four in the other car, two of which were young children. He was released from jail in 1988, moved to Philadelphia, PA, and went back to selling cars. He had no arrests on his record after his release from prison. Rocket was married briefly from 1990-1992, divorced, no children. He was hired by the AKC in New York City in 2009, and presently lived in an apartment in Queens, a convenient subway ride from the AKC offices. This seemed to be another strange resume. He didn't finish college and had a less than mediocre career. Although the success criteria for sales people might have been different than that used for the others, I still had to ask what was he doing on the leadership team? Could selling used cars define the cream of the crop in sales? He went on top of the growing PS pile.

The pile was down to the last two files Vincent had prepared. With half a cup of coffee remaining, I persevered and dove right into the next one. Henry Lodge was born in 1970 in Somerset, MA. He graduated from Colby College in Maine in 1992 with a degree in Computer Sciences. He moved to New York City where he got an IT job with a major investment bank and brokerage firm. He left the lucrative world of fraud and bonuses when his firm was dissolved a couple of years ago. It was merged with a larger bank under the friendly eye and shotgun oversight of the federal government, and apparently Hunter wasn't invited to stay. He resurfaced almost immediately as comptroller for the AKC shortly after his previous employer ceased to exist. Hunter was married in 1998, when he had the greatest of earnings prospects and the sky was the limit. Muffy, a former debutante and the most eligible bachelorette on the social register at the time, became Mrs. Lodge. They have two children and are seemingly still living happily ever after. No military service, no arrests, no criminal record. The family lives in an expensive suburban Connecticut community, a long, but easy, daily commute by railroad to midtown Manhattan. Lodge was another graduate from a top college with a successful career and a stable marriage. However, his career had taken a turn for the worse just before he joined the AKC. On an impulse and because of his computer science degree, I added him to the PS file.

One of my former partners when I was on the Los Angeles Police force, Harry, used to drink 7-8 cups of coffee, or more, a day. He used to say, "I don't really drink all that coffee, I just borrow it!" as he visited the men's room multiple times. I thought of Harry as I walked to our little lavatory, to bid fond adieu to some of the coffee I had been drinking while I read all these reports, and perhaps to make room for more.

This time I poured just half a cup, telling myself I really didn't need any more coffee this morning, but did need something to do with my hands. I picked up the last file to read. Stanley Morgan was born in 1956 in Brooklyn, New York. He graduated from New York University in 1977 with a degree in linguistics, and from New York University Law School in 1980 with a J.D. degree. He passed the bar on his first try and practiced business and corporate law as an associate in a large law firm. After 19.5 years, when he hadn't yet made partner, he read the handwriting on the wall and jumped ship to take his current position at the AKC. He was married shortly after finishing law school to a classmate who got a job in the New York City District Attorney's office. His wife Andrea, the former criminal attorney, was now a sitting Superior Court judge in Manhattan. Morgan had no military service, no arrests, no criminal record, a few parking tickets, but no moving violations. The couple lived in an East Side Condominium in New York City. They had three children and an apparently idyllic life. He had graduated from a good university and seemed to know his stuff. His wife had advanced pretty much to the top of her career pathway; perhaps he was content to stay in the background and support her.

On the other hand, he had struck an ambiguous chord with me at my interview. He was the most obvious member of the group to oppose Carswell's policies and was probably also the smartest member of the leadership team. He could easily have been the one who concocted the fancy schemes Suzanne's stalker had employed thus far. I didn't have any tangible evidence, but my intuition suggested some slight suspicions. On top of these concerns there was also that ambiguous drink he invited me to share when he visited Los Angeles. There was clearly an agenda behind his visit, but I didn't have a clue what it was all about. I put a bunch of question marks on the last page and added this file to the VUS stack, but with a big mental question mark attached.

I got up, stretched, and walked into Vincent's office. "Hey, Vincent, did you see anything that struck you as odd when you put together all these reports for me?"

Vincent smiled at me before answering. "Claro. Of course I did. You've got an almost perfect bimodal distribution of talent and background there. You could label the two piles you're making 'winners' and 'losers'. That's not what the Board of Directors of a big time corporation is supposed to look like. I'm surprised guys like Rosswell or Burnett-Smythe ever got hired by a big corporation like the AKC, much less that they ended up on the Board of Directors. Do you think there may be an agenda there?"

I sat down on the edge of his desk. "What do you think is going on here? When I took this job, I realized things were a little fuzzy about exactly what the AKC expected us to accomplish versus what they really wanted us to do. But the money was great and I was looking for a change, so figured 'why not?' Now I'm starting to wonder what we've gotten ourselves involved in."

Vincent fiddled with a ballpoint pen for a moment or two of thought. "Claro. The simplest answer is there are two factions on the board. You've got Carswell plus a couple of typical overachievers who probably do all of the heavy lifting, and you've got four more guys who are probably there to vote 'aye' on whatever Carswell wants. That setup gives Carswell the controlling majority so he can run the whole show his way. I think its pretty darn clear Carswell runs the whole operation, and does whatever he wants to do."

I got up from the desk and paced a little bit in the small office while thinking out loud. "Do you think maybe Carswell hired us to dig around until we got some dirt on someone on the board he wants to be able to control?"

Vincent looked up at me and replied, "Anything's possible. At this stage I don't think we know enough to make a good guess. My advice is you should watch your back, and especially Suzanne's back, while you're watching the dog shows. And maybe you shouldn't trust everything you heard when you were back in New York City. Claro. It looks like someone on that Board doesn't like you and Suzanne. It's possible you've been hired into the middle of some kind of corporate power struggle."

I went back to my office and put everything into my briefcase for future reference while I did some overdue work.

Back home, we had time to drink a little wine and study possible perverts before dinner. I explained to Suzanne about my PS and VUS system and who had ended up in which group. I deliberately didn't tell her my rationale for the choices so she could look at the PS files with a fresh set of eyes. Suzanne reached over and picked up just the pile of PS files to read. "Thanks, Roger. I'll trust your judgment and skip the VUS files for now. We can always go back and look at them if we rule out the others as stalker suspects."

She was lost in thought, taking copious notes until Bruce called us for dinner. Suzanne brought her notes and the files to dinner to share with us over chicken parmigiana, spaghetti and pesto, broccoli with an aioli sauce, and garlic bread. Robert had the jarred vegetables and fruit selection de jour with Cheerios. He was at an age when he could pick up individual Cheerios and put them in his mouth (at least some of the time). He enjoyed eating by himself and playing with the Cheerios for a short while, giving all of us a chance to eat the adult portions. Juliet had already eaten dinner, 1.5 cups of salmon flavored dog chow, served in a bowl a la crate. After finishing her dinner she was released from the crate to patrol the floor area under Robert, where she enforced the 3-second rule for all dropped Cheerios. Needless to say she loved Robert and he loved her. Neither boy nor dog ever seemed to tire of the game we called "drop the Cheerios".

Robert squealed with delight as each Cheerio he dropped brought a triumphant pounce and a small woof from Juliet, whose tail looked like a furry metronome as it wagged furiously. The extemporaneous entertainment seriously threatened to keep us from accomplishing our goal of reviewing all of the possible stalker files, but a laughing small person and a happy dog were a welcome distraction. Bruce finally intervened and picked up Robert for his bath and bed, with Juliet following at his heels in case any more Cheerios managed to fall from the sky.

We got back to work. Suzanne looked up from her pad full of notes, finished chewing a piece of chicken, and sipped her zinfandel. "I ranked the suspects based on the materials in the file. From the most likely to the least likely, I'd rank them as (1) Burnett-Smythe, (2) Lodge, (3) Rosswell, and (4) Forrest.

Suzanne reached across the table to pick up the wine bottle and poured some more into both of our glasses. "Burnett-Smythe is the most obvious possibility. He had a rotten childhood, a lost year to still investigate, two DUIs, which indicates a drinking problem and probably a propensity for erratic behavior and maybe violence, plus an unsuccessful marriage, which could indicate problems with women."

She took some more food and another sip of wine. "Lodge is my dark horse candidate. There's nothing damning in the file per se. He's got the computer science degree, which almost certainly makes him knowledgeable about hiding his tracks on the Internet. He's had an amoral, if not immoral, career track, so he could feel above the law. Lodge probably grew up wealthy, going to an expensive private college. Since graduating, he's made a ton of money, giving him the financial resources and status to get away with or buy his way out of crimes that would have given Burnett-Smythe or Rosswell a criminal record. I also have a hunch, or call it intuition, based on my fleeting impressions of him from our dinner."

Suzanne munched on a piece of garlic bread dipped in the aioli sauce. "Rosswell is third on my list. He had another rotten childhood like Burnett-Smythe. He has a failed marriage too. There's a hint of a drinking problem, but the accident could have been a one-off piece of bad luck."

She sipped some more wine. "Forrest has the computer skills, but that's about it. His second marriage seems to be pretty stable. He may get along perfectly well with the right woman, seemingly ruling out his fitting the stalker profile."

Suzanne finished her wine with a big gulp. "You know, this whole thing really pisses me off. We have a misogynistic stalker sending me anonymous threats from that old boys club we had dinner with in New York. Notice there aren't any women, people of color, or Asians on the Board. Just an old boys club stroking each other's egos and never being held accountable for what they do. I'd love to just walk in there and beat the crap out of all of them."

Suzanne stood up, walked around the table, gave me a big kiss on the mouth, and sat down next to me. "OK, I've vented and I feel better now. Let's get back to work."

I put my fork down for a moment, drank some wine, and faced Suzanne. "Your take is pretty much the way I saw them, for exactly the same reasons, except I had Rosswell ranked #2 and Lodge #3. I've learned to trust your hunches, so we'll tentatively go with your rankings here."

Suzanne took my hand and squeezed it gently. "So, what comes next?"

I finished the last of my wine. "Vincent looks a little deeper at all of the PS group. We try to hack into a few other databases to see if there are any incidents or complaints suggesting harassment or stalking by any of our suspects that didn't make the records. Maybe we can find a friendly cop to talk with back there. I wonder if Carswell knows anything; the AKC must have run background checks on all of the staff before hiring them. I wonder if Vincent could access those AKC personnel files. Or else, I could just call Carswell and ask him directly. That's all in my to-do pile. I have the better part of three weeks in which to get it done. What are you thinking, Suzanne?"

Suzanne got the look she always gets when she's about to jump into action. "I'm remembering that most stalkers are cowards, but they can be dangerous. Do you remember the serial killer we were able to identify in Chile with the help of a little disinformation? What do you think would happen if I sent thank-you notes for the flowers and plants to each of our four suspects on the PS list?"

I thought about the pros and cons of trying to get the stalker upset enough to take some thoughtless action. "Let's save that strategy for later, if digging around in the suspects' past doesn't get us any closer to the truth. I don't like the risks involved for you if they can be avoided and I certainly don't want to put Robert at risk. OK?"

She thought about my suggestion a bit, and didn't look too happy with it. "OK with me. I think we have the beginnings of a plan. But I've got to admit I'm getting awfully impatient with just sitting around waiting for things to happen rather than taking the offensive."

Suzanne stood up from her chair, leaned over me, and gave me a very long, lingering kiss. She sat crosswise in my lap and kissed me again. "I think we've discussed perverts and stalkers to death. Let's neck a little bit."

Chapter18.A break in the competition

Suzanne and I heard about a new dog park about ten minutes drive from our house. The park was fenced and allowed dogs to run around and play together off their leashes within the fenced area. That sounded interesting, so one Sunday morning we drove over there. There was a large parking lot in front of the fenced-in area, which must have been at least 100 feet wide and 750 feet long, an enclosed area of about 1.5 acres. I noticed a blue car I'd seen behind us for most of the short trip pull in behind us and park all the way back near the exit. The driver was just sitting there in his car, apparently in little hurry to start exercising his dog.

Most of the dog play area was grass, with an oval gravel track along the fence ringing the perimeter of the grassy area. There were perhaps two- or three-dozen dogs distributed within the park in different sized groups. The two most popular games being played were the ever-popular "chase me" and "keep away", the latter usually involving a coveted and well-chewed tennis ball or stick. As we walked into the fenced-in area with Juliet I looked back casually to see the driver stepping out of the blue car and walking in our direction outside of the fence. He was a complete stranger to me, most noticeable because he didn't have a dog with him. He loitered just outside the fence smoking a cigarette. Alarms were ringing in my head, but he might just be an innocent smoker taking a break to puff on a cigarette, which was pretty impossible to do anywhere indoors in California these days.

We walked through a double safety gated sally port into the grassy area and released Juliet from her leash. She immediately trotted over to a human stranger and rubbed against her leg, a clear request to pet her. After having her ears and head thoroughly scratched, she ran off to play with a group of five dogs all more or less her size---a couple of retriever types of mixed heritage, an Australian herding dog, a German Shepherd puppy who still had some growing to do, and a Vizsla.

It was a lot of fun to watch. Juliet made a few puppy-like moves and the race was on. Six dogs, all of which could run, ran. Juliet was the fastest by far, but made sure she stayed in third gear, keeping the pace reasonable.

All of a sudden there was another dog right in front of her and a messy crash seemed inevitable. At the last possible second, Juliet launched herself up and over the other animal, soaring effortlessly above her to land without breaking stride and keep running. Six dogs ran from end to end through the dog park over and over, Juliet in the lead some of the time and following the scrum at other times. We watched and socialized with a few of the other dog owners for ten minutes or so. The oft-asked question was "what kind of dog is that?" when people saw Juliet. Finally, some of the dogs got tired enough to drop out and the game came to an end. Juliet romped over to another group, exchanged polite nose to butt sniffs with a spaniel, and they were off once again. I checked out the parking lot. Our smoker had disappeared, and so had the blue car.

About an hour later, Juliet drank a lot of water from a convenient fountain, squatted to return some of the water to the local aquifer, and let us know it was time to go home. She sat in front of the gate waiting to have her leash returned before leaving the dog park, then navigated the double gates as she led us back to our car. As we returned home, I checked the rear-view mirror frequently. No sign of the blue car. Co-incidence or did he take off after I'd spotted him? I made a mental note to mention the car and the smoker to Bruce so he could keep his eyes open and decided not to worry Suzanne any more than she already was by giving her something else to be concerned about.

Bruce had a saying, or perhaps an aphorism is a better term. He'd tell us over and over, "Idle paws are the devil's plaything. You have to give your dog a job or she'll invent her own entertainment, and that's when shoes and furniture get chewed or she gets into other mischief."

Shortly after Sherry loaned us Juliet, Bruce started her exercise and training regimen. Actually, Juliet's supplemental training began the next day. This deliberately wasn't more conformation show training; Sherry had already done a great job on this and Bruce asked, "Why mess with success?" Rather, he told us that hunting or search, rescue, and tracking were useful skills he knew how to train for at the highest levels. The nose work involved in tracking and finding was a lot more convenient to perform in our urban setting and, perhaps, likely to be more useful for us in the future.

So, for 15-30 minutes a day, every day, while Robert took his nap, Juliet and Bruce worked on learning that there were other smells than pheasant and chukar that were worth pointing at. Bruce made sure Suzanne and I were included whenever we were at home, telling us, "There are a few principles and a lot of tricks that go into effective dog training. It's a lot easier with a well-trained and very smart adult animal like Juliet, who wants to please you. You only need her to understand what it is you're asking her to do. At some point we'll be training a new puppy. You might as well learn how just in case I'm not able to do it for you.

"The basic principles are simple. If you're teaching her to do something consistent with her hard-wired instincts, it's easy. For example, she instinctively hunts birds and upland game. She's mainly guided to birds and small game by sight and their scents. Training her to use her nose to find other things is just an extension of what she already knows how to do. Training Juliet to find a specific scent is just about making her understand what you want her to do, and she will. OK so far?"

We both nodded.

He knelt down to pat Juliet and scratched her special spots behind the ears and on her back, just in front of her tail. "It gets a lot harder if you want to train a behavior contrary to her instincts, but you can do that, too. As long as she wants to please her humans like Juliet does, she can learn. There are several breeds of hunting dogs. Some like the spaniels instinctively flush the birds they find. Pointers point at the bird before they flush it. Most pointers will instinctively "flash point". That means they'll point for a few seconds, then try to get the bird. It's a lot easier to hunt pheasant if the dog holds her point until the hunter gets close enough to take an easy shot. It's even easier if she is rock steady on point until you flush the bird yourself to shoot it. Then when you release her from her point, she'll retrieve the bird you've shot and bring it back to you. That's exactly what a well-trained German Shorthaired Pointer should do."

He played some more with the dog before he continued his explanation. "Most trainers break up complicated tasks into a series of simple ones, then design games and play to reinforce the behaviors you're putting together to complete the complex behavior. For example, I want to train Juliet to point, the same way she'd instinctively point a bird, at a new object or a specific scent I've introduced to her. Step 1 is playing a game of fetch. I'll throw a tennis ball or stick for her to retrieve to me. She knows the game and we'll have fun while she gets some exercise and learns she's supposed to work for me now rather than Sherry. Eventually we'll work on actually pointing the object I've introduced and to stay steady on point until I release her to retrieve it, just like hunting a bird."

We watched Bruce and Juliet play fetch for a while in the back yard. The first dozen or so times he threw it, Bruce let her chase the ball and to find it. When she picked it up in her mouth, he gave her a "come" command. When she brought it back to him, he made a big deal of rewarding her with praise and petting, then he took the ball and threw it again. He made sure to say "fetch" each time she started out to retrieve the ball to reinforce the association between word and deed. He was careful to gradually increase the distance of his tosses, eventually making the task more difficult by aiming the ball to land in some bushes behind Robert's new play structure. The increased distance or having to find the ball in a clump of bushes didn't faze Juliet, who used her nose to find the ball. The more complex the retrieve, the prouder she was for doing it. Juliet obviously loved this new game. As she returned the ball into Bruce's waiting hand, she started to do her happy dog prance, eagerly anticipating the next throw and retrieve. That completed our first formal session of dog training.

Bruce threw the ball for the final time and Juliet happily bounded after it. "We'll eventually change the game to my giving her an object to smell and then hiding it. I'll tell her "fetch" or "find" and she'll know she's supposed to look for it. When she eventually finds it, I'll make a big fuss, with lots of praise and rewards then we'll do it a lot more times. Like I said before, break the complex task into a series of fun and games that make up the complicated behavior. That's what dog training is all about. With this approach, you can do all of the training with positive rewards, making it fun for the dog and fun for the trainer. If she doesn't get it the first time we'll do it again some other time, until she eventually does. There's never punishment for making a mistake or forcing her to keep doing it until she gets it right. It's more important to have patience and to keep it fun. That's what gets rewarded in the long run."

Bruce continued Juliet's training whenever we were home. She learned to hold a point when she found the object she was sent to "find". It started with the simple technique of putting a 25-foot long check cord on her collar and "whoa-ing" her when she found the scent she was looking for. Just before she would try to "fetch" the object, Bruce gently pulled on the check cord, saying "whoa" until she learned to stand steady after a "find". She loved their playtime/training together. Bruce showed us remarkable progress on some complex behaviors coming together. Juliet was smart enough, and motivated enough, to be a quick learner. Bruce had the skills and creativity to be a superb "dog whisperer". The lessons went smoothly with positive reinforcement, praise and love. Negative reinforcement was never involved, keeping the training fun.

We could see Juliet bonding more closely with Bruce every day, and this shared intimacy carried over into success in the show ring. Juliet was not only a very happy little bitch in her new surroundings, but was also an ideal pet from the entire family's point of view. She was affectionate, obeyed commands (or requests if it was Robert) from all of us, and had become a full family member within a few weeks after we received her from Sherry. However, we didn't learn the real value of this additional training until a second dead body, another dog show judge, turned up at the "Woofstock" show.

In the meantime, Vincent had done a more in-depth investigation by computer and telephone of the PS candidates we suspected might be the stalker. We discovered a lot more about each of them, most of it useless trivia. But buried in the trivia were some potentially incriminating bits and pieces.

"We have an interesting problem with regard to your stalker, Suzanne," I said that night as we went to bed. Juliet had finished her late night visit to the back yard and was safely tucked into her crate. "Up until now, the bastard has only sent you flowers and plants. As far as I know there's no law against bad poetry, even if there ought to be one. When and if we figure out who he or she is, there's not a whole lot we can do about it unless we can somehow frame them for something criminal or catch them committing a crime. It's worth figuring out who the stalker is, but it's also worth giving some thought to what we plan to do about it when we find out their identity."

"I'd vote for capital punishment," she murmured sleepily. "Now hush-up and let me get some sleep, dear!"

Chapter19.Back to the competition

      It was time for Bruce, Juliet, and me to return to the dog show circuit. Many of the regulars had stayed in California to compete for a point or two here and there among the smaller shows with smaller entries. Although their class dogs already had their majors, some needed just a few points to get the coveted title of champion in front of their name. They were competing at these smaller shows with puppies or less competitive adult dogs and bitches. The rest of the regulars flew or drove out of state with their dogs, to the big major shows in Arizona or Oregon and Washington. Now it was time for us to rejoin them. We had formulated a plan to check out my current theories regarding the possible sources of skullduggery, both at the dog shows and at the AKC itself. I was beginning to think I had a pretty good handle on what was actually going on, but it was still far too early to report anything back to my client.

      Our stops this time around began at Vallejo, CA, just off I-80 about halfway between Sacramento and San Francisco, for the four days of shows known collectively as "Woofstock". Three weeks later we'd travel to Sacramento, Suzanne's old home town where she grew up. Then finally, the following week we'd be back to Vallejo again, which would bring us to the end of April and about the 4-month mark on our odyssey towards justice.

      "Woofstock" simultaneously paid homage to the 60s and to the aging hippies of that era and was a major happening, as well as an important cluster of dog show competitions. The show was a very big one, one of the largest on the circuit, drawing dogs of all breeds with owners hungry for majors. You could theoretically start a dog in their first show ever on a Thursday, and finish the dog's championship on Sunday by winning Best of Winners or Best Opposite Sex in your breed all four days of the competition. If the turnout was good enough, they could even become champions just by winning on three of those days. Owners and spectators wandered around all day in tie-dyed tee shirts or their best hippie outfits. After their last ring entry, handlers shucked their ties and jackets to join the "I Love Woofstock" tee-shirted crowd.

Everybody was having a big party, the barbecues were smoking, the wine was flowing, and the first day's show had gone well, when they found the dead body of another judge on Thursday evening. This time it was a judge from the Working Group, a Rottweiler breeder from Arizona named Jorge Guerrero. He was also strangled with a show lead, so the modus operandi matched the unfortunate demise of Orval ("Awful") Krause.

The local police and highway patrol officers who responded to the call sealed off the crime scene and made the dog show people, myself included, feel decidedly unwelcome anywhere within a hundred feet of the body. Sketchy details were available from a couple that had been there when the body was found. They immediately became the center of attention at one party after another in the RV parking area. I called Stephen Callahan on my cell phone at his personal number. Wonder of wonders, he answered his phone on the second ring and remembered who I was. I told him what was currently happening at the Solano County Fairgrounds in Vallejo and suggested he drive out and see if the police had found any clues that might be useful for his case.

There was a short interval of silence on the line before he replied. "I can be there in less than an hour. I've passed the Solano County Fairgrounds dozens of times on my way to Lake Tahoe or Sacramento, but I've never actually been there before. That's the same exit from I-80 as Six Flags Discovery Kingdom, isn't it?"

"Yep. It's right across the road from the Amusement Park. We can meet to compare notes at my motel room after you've talked to the local police. Give me a call on my cell phone when you finish with the cops. I'm staying at the Marriott Courtyard across the street from the Fairgrounds, Room 116."

About two hours later Detective Callahan, Bruce, and I were sitting in my motel room sipping Scotch and talking. Juliet lay adoringly at Bruce's feet. She was still too young to drink Scotch legally and we had a working cop in the room, so we didn't offer her any.

Callahan, still wearing his San Francisco police detective's working clothes consisting of a suit and tie, got pride of place awarding him the chance to go first. "The victim was strangled with a show lead, same as the judge at Golden Gate. They both looked a lot alike---tall, skinny, balding, 60-ish, mustache. No obvious clues, but forensics still has to do its thing and that won't really happen until tomorrow. I'd guess it was the same killer from the similarity of technique, but that's for the experts in crime scene reconstruction to say for sure. The local police weren't too pleased to hear we have a multiple murderer, since it's bad for tourism and conventions, but liked the idea of sharing the responsibility for what might be an unsolvable case. I didn't mention you, so they shouldn't be knocking on your door tonight. Likely time of death was about 6:00-7:00 PM. The corpse was lying in a grassy area to the west of the dog show venue, partially hidden by a couple of trees. The dead man was discovered by a gay couple who were walking around the site. They were probably looking for a little privacy where they could do their thing. Otherwise the body most likely wouldn't have been found until tomorrow morning."

Callahan loosened the knot on his tie and relaxed back into his chair. "It's too soon to know anything about the victim except for what was in his pockets and wallet. He was one of the judges, as you know. The address on his driver's license was Bisbee, Arizona, a small town near the New Mexico border that was famous in the 1880s for its silver mining. He had papers from the AKC that said he was a judge, a round trip electronic plane ticket from Tucson to Sacramento, and a rental car receipt from the Sacramento airport. I'll e-mail you all of the background material they share with me, but it'll probably take a few days. That's about all I can tell you. What'd you find out?"

We both turned towards Bruce as a cue he was next. Bruce asked, "Have they removed the body yet or are they still collecting evidence?"

Callahan looked surprised, but answered immediately. "The body is still there. Why?"

Bruce smiled and reached over to pat his dog's head. "Because I've been training Juliet for search and rescue work. If you can get her a sniff or two of the show lead used as the murder weapon, we can walk her around the fairgrounds and watch her. She'll give us an alert signal if she smells whoever handled the lead, or if she finds the same smell on any other item, such as another show lead from the same batch, that's been touched by whoever it is that has the same smell."

Callahan looked directly at Bruce with an incredulous expression on his face. "You've got to be kidding. That's evidence and off limits for us or for a dog to touch."

Bruce sat up straighter. "She doesn't have to touch the lead, nor do I. She can just sniff it in an open plastic bag or even around the dead man's neck. After I give her a specific command, she'll do the rest."

The Lieutenant gave Bruce another look that said, loud and clear, "that's got to be a load of BS."

"I don't believe that's possible!"

Bruce just smiled while his body language said, every bit as loud and clear, "Just watch."

"That's part of what I trained dogs to do in Iraq and Afghanistan and I was very good at it. Juliet has a vastly better nose and is a whole lot smarter than the mutts I worked with back in the desert. Trust me, she can do it, and we won't charge for the service."

It took a while, but eventually we were part of a group standing around a dead body lying on the ground with a show lead embedded deeply into his throat and neck. Bruce had Juliet on a regular leash and led her towards the body. Juliet was quivering with anticipation, tail wagging at a dozen beats per second, or so it seemed. We all watched the show---Callahan, me, a number of uniformed local police, a couple of local detectives, and several CSI staff wearing CSI emblazoned vests as their special I.D. Bruce instructed one of the CSI staff exactly what he wanted done. A cute blonde in her early thirties had volunteered for the job, and listened carefully to Bruce. She stood next to the dead body wearing a windbreaker with CSI printed on the back over her CSI vest. She was to kneel by the body, trying not to move too much, and lift the loose end of the show lead away from the corpse's throat with her gloved hand, extending it towards Bruce and Juliet. Bruce would do the rest.

Bruce stood up straight and gave Juliet a very light correction with the leash. "Sit!" commanded Bruce in a gentle tone.

Juliet looked at him and at the CSI technician kneeling by the body for less than a second and sat, watching the body and the technician carefully. She was in full working dog mode now, with all of her attention focused on the body. She knew something was going to happen and listened carefully for Bruce's command.

"Find," was Bruce's next command as he stepped even closer to Juliet, creating some slack in her leash.

Juliet sniffed the wind and walked carefully back and forth in the general direction of the CSI technician, quartering into the light breeze to make sure she picked up all of the scents coming towards her. When she finally got to the kneeling technician Bruce stopped and said "find" once again, in a firm but calm and quiet voice. Juliet, her tail going back and forth like a miniature metronome, took two sniffs of the extended lead, and sat directly in front of the technician waiting for Bruce's next command.

"Heel." They walked away from the body directly toward Callahan and me, where we stood off to the side, away from the main group. Bruce stopped a few feet from us and Juliet sat beside him, waiting for further instructions. Her entire demeanor continued to express she was alert and working. Bruce rubbed her head and ears while telling her what a good girl she was.

Bruce gave our police colleague a look that spoke volumes about his obvious pride in Juliet. "That's it," said Bruce to Callahan, "Let's take a walk."

"Where to?" asked the detective, with a look on his face that said, "This is still all BS!"

"The last time I saw a routine like this was when one of our Lieutenants tried to crack an unsolvable case. The Department hired a psychic who had done some kind of a con job to get paid to have a vision of where to find clues. Needless to say, the case wasn't solved even if our psychic got paid a small fortune to mumble New Age nonsense!"

I had a very specific suggestion as to where we should let Juliet do some finding. "Let's start over at the RV parking area if nobody has any objections."

Nobody had a better idea. Off we went with Bruce calmly leading Juliet to the parked vehicles. Juliet was intensely eager, tail still wagging as fast as she could, head up and nose in the air seeking the specific scent she'd been told to find.

As we walked towards the RVs, I spoke directly to

Callahan. "Since I suppose you haven't ever done this before, let me explain the relevant rules of evidence here. If we find something you can decide what, if anything, you want to do next. Remember I'm not only an ex-cop but I'm also a licensed lawyer. You can assume what I'm telling you will be accurate and will help you keep any evidence we find admissible in court when this case comes to trial. If Juliet alerts at a car or RV, we have the option of doing nothing else and just quietly keeping on walking. In that situation, you have adequate probable cause for a search warrant and you can get one from almost any judge. If you do search the vehicle, I'll guess you'll find matching show leads from the same batch used for the murder or murders, but that alone isn't enough evidence to convince a D.A. to go forward with an arrest. You could perhaps link the leads to a killing or two, but it's insufficient to accuse any specific person of being the killer even if their scent is on the leads.

"Or, we can keep walking and do nothing. However, we'll have defined a person or persons as a suspect and can focus your investigation on them to look for motive and evidence.

"Or, we can knock on the door, go in, and bluff about how much we know and hope for a confession."

Callahan nodded acknowledgment to me. "I suspect I already know the answer, but which option would you suggest?"

"I like what's behind door #2 the most. If we can define a suspect or two and focus on them I can't think of any reason we should tip our hand at this stage of an investigation."

By that time we were almost at the RV parking area. "I agree. Now let's hope she finds something."

Bruce leaned over to pet the dog on her head and neck and gave her a new instruction. "Seek!" He disconnected the leash from her collar, tapped the back of her head to release her, and started walking slowly along the row of parked RVs. Juliet figured a course along the same general direction we were walking. Bruce moved to keep her quartering into the breeze, as she loped ahead of us, head high and nose pointed into the wind, making broad casts between and around the huge vehicles,. She looked like she was just having fun while she exercised. Anybody who noticed her wouldn't have any idea of why she was really there.

It was almost an anti-climax when Juliet alerted as we came to the seventh RV. The dog abruptly sat, her body frozen in place, ears cocked forward, nose pointed towards the door of the seventh RV.

We caught up to her. "What now?" Bruce asked.

I had thought about our moves in advance. We didn't want anyone watching to figure out what we were doing, or what Juliet's behavior actually meant. "Keep going," I replied.

Bruce rewarded her with praise and a few well-placed scratches on her ears. "Good girl," Bruce told Juliet, who visibly relaxed. "Heel!" They walked several steps further along the path by the parked RVs. "Seek!"

Juliet bounded off again, nose in air, checking the remaining vehicles. As it turned out, there weren't any more RV alerts. We kept walking until we came upon the same group we had partied with in Woodland, sitting at a table drinking wine. There was also the telltale odor of marijuana smoke in the air, but that was typical of many of these tailgate parties and we were all used to it. Juliet sat and came to full alert again. Bruce casually took her off alert by telling her what a good girl she was and walked her past the party towards our motel.

"I'll just finish Juliet's walk and take her back to the hotel. She's had plenty of exercise, Roger. I'll see you back at our room."

I introduced Steve Callahan to the Breeds, Schlecks, Todds, Schaefers, Pete and Jewel Harris, and the Cords as a local friend who had stopped by to say hello while we were near his home. We each took the cup of red wine offered to us, then excused ourselves saying we had an early ring time the next morning and had to find Bruce.

Back at our room we caught up with Bruce and Juliet. I played tug of war and fetch for a few minutes with Juliet and one of her dog toys, a squeaky green snake-like thing made of furry cloth. After that, I introduced Steve Callahan to our dog, gave him a tennis ball, and encouraged him to play fetch with her. She was quite full of herself, as if she realized how important her earlier search and alert mission had been to us. She threw herself into the game with Callahan, a complete stranger until a couple of hours ago. He sat on a comfortable chair while Juliet barked happily every time he threw the ball for her to retrieve. On the final throw she retrieved the ball to his hand, stood on her hind legs with her front legs on his lap, and planted a big doggy kiss on his face. Finally, we discussed what Juliet had done earlier.

Callahan offered a handshake to Bruce. "If I hadn't seen it, I wouldn't have believed it. But I did and I do. OK, Roger, whose RV was it and who was she pointing to in the party crowd?"

"The RV belongs to the Schaefers, Albert and Sadie. They're a couple from West Texas, not too far from San Franciso de Texas where Orval Krause grew up. People were standing close together so I can't be sure enough to testify under oath that Juliet was pointing at Albert Schaefer when she alerted at the party. But I'm pretty sure that was how she lined up. Did you see it any more clearly from your angle, Bruce?"

"Yes I did. She pointed directly at Albert, which I would testify to under oath in court if it ever comes to that."

"Well Steve, we have a person of interest, if not a real suspect. Can you check him and Sadie out?"

"That'll be my top priority tomorrow morning when I get to work."

"As I remember from my days as a homicide detective in Los Angeles we never got a lot of cooperation from law enforcement in the Texas agencies, especially the Sheriff's offices in the rural areas. We were lucky if they even returned our calls. Maybe if you make it a point to tell them in San Francisco de Texas you're from San Francisco de California, they'll feel neighborly enough to give you some professional courtesy. Another word of advice: Earlier this year I learned in Valparaiso, Chile that you don't want to shorten their name from San Francisco to Saint Paco or just to Paco. Small towns are sensitive about things like that." I hoped my grin wasn't too obvious.

We shook hands, said our good-byes, and went to sleep.

The next day was an early ring time for GSPs, 8:30 A.M. Juliet was in a great mood. I anthropomorphized her thought process a bit, and ascribed her self-satisfaction to her feeling very, very good about her near-perfect performance as a police dog the previous evening. She was positively prancing in the show ring. Her body language clearly shouted "Look at me, look at me!" to the judge. She was absolutely unbeatable under these conditions and sailed through to Best of Breed by a large margin. The good mojo continued to a Group 1 rosette and a trophy, her first ever Group 1 victory with Bruce handling. The third judge of the day actually gave her a long look before awarding Best of Show to a lovely Schnauzer. All in all, it was a great day for Juliet as a "Special", lots of Grand Champion points, lots of congratulations, and lots of invitations to parking lot parties for the two of us. Coupled with her getting major "select" points in Thursday's competition, she was on a roll this weekend.

Saturday and Sunday featured two new judges awarding

Juliet one Best of Breed and a Best Opposite Sex, a mild disappointment after Friday's victories, but good for more points and two more rosettes and trophies with no shame in the result.

Also on Friday afternoon, Steve Callahan e-mailed to my iPhone several scanned pages of fascinating background material about the murdered judge and the new persons of interest Juliet had found. I skimmed the material while Juliet was waltzing through the breed competition on her way to the Group. Then I read everything again a lot more carefully while I waited for Juliet's appearance in the Group competition. I studied the relevant pages two or three times, particularly the sections on Albert and Sadie Schaefer's background and criminal records. Both had grown up in West Texas, which is a big part of a very big state. Texas west of the Pecos River sprawls over a larger area than most of the states in the eastern USA. However, in the words of the popular song, it was a small world after all. The Schaefers had grown up at about the same time in the same small town where Orval Krause had been raised. They must have known each other back in the good old days.

I had a crazy hunch so I cross-referenced dates and places of birth for Judge Guerrero, the murder victim from Arizona, the Schaefers, and Orval Krause. Bingo! Guerrero was another West Texas product and had also grown up at the same time, near the other three people. The odds had to be something like 1,000 to 1 they all knew each other both from growing up in close proximity and from their shared interest in show dogs.

Both of the Schaefers had criminal records in West Texas. Sadie had been arrested several times for prostitution in her younger days but had never done any prison time. Albert had been arrested multiple times for allegedly using or selling drugs, mostly grass and crank. The only charge progressing to a conviction with time in prison was when he was caught in a trailer with a methamphetamine lab setup, brewing crank. That was way back when he was still in his 30s, and cost him a year in the local county jail. Nobody had arrested either of them in the last 20 years or more, but the couple had a lot more money than either of them could possibly have earned legally. In a Texas border area awash with drugs imported from nearby Mexico by heavily armed cartels, they were small potatoes.

"Son of a gun!" I said out loud to no one in particular. Juliet may have found us the candy man who was supplying recreational drugs to the RV crowd on the dog show circuit. All of a sudden, for the first time, I had circumstantial evidence the murders might be directly linked to the original job the AKC had originally hired me to do. The judging, the drugs, and the murders could all be connected. The AKC's revenue shortfall could be due to disillusioned dog owners dropping out of competition because of unfair judging by the two dead judges, and perhaps by other judges as well. The vague sense of something being wrong with the judging might be collateral damage from the active and lucrative recreational drug scene ongoing at these shows. What kind of corrupt judge wouldn't give their drug dealers preferential treatment in the show ring?

All of that money the AKC was paying us to chase shadows may have finally led us to something tangible to investigate. It made me think solving the two murders might actually be related to what the AKC was looking for in the first place. When things go wrong in the drug world, murders happen.

Going forward, the murders were likely to have a further negative impact on attendance at the dog shows, and therefore on revenue coming to the AKC. It should make the AKC very happy indeed if we solved them and showed the spectators they were safe. For the first time since we'd started the dog show circuit with Juliet, I had a sense of actually knowing what I was doing and the beginnings of a real plan for what we should do next.

None of this theorizing meant that the show lead scent Juliet had tracked to the Schaefer's RV, and to Albert Schaefer himself, wasn't a clue to the identity of the killer. However, it made a lot of sense to investigate whether the drugs that were so freely available at the shows were a motive for the two murders. The dog shows provided a convenient gathering place for potential customers with plenty of cash and time on their hands in the evenings. A lot of money was changing hands in this profitable market for recreational drugs. In my experience, where there's easy money to be made somebody will always find a way to exploit the situation.

This train of thought brought me to wondering about the possible drug connections between all of these present and former West Texans meeting again at the California dog shows. Like the Sherlock Holmes story with the famous dog that didn't bark in the night, it seemed more suspicious that none of the dog show participants from West Texas had been arrested for recent drug dealing than it would have been if they had been arrested regularly. With their records, all of them should have been on someone in law enforcement's radar. The lack of any recent record of arrests for selling pot, crank, and crack during the intervening years among all of these shady characters suggested some powerful protection going on behind the scene here. In West Texas along the turbulent and notoriously leaky Mexican border, the source of the protection could be either the bad guys or the good guys. The bad guys were the drug cartels, while the good guys were the federal law enforcement agencies, like the DEA.

I forwarded the e-mail from Detective Callahan to Vincent with a covering note, asking him to work his computer magic and see if he could amplify the sketchy parts of this scenario. I also asked if he had a friend at the Drug Enforcement Agency or the CIA who could add to our available data. I was especially interested in whether the Schaefers' apparent immunity from the local law over the last couple of decades might indicate that they were DEA informants or had protected status for some other reason.

My timing was good. I finished all of this just in time to watch Bruce and Juliet enter the ring for the Sporting Dog Group judging.

Chapter20.A stalker unmasked

An excited Vincent greeted me as I entered the office Monday morning, after the drive back from Vallejo the night before. "I think we've found something. I love the three-hour time difference in Washington, D.C. When I send a request for something at the end of the day here, I sometimes actually have an answer waiting for me when I get to work the next morning. In this case, I got some answers from my contacts at both the DEA and the CIA. Claro. You guessed exactly right. The Schaefers are indeed confidential informants for the DEA and protected by the agency from the local law enforcement groups. According to my CIA contact, it's more than just keeping the Sheriff's deputies off their case. Claro. The DEA is actually bankrolling them as mid-level drug dealers to troll for bigger fish. Albert and Sadie get to sell their drugs locally in West Texas and on the dog show circuit, courtesy of the U.S. Drug Enforcement Agency and backed by the full faith and credit of the United States Government."

Vincent stood up. He looked like he was ready to pound on his desk in frustration. "You know what? That really pisses me off."

I was suddenly getting a headache. I rubbed my eyes and head. "Did you find out anything else I should know about?"

Vincent calmed himself a bit and sat back down. "Claro. Yes I did. The CIA connection says there's a lot of suspicion and no actual proof that both of the dead judges, Krause and Guerrero, were connected with the Mexican drug cartels, probably as fairly high-level drug dealers in their regions of Texas and Arizona. Krause seems to have had ties with the Sinaloa Cartel, while Guerrero was apparently in bed with the worst of them, The Zetas Cartel. There's a lot more detail stuff about who knows whom, but that's the short summary."

The plot was thickening. I turned to look directly at

Vincent. "I've got another hunch. Check all of the dog show winners in every AKC event, from the puppy classes in breed through best of breed, group, and show, judged by either Krause or Guerrero over the last three years. Look for any patterns you can find. Start by matching up the winners with who owned or bred the dogs, and use your imagination after that. All of this information is on-line and publically available via a site called infodog.com. Anything you can't find on Infodog will be somewhere on the AKC site, even if it isn't organized quite as conveniently. You'll just have to download the pertinent data and look for correlations."

Vincent looked even more excited, if that was possible. "I've got some fun software to do the hard parts for me. I just program it to look for key words on the web site. Claro, I can have this done for you by the end of the afternoon. Would you like to buy me dinner while we look over the results?"

That was easy, thanks to our Beverly Hills Nanny and dog trainer. "It's a deal. Plan on coming home with me for one of Bruce's patented dinners. You haven't seen Suzanne in a while and she's been asking about you. We can get eight eyes on the results and double our chances to see whatever jewels might be buried among the doggy litter."

I called Bruce and Suzanne to warn them we'd have company for dinner and got back to work. After hanging up I phoned Harold Carswell in New York using his personal cell phone number. Even with the three-hour difference in time zones, it was still early enough in the day in New York City to catch him at work. Once the social amenities were finished, I told him I didn't have anything in particular to report, but I needed some information. I asked him to keep my request completely confidential.

A short pause was followed by "Don't worry. I can respect your confidences."

That sounded like the right answer, but I wondered a bit about the pause. Maybe this was typical CEO behavior---think through all the angles before you answer. Whatever, it was time to ask my question. "Did any of your staff that we met in New York City object to hiring me for this job, or vote against hiring me at crunch time?"

Another pause, but it was longer this time. "Now that's a strange question. Is there something you should be telling me?"

Clearly Carswell was stalling while he thought through the implications of honestly answering my question. I made a note to myself, he was definitely a cagy bastard and it was a good thing we're on the same side. "No, not now. I just want to dot all of the I's and cross all of the T's, before I prepare my first report."

No pause this time. "I think this is the sort of information that a real gentleman keeps confidential."

I noted that he still hadn't answered my question. Could there be some kind of agenda here, or was he just protecting his employees like an honorable boss should? It was time to be a little less deferential and more to the point. "No, it's the sort of information you give a private investigator that you hired when he asks for it and you don't give him a hard time about it."

There was another long pause while he considered what I said. Finally, he seemed to make a decision and the floodgates opened. "Still a bit feisty, are we? OK, we'll do it your way. The vote to hire you was four in favor, three against. The no votes all said they were concerned about the cost. The three who voted no were Nathan Forrest, Hunter Lodge, and Rocket Rosswell. In addition, even though he voted yes for hiring you at crunch time, during our discussions before the vote Stanley Morgan expressed a great deal of doubt about the wisdom of hiring you. He thought you were the wrong man for the job, based upon what he called 'your undistinguished record' and the lack of input from the Board members in the preliminary selection process."

He paused for a few seconds before asking, "Does any of this information mean anything to you?"

"I don't know yet. But I think things are coming to a head here, and I appreciate your information. I should be back in touch soon."

We said our good-byes and hung up.

At dinner that night at our house, Bruce prepared a heart healthy and flavorful meal to honor Vincent's long residence in Chile, baked Chilean Sea Bass in a fresh salsa, baked yams, and a large salad. A crisp chilled Washington State Riesling complemented the fish nicely. Dessert would be fresh baked apple pie a la mode. We were all sitting around the big dining room table. Suzanne and I sat across from each other, with Vincent and Bruce sitting between us. Robert sat in his high chair between Suzanne and Bruce. Juliet lurked under the table to pick up any food Robert or an adult might drop towards her. Bruce quadrupled up on jobs as cook, waiter, nanny, and detective. He juggled all of these tasks with grace and aplomb.

The first half of the meal consisted of social niceties. Vincent updated us on his family. His two sons were at UC San Diego and UC Berkeley, doing very well, and his daughter was graduating this year from Santa Clara University. Robert's thus far less extensive, but by no means less important, achievements were appropriately noted, as were Juliet's.

The second half of the meal and dessert were used to talk business, and it turned out we had a lot to discuss. Bruce and Suzanne put Robert into his playpen in the family room and returned to the table. Juliet stayed with Robert to make sure he was protected from any monsters that might sneak in while Bruce wasn't on guard. As evidenced by the occasional barks and gurgles, they seemed to be entertaining each other quite well.

Vincent sipped some wine and leaned towards Suzanne, who had a pen and pad of paper to scribble random notes. "Just to update all of us so we're on the same page, I found some very heavy drug connections in this case. The Schafers are both mid-level drug dealers and protected DEA informants, while the murdered judges were each connected with a different major Mexican drug cartel. Claro. Interestingly, both judges and the Schaefers lived in the same small town in West Texas at the same time, when they were younger. Between drug deals and dog shows they had to know one another. Claro, it's a good guess the killings are tied in some way to the drug dealing. Bruce tells us recreational drugs are passed out like candy at the parties after the shows, and as I understand it, the AKC hired us because something seemed to be wrong at the dog shows. I assume all of this is interrelated."

Vincent took another sip or two of his wine and turned toward Bruce, looking directly at him. "Roger suggested I look a lot more closely at which dogs were chosen as winners when either of the two murdered judges were working at a show. I have some special software left over as a souvenir from my CIA days that isn't standard issue for police forces. It lets me do some tricks with very large data sets, so I can sometimes find things the police can't. This seems to be one of those times. Claro. My program looked at the winners in every AKC-sponsored event judged by either Krause or Guerrero in California, Arizona, Nevada, Oregon, or Washington from the smallest puppy classes through best of breed, group, and show over a span of three years. It matched up the winning dogs with who owned, handled, or bred the dogs that won. Guess what I found? There was a significant and moderately strong correlation between who was the Chairman or Chairwoman of the local sponsoring kennel club and whose dog went "Winners Dog" or "Winners Bitch" in the competition. There was also a weak, and not quite statistically significant, correlation between a dog belonging to the local club chair and its winning "Best of Breed."

Suzanne, Bruce, and I shared a brief laugh, which I explained to Vincent. "So all of the anecdotal bitching by the owners and handlers might have a basis in fact. A few of the judges, like Krause and Guerrero, do pay tribute to whoever invited them to their lucrative gig at the dog show. That is very funny. I'll have to include this in my report to Carswell, even if it does only look at the behavior of two specific judges, who we already know were crooks."

Looking briefly at his notes to refresh his memory Vincent continued. "Claro. Something else very interesting popped up. Over time, there's a statistical probability that any specific dog will win at a specific event. If we add up the total number of dog shows a specific dog has entered over the years, then factor in all of the judges the dog has encountered, we can calculate the "average chance" for this dog to win, pretty accurately and very precisely. Within a small margin of error, we can assign each dog that competes at AKC dog shows a specific average chance to win an award. The owners can skew these results a bit by picking which shows to enter, or not enter, their dogs into based on whether the judge has favored the dog in the past or not. However, the bias introduced into the calculation by owners picking which judges to show under is not a major source of error as long as the owners behave consistently. Based on my statistical analysis, several of the dogs owned by Hunter Lodge, the AKC comptroller, won significantly more often than they should have when Krause or Guerrero were judging."

Vincent, with a good sense of the dramatic, paused briefly to let that little piece of detection sink in.

"Do you think you might have seen a similar correlation with any invited judge from Texas or Arizona, Vincent?" asked Suzanne, who knew quite a bit about statistics and the scientific method.

Vincent smiled a big grin. "Good question, Suzanne. I thought about that too. So as a control, I picked a dozen more judges with addresses from the southwestern states or Mexico, more or less at random, and ran them through the same analysis. Two of them showed this same pattern of correlation as Krause and Guerrero, while the other ten didn't. What makes those two judges very, very interesting is they're the same two judges who didn't show up at the Golden Gate Show where Orval Krause was murdered. Their names were in the program as the judges for the show, but there were footnotes on the web site flagging the substitutions. If I remember correctly both judges were replaced by women who had addresses in the San Francisco Bay area. I think we can theorize their visa problems arose because Hunter Lodge knew Roger would be there. To avoid giving him anything to work with, Lodge may have cancelled the fixed competition portion of the competition so as not to give Roger the chance to see a crooked judge in action. The odds of those two specific judges being the only ones out of a panel of twelve potential judges not to show up for their shows by random chance are too low to believe this was a coincidence!"

I looked over at Vincent and Suzanne while I reacted to these new observations. "It never ceases to amaze me how arrogant the average crook is, and how often they make the stupidest mistakes because they're greedy and want it all right now. I had another idea I wanted to check out too. I started wondering whether Suzanne's stalker was really a sexual pervert or whether he might have another motive for trying to scare her. I'm sorry, Suzanne, but the possibility that you were irresistible to one of the seven older men who run the AKC after just an hour or two at dinner seemed less likely to me than that someone in that group didn't want me investigating those dog shows too closely. I called Harold Carswell to ask who voted against hiring me when he put the suggestion to his advisory board. Three of them voted against hiring me. Forrest, Rosswell, and Lodge, were the "no" voters, while Stanley Morgan seemed to be ambivalent. It looks like Lodge's name keeps coming up, over and over, at or near the top of our suspect list.

It was my turn to enjoy a moment of dramatic announcement. I paused a bit to enhance the suspense before telling them my plan for dealing with the stalker. "If my theory is right, Lodge sent the flowers and plants, but his motive wasn't stalking you, it was trying to divert me from learning what we've just found out thanks to Vincent's computer skills. I've thought a little bit more about what we can do to see that he's punished for his stalking escapades. I picked up some vibes from Carswell back in New York. He doesn't completely trust his staff, and may not be surprised if one of them was mixed up in something criminal. We know Lodge is too greedy for his own good, from his previous job history. Given that Lodge is the comptroller, I'll suggest to Carswell the AKC runs an in-depth audit to look for any embezzlement or diversion of funds."

Suzanne seemed to be lost in thought for about 30 seconds before asking Vincent, "Can you run the same computer program you used, backwards, so to speak? I'd be curious to find out whether any other judges show the same kind of bias a significant percentage of the time."

It was Vincent's turn to stop and think a moment before answering. "Claro. That's an enormous amount of data to crunch, Suzanne. It would require a huge amount of computer time and raise a lot of questions about the proper statistical handling of multiple comparisons within the same data set. I think we can get the same information more quickly by running all of the judges sequentially, by name. If we limit the data search by choosing only those individuals who have judged more than, say half a dozen shows, I think we can get through that problem in a weekend or two of computation time. It should take me about ten minutes to make a slight modification in the software programming and we could begin this task. If I set a criterion of significance to be more stringent than the 5% probability of an observation occurring by pure chance, I think we can get a reasonably small number of false positives. Claro, we can re-run all of the apparent positives another time or two and eliminate random chance as a cause of false positives. By that time we should have a small enough data set to just look at the results. We should be able to see if anything jumps out at us as egregiously as Krause and Guerrero did the first time."

Suzanne nodded her assent before she stood up abruptly and got a card and a fancy calligraphy pen from a desk in the study. She returned to the table and wrote carefully for a moment on the card. "Vincent, can I ask you for a favor, please?"

Vincent looked up at Suzanne and smiled. "Sure, Suzanne. What can I do for you?"

She looked the card over one more time before handing it to Vincent. "Tomorrow can you send a floral arrangement, completely anonymously, to Hunter Lodge at the AKC and include this card?"

Vincent took the card from Suzanne, read it, and chuckled. "Claro. It will be my pleasure!"

Suzanne leaned over and gently kissed his cheek. "Thank you."

Vincent read the card to us.

"Smart phones are handy,
Computers are good.
Thanks for the flowers
But you sent more than you should."

We all shared a good laugh.

The next few steps for our investigation seemed obvious. "It sounds to me like I'm finally ready to send my first report to the AKC. I suspect Carswell will feel he's gotten his money's worth, based on our finding a rotten apple in the corporate barrel for him. But we still have only theories, so I'll also make sure to emphasize that the job isn't completed yet. There are two murders to solve, and a heavy-duty drug scene to do eliminate, before the feeling something is wrong at the dog shows will go away for most of the regulars there."

I asked the big question. "What do you all think? Was Lodge involved in that part too or do we have two different sets of crimes and criminals doing parallel play here?"

Suzanne looked very thoughtful. "I'd guess the answer to that question is going to be two groups doing parallel play, Roger. The difference in the level of violence between Lodge fixing a couple of dog shows and stalking me versus the two brutal murders of the judges makes me think that different people are involved."

After a pause to let the significance of that comment sink in, she continued a lot more forcefully. "The apparent overlap between Lodge fixing shows with the two corrupt judges and both of the judges being murdered at dog shows may be pure coincidence, no matter how improbable. But a corrupt judge is a corrupt judge, whoever paid them to pick certain dogs as winners. Lodge may have had more judges in his pocket, or the drug dealers may have had their own set of crooked judges. The second set of criminals seems to prefer solving its problems by killing them, which sounds more like the drug cartels' modus operandi to me. They may still be hypothetical from a standpoint of the kind of proof that would hold up in a court of law, but I'm convinced they really exist."

She paused again to let us absorb her logic, then continued earnestly. "Lodge acted like a typical white-collar criminal, with his tools being non-violent intimidation and trying to scare you off, not murder. He certainly has the financial capacity to hire some serious muscle to slow you down, but he didn't try that route. If my theory is right, he'll still pay a very high price for seriously underestimating Vincent's and your capabilities.

"On the other hand, he could be in a lot worse trouble than he already is if my theory that there are two different groups working independently here is wrong, and we find a link between Lodge, the murder victims, and the killer we haven't identified yet."

We switched to dessert and a lot more discussion while we rehashed what we knew, making little progress. We had to learn a lot more about the murdered judges and their connections with the Schaefers, before we could move this part of the investigation forward. It was a sticky situation, because there was a pretty good chance we might run afoul of the DEA and whatever undercover operation they were running when we tried to do that.

Later that evening, I was lounging on a couch in front of the TV. Suzanne and Bruce relaxed in nearby chairs, reading or watching the show with me. It was one of my favorites, "The Glades", a mystery series set in southern Florida starring the Australian actor Matt Passmore as the unconventional police detective hero. As our hero was busily solving crime on the screen, Juliet slipped over to the couch and crawled up to share my space. After a particularly slurpy kiss or two, she made a typical GSP move to maximize body contact with one of her humans. Her head was draped over my leg, while her body was gently pressed against mine for pretty much the entire length of the dog. She pretended to watch the show, but I could hear her snoring contentedly during several of the shoot-'em-up scenes. It was a one-hour show with commercials and she barely moved the entire time. I scratched her ears and tummy off and on and was rewarded with a series of gentle purrs from a contented dog when I did. This particular bonding behavior was pretty typical of Juliet. Whichever one of us had the couch, Suzanne or I, generally also had Juliet as a couch mate. It was tough duty, but one of us had to do it.

Chapter21.More detective work

For security reasons, we sent the first formal report by U.S. Postal Service Priority Mail to Harold Carswell's home address. It was on our new agency letterhead from the recently renamed Bowman-Romero Detective Agency. The report was several pages long and contained a moderate amount of dynamite, at least as far as Hunter Lodge was concerned. Vincent and I decided to delay Suzanne's floral gift for a couple of days, until Carswell received this report some time the following evening. I suggested Vincent might want to frame a copy of the report for the wall at the entrance to the office to prove he was a full partner. He settled for the privilege of designing and printing our new letterhead on his computer. We celebrated his promotion with a strategy meeting over lunch to plan our next few moves.

Picking a restaurant for lunch within walking distance of our office wasn't a trivial decision. We're in Century City, the heart of the financial component of the Hollywood entertainment industry, a place where people did power lunches and A-list appearances. Nobody walks to a destination here. They rent limos to show off their status. Finding a restaurant that served good food at a reasonable price, where we wouldn't have to kill for a table, or pay the maitre d' a large ransom to seat us, was the challenge. Fortunately, such a place not only existed right around the corner from our office but hadn't been discovered yet by the in-crowd. We were regulars there. Over cheeseburgers and beer at our local yuppie restaurant, we strategized.

Between bites of burger and gulps of brew, I got to the point. "We have to learn a lot more about the Schaefers. The obvious distribution of labor is you on the computer, and me in person at the next dog show with Juliet. Is that OK with you?"

The junior partner nodded agreement with his mouth full of burger and roll. A little bit of beer and a big swallow preceded his next suggestion. "How about me flying to El Paso, renting a car, driving to San Francisco de Texas, and discretely asking around about the Schaefers and Krause? Claro. I can't pass as a Mexican when I speak Spanish with my Chilean accent, except with some dumb gringos. But I'm as fluent as any native Spanish speaker and nobody will question me if I claim to be Colombian. I could also check out the drug dudes across the border."

This suggestion came as a surprise to me. My partner had obviously been thinking, and he obviously could think out of the box. I nodded that I heard him and understood, then thought through Vincent's idea. "That could be dangerous. Somebody has already killed twice. I'd stay out of Mexico and be very, very careful in Texas, if I were you. Do you really think it's worth the risk to ask direct questions in Texas?"

Vincent snorted in derision. "What risk? Claro. With all of my CIA training, I should be able to take any two guys with bare hands or knives, and I'll take a pistol with me. I have a California carry permit. It's legal for me to take a gun in my luggage when I fly, and I can carry a concealed weapon in Texas. I'm not expecting to run into any pros. If I do, I trust my instincts to recognize them before I get into any trouble."

Uh-oh. I had to slow Vincent down before he got himself into a kill or be killed situation. And I had to do it without insulting his machismo. "I know you can take care of yourself, Vincent, but private detecting isn't a macho career track in real life. If you shot anyone in Texas, you'd rot in jail there and I couldn't help you. The agency rules for both of us are no guns on airplanes or in other states."

I motioned to the waitress for fresh beers, made an elaborate production of finishing mine just in time to refill my glass with the new beer arriving at the table, and sat back to savor the fresh brew.

I got back to the conversation with Vincent, looking

directly at him and trying to look decisive. "OK, then, you have my blessings and full access to the AKC expense account to take a trip to West Texas. How about your old CIA connections? Can they hack into the DEA computer and get us a copy of the Schaefers file? Or do you think you could do that on your own?"

He looked right back at me and answered pretty quickly. "No to both. My gut is telling me to stay as far away from the DEA as we can. If we can avoid it, we shouldn't leave either of our footprints anywhere near this mess. Claro. I don't think this investigation is going to have a happy ending for the Schaefers. I also don't think the DEA is going to be at all pleased to lose a couple of their long-term assets. We'll both be a whole lot happier if we stay way down under the DEA's radar on this investigation."

We finished lunch, I paid the check, and we walked back to the office.

The next morning Vincent was on a Southwest Airlines plane to El Paso, with a stop to change flights in Las Vegas. Then he rented a car to drive down I-10 to San Francisco de Texas, across the border from the Mexican state of Chihuahua. He arrived at his destination in mid-afternoon and checked into a motel that was part of a well-known chain. He quickly found a restaurant to grab a Tex-Mex lunch and practice his Spanish. After a couple of chiles rellenos, baked pasilla chiles stuffed with cheese and covered with a flavorful sauce, he visited the local high school library. The library was dusty and had an unoccupied feeling, as if it hadn't seen a student for months. All the books were on the shelves, with the ubiquitous local dust accumulating along their spines and tops. A gray-haired matron was puttering around behind the counter, looking quite bored, with a sign displaying the name Saundra Clyde. She looked like she might be in her early 60s, about the perfect age to have been a classmate of our targets.

Like any successful salesman, Vincent knew the first step

in getting what he wanted was finding someone to help and making them want to assist him. "Hello there. I'm new in town and wondered if you could help me out."

Saundra Clyde looked at him sternly. "Good afternoon, Sir. It's a hot one today, isn't it?"

Vincent got the hint. Small talk first. After the social amenities had been attended to, he could ask for help. "Yes indeed it is. I'll bet you could fry eggs on the sidewalk if you wanted to. This seems to be a nice little library and a pretty comfortable spot, even if it is hot outside."

Saundra patted her hair. "Are you visiting us here in San Francisco today for business or pleasure, Sir?"

Vincent leaned towards her, body language for, 'I come in peace, friend.' "Some of each, but mostly business today. I was hoping you might be able to help me with some of that business."

Saundra smiled, signaling the rules of behavior had been followed and they could get down to business now. "What can I do to help you today, Sir?"

Vincent introduced himself to her. Well, one of his many selves. "My name is Vincent Romero. I'm a party planner who's been hired to organize a mini class reunion for a small subgroup of classmates from the late 1960s and early 1970s. My client has lost track of a few former students he knew back then and he's eager to reconnect. I've got to confirm their attendance at the school and copy the relevant yearbook pages to select old images we can use for our program. I need your help finding years of attendance and a picture or two for each of the names on my list. Then I'd like to do some Xeroxing for each student we can find."

Saundra looked at him for a moment, without saying anything. Then she disappeared through a small door behind the desk, returning 5-10 minutes later with a cart piled high with stacks of old and dusty yearbooks spanning from 1960-1980. A moment later, she was helping him find the yearbooks he was looking for while she chattered away about the good old days in her hometown, where she had spent her entire life. Her hair was tied up in a tight bun and she wore an old-fashioned dress, complimenting her strict school-marm image. Her posture still said no-nonsense, but her eyes had a twinkle they hadn't had when Vincent first introduced himself. He sensed that she might not really believe his cover story, but had decided to help him for some reasons of her own.

"That's a few years ahead of me, but ah have an older sister and brother, so ah'd know whoever y'all are looking for. Can y'all tell me what names they went by back then?"

His first selection was good old Orval Krause. She pulled the book for 1969-1970 from the pile and they started looking. There were no indexes, so the easiest way to find what he wanted was to page through the book. It could have been much worse. The high school was small in those days, with a graduating class of only about 50 students. At least the pictures of the graduating classes were in alphabetical order. Sure enough, there was Krause in a cap and gown smiling out of a photo on page 35 of the book.

"Orval wasn't born here as ah remember, but he went all the way through school from first grade to graduation here in San Francisco. He wasn't much of a student and he wasn't a jock. Y'all might want to check out the school band. If mem'ry serves, he played some kind of horn. Not a bad choice. As ah recall he was pretty horny in those days." And she grinned an evil smile.

Vincent asked Saundra about making copies. She led him to an old Xerox machine with a counter attached. "Just go ahead and make all the copies y'all need. But be sure to be real careful with these books. They're all kinda stiff, so y'all make sure to treat 'em real gentle. When y'all are done we'll settle up. It's a nickel a page, so let's just write down where the counter's at now afore y'all start. Are y'all a-gonna need more pictures of Orval, or are y'all ready for the next one from the class?"

Pulling a notebook from his pocket, Vincent replied, "This will be just fine for Orval. Let's see who's next on the list." Vincent made a big production of looking up the name. "Claro. How about Jorge Guerrero?"

She happily bounced back to the yearbooks. Vincent made copies of the yearbook cover, the copyright page with the date shown, Orval's graduation mug shot and a photo of him playing the saxophone in the full marching band uniform. He also copied a couple of pages of text, one about Awful Krause's band activities and the other by his graduation photo, about his future plans (to be a world traveler and make a ton of money selling new cars).

Saundra still had the entire stack of yearbooks on the cart, with none of them pulled out, when she got back to where Vincent waited. "It's probably 'cause of all the cattle ranching we do locally, but we've got an expression 'round here that y'all should never try to bullshit an old bullshitter. Are y'all about ready to tell me what y'all are really doing here at the school so ah can help? Y'all just asked me to find out about two men who were here 40 years ago and both just got murdered in California in the past month. Are y'all some kinda cop?"

Vincent thought about things for a bit and opted to tell her the truth. He already had what he'd come for and now saw a chance to get a whole lot more.

"Thanks," replied Saundra. "That sounds a whole lot better. I'm just an old lady who doesn't mean much of anything to anybody 'round here, but Ah'd like to help y'all nail them-there bastards. One of the men who got killed by those drug runners a long time ago was my Pa. Ah'll help anybody who wants to see 'em in jail or dead. The next name up is Jorge Guerrero. He never went to high school here in town. They moved a few towns over when he hit his teens. But he had a pickup truck and was part of the social life, so ah knew him. Average student, played some football, did a bit of bird and deer hunting, and was into raising dogs he hunted with."

Vincent continued by asking, "Claro. I've got two more names on my list. Can you help me with Albert or Sadie Schaefer?"

"Y'all are into some purty heavy stuff, ain't y'all, mister? Those two are big-time trouble. They were both in school here 'bout the same time we're talking 'bout. Albert was in and out of trouble all the time. If y'all wanted to see him, the best place to look was detention. He was the guy to go to for beer or weed if y'all wanted to party. Lousy student, just got by 'nuff to graduate. Sadie was a wild little thang. A lot of the boys went out with her once, if y'all take my drift. She and Albert were together for most of high school.

"Ah suppose y'all wants to pick my brain 'bout what happened to all of them after graduation too."

Vincent nodded. "Claro. I'd appreciate hearing anything you could tell me about them."

"Jorge Guerrero's easy. The whole family moved to Arizona 'bout that time and we all lost track of him. Ah've heard rumors 'bout drug dealing and Jorge, but don't know nothin' for sure.

"Orval stayed 'round here fer a year or two after graduatin' before he moved to El Paso. He made a livin' sellin' used cars and trainin' guard dogs he bred. Orval was married fer a couple of years a long time ago, but that ended with a divorce and no kids fer him. There were lots of rumors 'bout him makin' and sellin' weed, meth, and crank, but he stayed out of police-type trouble. His Dobies have been a big item for the local meth lab owners on both sides of the border for the last thirty years.

The word is he got paid top dollar for his guard dogs by the local trailer park chemistry industry. His dogs were well trained and real mean, just right for protectin' a small meth lab on yer property.

"The Schaefers were real good customers for Orval's Dobies through the years. They were his friends as well as his customers. This is a rough area. We've got a purty large rural area with just a small Sheriff's department to patrol it, so there's lots of drugs comin' over the border headed north 'round here. This is one of the biggest drug smugglin' routes in the country. There's a whole lot of killin' 'cross the border in Mexico while the different drug cartels fight it out for who controls the transport route. Scuse me a minute, honey."

Saundra took a break to walk over to a nearby water fountain, drank a bit, and came back to continue from where she'd left off. "The Schaefers are a big part of our local drug problem. There've been rumors the Schaefers work for the DEA as informants and that the DEA protects them from the local law in return. There were also lots of rumors they were loyal to the Sinoloa Cartel, which used to be in charge of all the drug traffic on the Mexican side of the border. Somehow all of their tips to the DEA resulted in grabbin' drug shipments from, or arrests of, the Gulf cartel members, who were the rival gang back when there was a big turf war goin' full blast in Mexico. The Sinoloa cartel's mostly gone now, or in jail, or killed, but the Zetas are takin' over. They're worse killers than the Sinoloa hombres ever were. And there was a lot of whisperin' goin' on, suggestin' the Schaefers did some of that killin' for the Sinoloa Cartel and the Zetas, on our side of the border, durin' the big gang wars."

"Can any of this be proved or is it all just rumors?" asked Vincent.

"The only way the Schaefers are still runnin' around loose and not dead or in jail after all this time has to be the protection they get from the Federal Narcs. Y'all need to try pullin' at the loose threads from that end, if y'all want to nail Albert and Sadie. Ah'd guess there's been half a dozen different murders tied to Albert Schaefer, but the local crim'nal investigations went nowhere after the Feds got involved. Someone needs to put an end to that stuff. Murder is murder and drug runnin' is drug runnin', no matter who's payin' y'all to do it."

Vincent thanked Saundra Clyde for all of her help, and made a big donation to the high school library fund despite her protests. Next, he drove back to the motel, parked his car, and walked over to the local Sheriff's office to talk with the local law enforcement folks.

A short walk took Vincent from the motel to the Sheriff's Office. Vincent showed his credentials to a deputy at the front desk, which earned him an interview with Tom Hawks, the Chief Deputy, after a 15-minute wait. Hawks was several inches over 6 feet, in his 30s, with the heavily muscled upper arms of a serious weight lifter. He wore a standard issue uniform, addding a 10-gallon Stetson hat placed casually on a convenient hook on his wall. He stood, offered his hand for a shake. "What can I do for y'all, Mr. Romero?"

Vincent shook the proffered hand before taking a seat in the chair in front of the deputy's desk. To introduce himself he handed Deputy Hawks his business card, which Hawks examined carefully. "I'm trying to get some information about a couple of your current residents in connection with a case I'm working on in California. I was hoping you might be willing to share some information with me. Of course, it's up to you to decide what you might want to tell me about my suspects. However, I think we're talking about two of your less desirable citizens here in San Francisco, Texas. You might want to help see them be prosecuted in California, where they may be more likely to actually come to trial than around here."

Hawks looked at Vincent with an expression of curiosity on his face. "Y'all really know how to get my attention, Mr. Romero. Why don't y'all tell me who these illustrious citizens of my town are, and what sorts of crimes y'all allege they've committed in California?"

Vincent relaxed and sat back in his chair. "The crimes I'm talking about are the murders of two of your former citizens, Orval Krause and Jorge Guerrero. There are also probably some drug-related felonies involved, but for now I'd prefer to focus on the murders. The illustrious citizens of your town, to use your phrase, are Albert and Sadie Schaefer. Claro. I gather they've been on your radar for a long time, but are somewhat untouchable around here. I don't think we'd have that problem with the jurisdiction involved in California. Ironically enough, the first killing occurred in San Francisco de California."

Hawks' face took on a pained expression as if he'd bitten into something with a bitter taste. "Officially, I can't talk to y'all about anything to do with an open case, so the Schaefers are off limits. Unofficially, I go off duty at 7 P.M., and I'd be open to the suggestion that y'all buy me a beer at the San Francisco Bar to celebrate the remarkable coincidence that we both come from cities with the same name." The deputy stood, shook Vincent's hand, and gave him directions to the bar.

Vincent spent the remaining time before his appointment walking around the small town to get a feeling for the place and a little bit of much needed exercise. He walked into the front door of the San Francisco Bar promptly at 7:00. It was a narrow, deep building with the bar running the length of the wall on the right. Most of the stools in front of the bar were occupied, almost all of them by men sitting alone or in pairs, quietly drinking beer a glass at a time. The lighting was dim as compared to the sunny street, but you could see who the people were after your eyes adjusted. The wall on the left was set up as a line of booths, most of which were occupied by couples or by groups of four people. Beer in pitchers was the drink of choice at the tables, some of which also had tubs of peanuts to accompany the beer. Between the booths and the bar were a couple of aisles to walk from the front to the back of the bar, with a series of tables and chairs down the middle, wherever they could fit in. There was a good-sized crowd at the tables. Immediately to the left of the door was an old-fashioned jukebox spewing out country-western ballads. This was a drinking crowd, not a dancing one, as evidenced by the thick layer of broken peanut shells coating the floor under and around the tables.

Tom Hawks waved Vincent over to a booth near the back of the bar. A pitcher of beer and three empty glasses sat in the middle of the table, probably waiting for him. He noticed the deputy's hospitality didn't include peanuts. Vincent slid onto the bench across from Hawks.

"Good evening, Deputy Hawks. I assume you had enough time to check me out since we talked this afternoon. Is everything OK?"

"Your identity checks out. Y'all seem to be who y'all say y'all are, at least as of last year. Nobody in Los Angeles or San Francisco knows much of anything about y'all and it's impossible to find any paper 'bout y'all that goes back more than a year or two ago. On the other hand, your boss Roger Bowman gets glowing reviews from several police detectives I talked to and that's good enough for me. I think that translates to my talking to y'all tonight is OK with my boss. I've invited the Sheriff to join us. He goes back a lot further than me in this town, so should know a lot more about the history of things than I do. In the meantime, we can talk 'bout our most frustrating criminal problem and try to help y'all help us to solve it."

Deputy Hawks poured two glasses of beer for himself and Vincent. "The Sheriff will want to talk to y'all about some of the things y'all been askin me 'bout earlier. While we wait for Sheriff Harkins to join us here, let me tell y'all some background about what law enforcement is like when a small Sheriff's department has the responsibility to patrol a rural area larger than many whole states back east. Most of it's empty space, sandy desert, canyons, and small mountains. A lot of it is unfenced ranch land and now windmill farms generating electricity. We're understaffed, underfunded, and asked to do the impossible every day."

He took a long draught of beer from his glass and wiped his mouth with the back of his hand. "There are substations managed by a deputy in each of the towns in our county, but most of these are one-man operations. We have a couple of small planes to patrol large areas of empty space, but if they spot anything that looks like it needs investigation, the response time for a patrol car can be hours. The border basically runs on the honor system and leaks like a sieve. There aren't enough Federal Border Patrol officers in the entire county to make any difference. Directly across the border is a war zone where rival drug cartels are better armed than the Mexican Army. Some of that violence spills over across the border and affects us. This is a poor county, except for a few wealthy ranchers who own most of the land, so we have all of the crime that goes with poverty. Cottage industry out here is often a trailer in the middle of nowhere that serves both as a home for a family and as a meth lab. The meth makers compete with each other and with the Mexican cartels for the local customer base. And I mean competition with automatic weapons and shotguns."

Hawks poured the second round of beers. "So now y'all know part of why we haven't arrested and tried all of the locals that we think are involved in drug trafficking. There are other reasons too, which the Sheriff will talk about with us shortly. I see him comin' in the door, so y'all will finally get to meet him."

The deputy did the introductions. Sheriff Harkins was shorter than his deputy by at least six inches, in his late 50s or early 60s, deeply tanned, wore western garb rather than a uniform, and sported a large mustache with long sideburns. The deputy filled the third glass of beer while Harkins sat down at the booth. Vincent noted the Sheriff chose to sit on his side of the booth, effectively pinning him in place on the bench they both occupied. Whatever his intent, Harkins" move definitely seemed more intimidating than friendly.

"We're not very big on small talk hereabouts," the Sheriff began. "There's a couple of things that bother me about y'all. If y'all can explain them we can talk 'bout our local problems a lot more frankly than if I'm still bothered by them. Do y'all get my drift here?"

Vincent turned around to look directly at him, trying to give an image of confidence. "Loud and clear. What do you want to know, Sheriff?"

Harkins returned the look, staring directly at Vincent. "When we called back to check out your story with the local police in California, they told us y'all were who y'all said y'all were and your detective agency is on the up and up. But, and it's a big but, nobody knows anything about y'all before last year. Do y'all want to explain?"

Vincent tried on an aw-shucks, gee-whiz look of total innocence. "Claro, there's no mystery about my past, Sheriff Harkins. Until last year, I was teaching biochemistry at the University of Chile branch campus in Iquique. I worked there for most of my adult life."

Harkins continued to stare directly at him. "Are y'all a Chilean citizen?"

Vincent sipped some beer and leaned forward directly towards the Sheriff. The body language said, 'we're just two guys talking here'. "No, I'm an American, born and raised in Wisconsin. I moved to Chile when I married my wife, after we finished college here in the United States. She has dual citizenship, American and Chilean."

Harkins visibly relaxed a bit. "Good answer. Is there someone I can check it out with?"

Vincent leaned back, sipped some more beer, and responded, "Yeah, you could check this out with my partner in the detective agency, Roger Bowman, in Los Angeles. Or you can call the University of Chile in Iquique, but that would take a bit of time or somebody who can speak fluent Spanish on the phone."

Harkins finally picked up his beer, drank some, and leaned back a bit. "That's no problem. Most of the folks here, around the border, know some Spanish. I may just do that tomorrow. For now, I think I believe y'all enough to have that talk y'all wanted to have. What do y'all want to know from me? And is this all 'bout me telling y'all things y'all want to hear, or do we get some information back in return?"

Vincent looked thoughtfully at the Sheriff and his deputy while he decided how much he wanted to tell them. Finally he decided when in doubt telling the truth was a good policy, but only as much of the truth as he had to. No more. Neither of these two lawmen was either naïve or gullible.

"Claro. My partner Roger Bowman is working undercover for a major national corporation. He's investigating alleged criminal activities at the large dog shows that are held more or less weekly in California and its surrounding states through most of the year. There have been a couple of murders recently at the dog shows. They seem to be connected because both of the victims originally came from around here. I assume you're both aware that Orval Krause and Jorge Guerrero were killed at California dog shows where they were judges?"

He paused to let that sink in then continued. "Roger has obtained evidence a couple of other citizens from here may be involved in drug dealing at these dog shows. If that were true, it puts them near the top of the suspect list for the murders. I'm talking about the Schaefers. I also know it's an open secret around here that Albert and Sadie are drug dealers and probably killers, and they could be connected with the Zeta cartel in Mexico. I've been told the Schaefers seem to lead a charmed life because they are DEA informants. For whatever reason, it appears the DEA is protecting them from the law, which would be you two here in town. That's why I came to talk to you."

Vincent took another sip of beer, hoping the Sheriff and deputy were ready to believe he was as stupid as he sounded. If he came across as dumb enough not to be a real threat to them, they might let something slip out. Deputy Hawks refilled all three glasses. "What I'd like to know is how much of my information is true, and whether you two would like to help me build a case that'll get the Schaefers in jail for life in California, well out of your jurisdiction, no matter what the DEA thinks it wants."

"Y'all are well informed, Mr. Romero," replied Harkins. "The broad picture is exactly as y'all described it. And nothing would make me and Deputy Hawks happier than seeing both the Schaefers in striped uniforms at a maximum security prison anywhere y'all want to put them. So I'll fill in some details for y'all. We knew about Krause's death, which was big news around here. We hadn't heard about Guerrero being killed, but he lives in Arizona these days and there's no reason we should have been notified about his murder. Was it done the same way?"

Since he could find that information on the Internet, Vincent had no reluctance to tell him. "Yes, he was strangled with a dog leash, just like Krause."

The Sheriff had another question. "What makes y'all think the Schaefers did it?"

This time he didn't need to know. "I really don't know the answer to that question. Roger hasn't had a chance to tell me yet. Before I left Los Angeles this morning, I didn't hear about any arrests in this case. There's clearly a need for more evidence than they already have against the Schaefers. Which is why I came out here to talk to you and where I hope you can help."

The ball was back in Sheriff Harkins' court and the expression on his face let Vincent know that he knew it. "OK, let me explain to y'all how things got so messed up out here. We arrested the Schaefers more than a dozen years ago for making and selling methamphetamine. It wasn't the first time either had been arrested, but this time we had them cold. We caught them red handed with a lab in their trailer and several kilos of meth all neatly weighed and packaged ready to sell. Less than an hour after we arrested them, their lawyer showed up and advised them not to say anything to us. They hadn't talked at all until then and they sure weren't about to after the lawyer told them to shut-up."

The waitress passed our table and put a bucket of peanuts on it. The Sheriff picked up a handful of the nuts and started to shell them and pop the nuts into his mouth while he thought about what he was going to tell me next. "They were sitting in a jail cell here in town a few hours later when a couple of suits showed up in a government issue Ford. The suits were obviously feds and pretty darn sure of themselves. Their ID said DEA and they said they owned the Schaefers and we couldn't have them. It seemed like the Schaefers' crooked lawyer had made a deal with the DEA to swap information for immunity. I said 'no'. Then they waved a piece of paper in front of me signed by a Federal Judge that said 'yes'. That piece of paper said I had to release the Schaefers into their custody or be in contempt of court. There wasn't a whole lot I could do about it. There still isn't. My guess is both the local DEA and the judge who signed the writ were all being paid off by the drug cartel, but there's no way to prove it. Now, here we are a dozen years later and nothing has changed."

After another momentary break to shell and eat a few more of the peanuts, he continued. "The whole deal stank to me. The Schaefers were back in business down here within a matter of days, figuratively thumbing their noses at us. The DEA, who we had never gotten any help from before, was suddenly making headlines with all of their drug raids and seizures. This all went on during the big gang war between the Sinoloa and Gulf cartels in Mexico. The Gulf cartel was the larger and stronger gang. After a while the pattern became obvious. All of the drug interdictions and arrests in the United States seemed to target the Gulf Cartel members. Meanwhile, the Schafers were working with the rival gang, the Sinoloa Cartel. The Gulf Cartel were able to kill most of the leaders of the Sinoloa cartel that didn't end up in Mexican jails, but the gang war made them lose their power in Chihuahua State and became a smaller cartel based further east. The Gulf cartel finally won the battle, but lost the war. The Zetas took over the vacuum left after the Sinoloa leadership was killed or jailed, and the Schaefers became Zetas."

The last of the beer in the pitcher disappeared into our glasses as the story came to an end. "That sounds pretty much exactly like what I expected. Claro. I'd like to help. What would you like to see me do at this point?" asked Vincent.

Harkins emptied his glass in two big gulps. "I thought y'all'd never ask," replied Sheriff Harkins. "I think y'all 'll like my idea. There're some things y'all can do as a stranger hereabouts that would cost me my job as Sheriff if I ever tried to do them myself. The DEA agents have as much as told me that a few times, whenever I was tempted to arrest the Schaefers again. I'm not quite ready to retire, but maybe you could make some things happen that I can't. "

Vincent finished his beer to keep pace. "What do you have in mind, Sheriff?"

The Sheriff scratched his mustache to remove a bit of peanut debris. "I know a young, ambitious, and fairly honest reporter who works for a good-sized paper in El Paso, as well as writing stuff for our local weekly paper here in San Francisco. How would y'all like to give him an interview on your way home tomorrow morning? The story I have in mind is the one where y'all leak to this particular reporter about the DEA being an accessory to multiple drug dealing felonies and several murders via the Shaefers. Y'all can tell him to quote you as an anonymous source and say anything y'all want to imagine, out loud, including how they're making, manufacturing, and selling drugs, plus killing the competition. The article can focus on morality versus situational ethics, for a big Federal agency, and can skip most of the actual details. That should stir the pot. It might even get some of the DEA bosses back in Washington to take a good long look at our local DEA operation. I don't think they'll like what they see. They certainly won't like all of the bad publicity they'll be getting in the media."

Vincent smiled sardonically. He especially appreciated the "on your way home tomorrow morning" line. That was a very cute way of saying he'd worn out his welcome in West Texas. "Claro. It's very kind and thoughtful of you to let me have the chance to do this, Sheriff. That way, if there's any fallout from a very pissed off and powerful federal law enforcement agency, it's on my head, not yours, right? I assume you've been waiting patiently for a potential sucker like me to roll into town for the past twelve years or so, haven't you?"

Sheriff Harkins smiled back. "I wouldn't call y'all a sucker, Mr. Romero. I prefer to kinda think of y'all as a public spirited citizen."

Vincent did some mental calculations of time and his window of vulnerability. "Set the interview up for the El Paso airport, tomorrow morning just before my mid-morning flight back to Los Angeles. And make sure there aren't any leaks. If I can get out of Texas without meeting your DEA friends, I should be pretty safe from reprisals. I have some old friends in Washington who should be able to discourage the temptation for any retaliation, once I'm back home in California."

The Sheriff nodded. "So you have some powerful friends in the Nation's Capital. What did you say y'all were doing while y'all were in Chile?"

"I was just a simple college teacher," replied Vincent, humbly and insincerely.

They shook hands and said their good-byes. Later that night, back at his motel, Vincent called Roger on his cell phone to bring him up to date on what was happening. Roger listened attentively without interruption until Vincent had finished.

"What do you think I should do now?" Vincent asked. "Or should I say y'all while I'm down here?"

Roger was silent for about half a minute while he thought things through. "I assume you've already paid for the motel in San Francisco de Texas with a credit card. I'd sneak out of the motel and drive to El Paso right now to spend the night anonymously. No credit cards. You need to pay cash and to use a phony name when you find a motel somewhere near the airport. Just in case, return the rental car tonight at the airport so the local DEA agents can't ambush you at the rental place tomorrow. I would assume there could be some leaks. You don't want to bring the DEA into this if it can be avoided, particularly while you're on their turf. Check with the airline whether you can get an earlier flight out tomorrow morning, or better yet, a late flight tonight, at least as far as Las Vegas. You can stand the reporter up tomorrow morning; it won't be the first or the last time its happened to him. After the Schaefers have been arrested and charged with murder, you can do an interview, if you think that's a good idea. But let's not do anything to spook them before the case is airtight in California. I'm not 100 percent sure how secure your phone line is down there. I'll fill you in on what's happening here when you get back to the office tomorrow."

"Claro," replied Vincent.

The trip to El Paso was quick and uneventful. Rather than testing the system to see what would happen if he missed the scheduled meeting with the reporter at The El Paso Airport, Vincent caught a late night flight to Las Vegas, connecting with a flight to LAX arriving very early the next morning. He spent a lot of time en route thinking about all he had seen and heard that day. He concluded, inevitably, that the odds were about 5:1, maybe as bad as 10:1, he'd have been met by at least two or three cartel killers with Uzis if he'd shown up for the appointment Deputy Hawks had arranged for him. The switch in flights he made might be traceable, especially with help from the local DEA agents. But the power of the various drug cartels or the Zetas was a lot less to worry about in California than on their own turf along the Texas, New Mexico, and Arizona borders or in Northern Mexico itself.

Vincent's previous training as a CIA agent kicked in, especially the lesson that you get your sleep whenever you can while you're on a case. He got some sleep on both legs of the flights west.

Chapter23.Back in California

Vincent returned safely to Los Angeles with no further incidents and was at the office to greet me when I came in, shortly after eight. Over coffee and croissants, catered by yours truly, the senior partner, I updated Vincent on what happened while he was gone.

I leaned back in my chair with my feet on the desk and my hands interlocked behind my head, looking directly at Vincent. "I should probably explain where the stuff I told you yesterday came from. Part of the reason I got so conservative with my advice to you last night was a phone call I got from Steve Callahan, just before we spoke to each other yesterday afternoon. That morning, Steve got a visit from the local agent-in-charge of the DEA in San Francisco de California. The DEA guy, who was a real schmuck and starting throwing his weight around, told him that the Schaefers were strictly off limits on grounds of "National Security". The agent-in-charge, a dork named Napelli, blustered about putting Steve in jail if he didn't cooperate. Callahan must have seen a couple of Clint Eastwood movies since we worked with him in Vallejo. He put Napelli in handcuffs, threw him into a cell, and charged him with being an accessory after the fact to murder. I'd have enjoyed seeing that; maybe there's a tape somewhere we can get a look at."

Vincent and I both had a good laugh as we replayed the scene in our heads. "A few hours later, Steve let him out of his cell just long enough to remind him the SFPD was the law in San Francisco. The federal authorities have no jurisdiction in a local murder case. The agent in charge, who was a very pissed off dork by that time, borrowed his phone and called his superior in Washington to explain what had happened to him. Steve thinks he may have expected to get an Air Force flyover and a Special Forces battalion to help him restore his authority. It was a very one-sided conversation, with Napelli mostly listening and quite obviously being reamed out by long distance phone. He was a very changed man when he got off the phone. It looks like the

DEA may be ready to throw the Schaefers to the wolves, at least in California. Our friend Detective Callahan is very pissed off and ready to go after Albert and Sadie with everything he's got. The last I heard yesterday, he was just waiting for warrants to serve and cooperation from the local cops."

Vincent got up and refilled his coffee cup at the pot. He gestured to ask whether I wanted a refill, which I didn't want or need. I nodded no. He came back to sit down while I continued, "We need to call Steve Callahan and bring him up to date on all you found out in our sister city of San Francisco de Texas. It paints a very nasty picture of Krause, Guerrero, and the Schaefers, as well as the DEA down by the border and whoever their supervisors are. What's your best guess, are Sheriff Hawkins and Deputy Hawks dirty, or just stupid and incompetent?"

Vincent had obviously thought about this and answered immediately. "Those two have got to be dirty. It's a very, very small town in San Francisco de Texas, where there aren't any secrets. Sheriff Hawkins and his deputy have to know everything that's gone down. They've covered it up and let it happen. No se. Whoops, I mean I don't know. It could be greed or fear of the cartels or fear of the DEA, or all three things, keeping them from arresting known murderers and drug dealers. They've got to be making quite a few dollars or pesos while they're looking the other way. Damn, I was in a Spanish speaking town for just a day and I'm already thinking in a mix of Spanish and English."

There was a croissant beckoning me from the paper plate where I'd left them. It practically jumped from the plate to my hand, and from my hand to my mouth. Mom would have chewed me out for talking with my mouth full, but it tasted pretty good.

I had of course reached exactly the same conclusions as Vincent, just sooner. "That's one of the biggest reasons I wanted you out of there and safely back in L.A.. I didn't buy the story you were actually going to meet a reporter in complete safety at the El Paso airport. Especially the part where you'd get to discuss the DEA cover-up, when they'd only just met you and didn't have enough time to check you out thoroughly. My guess is you'd have met a couple of killers from the Zeta Cartel instead, and you might not have won that particular battle. Those guys use machine guns in the middle of crowds and couldn't care less about the collateral damage. I wasn't ready to lose my new partner this soon."

Swallowing the last bite of croissant, I continued, "I think we should call Steve Callahan to update him on what you know. I don't know when or where, but I assume he was getting ready to arrest the Schaefers more or less immediately. I also don't know whether he's ready to take on the DEA singlehanded. Remember, we're talking about some serious crimes getting committed under their supervision, if not direct orders. They have a lot more motive for a cover-up than a big PR disaster. The DEA may need some guidance to develop the motivation to do the right thing in this situation. It might be worth our checking with Callahan to see if he knows a friendly reporter out here to whom you could give your story."

Vincent nodded in agreement as I went on. "Why don't we call him as soon as you get back to your desk and have your notes organized? You take the lead, but it's probably a good idea if I listen in, without mentioning I'm there. Then you'll have a witness in case he suddenly decides to switch over to the wrong side."

Vincent introduced himself to Steve Callahan over the phone, and made small talk to break the ice for a minute or two. After he described the vast emptiness that is West Texas and the amusing name of our California San Francisco's little brother Pancho, they got to the point. Vincent repeated everything he had told me, pretty much the same way he told the story the first time.

Callahan had a question. "Why do you think they told you so much of the truth, Vincent? I'm thinking just about everything they told you is true, except the part where they claim to be innocent bystanders, who didn't take part in any of the crimes being committed."

Vincent thought for a short moment. "I asked myself the same question several times while I was flying back home. The only logical answer is, they didn't expect me to live long enough to tell anybody what I'd heard."

Steve asked, "Are you listening in on the line too, Roger?"

So much for my clever strategy of not taping the call so I didn't break any laws. "Yes, I'm here".

Callahan's voice came back on the line. "Good. That way I'll only have to say all this once. We arrested the Schaefers at 4 AM this morning at an RV Park in the Kern County Fairgrounds, where they were staying for a local dog show. CSI-Bakersfield is going over the RV to look for evidence. Our murder case is still pretty thin. We could use some forensic evidence that connects the two victims with the RV. The Schaefers are on their way back to San Francisco via a very slow and bureaucratic route. They won't have a chance to lawyer up for another 10 or 12 hours, maybe longer. That should give us plenty of time for the CSI crew to completely examine the RV.

"Former DEA Agent-in-Charge, Napelli, is on his way back to Washington, DC. A couple of federal marshals are escorting him so he doesn't get lost during the trip. He's technically not under arrest until he gets to the jurisdiction where they want to charge him. He'll either be arrested or an unemployed civilian by this time tomorrow. The FBI is urgently putting together a task force out of El Paso to investigate charges of municipal and federal law enforcement agency corruption in West Texas. They'll have boots on the ground later this afternoon. Harkins and Hawks are under surveillance. Neither of them is going anywhere before the FBI gets there. If they try to run, the orders are to use whatever force is necessary to restrain them. The FBI isn't fooling around here."

There was another short pause on the line. "Things seem to be under control here, at least for the moment. The short-term, worst-case scenario is the DEA chickens out and decides to cover up the whole mess. Do you have any suggestions about how to make sure they can't, Roger?"

I sat up straighter and tried to sound more confident than I felt. This case seemed to be coming into the home stretch, and Vincent's quick trip to Texas was going to play a big part in its solution. "As a matter of fact, we do. We like Sheriff Harkins' and Deputy Hawk's idea of turning up the heat under DEA Washington. However, we'd rather use a real reporter and a real newspaper. Vincent can freely share the results of his investigations in West Texas and the DEA's role in murder and drug dealing down there. The arrests of Sheriff Harkins and his deputy will confirm Vincent's story for the reporter. I imagine they would run with it, especially if they get Vincent's interview near the late afternoon deadline. What do you think, Steve? Do you know a good crusading reporter who would write this story based on a telephone interview with a private detective using a phony name?"

There was another short pause from Callahan's end of the line. "I think I do. Give me the headlines and please make sure Vincent is at the telephone from 2 PM on. Use a burner cell phone, if you want to be untraceable, and give me that number when you get it."

"Let me get this part, Vincent," I volunteered.

"The headlines will be:

(1) Vincent can tell him about Orval Krause's Dobies being the pick guard dogs for all of the meth lab proprietors in

that part of West Texas and along the border there in Mexico. That should imply a motive for one of the murders.

(2) He can talk about who were high school classmates from the Yearbooks, including both murder victims and the accused killers, and about who was a known drug dealer back in those days.

(3) About how other drug-related murders have been tied to Albert Schaefer, but the investigations were squashed by DEA.

(4) About the Schaefers being known as DEA informants."

"That's kind of circumstantial, isn't it Roger? As you well know, you couldn't get a D.A to go to court with that alone. Why do you want to hold back the real evidence?"

"Because there's a lot more going on here that you don't know about yet. Why don't you fly down this afternoon and have dinner with us? We can tell you what we both know and what I suspect, and decide what we should do next."

We made arrangements to meet his flight and I rehearsed Vincent for his big dramatic role as an anonymous informant to the media. Then we left the office for a working lunch to discuss all of our other pending cases, and who would be doing what on each of them.

Our office is on the second floor of a high-rise office building in Century City. As usual, we took the stairs and went out the front door, heading towards our favorite upscale burger restaurant, a block to the south of the building. The first indication that something was wrong was the squeal of brakes as a speeding SUV roared towards us. Vincent acted instinctively, based on decades of training and practice in the spy business. He shoved me back and down violently, as he also dove for cover behind the giant potted plants at the entrance to our building. The squeal of brakes was now accompanied by the chatter of a couple of Uzis spraying the area where we had been standing a few seconds before.

The area a few feet above our sprawled bodies was sprayed with 9mm slugs at a rate of 600 rounds per minute while two shooters emptied two clips at us. The usual clip for an Uzi holds 32 rounds, so it takes a bit less than 3 seconds to shoot a full clip. It felt more like 3 minutes while it was happening. I got a quick look at the SUV and the shooters while all this was going on. Strangely enough, I immediately recognized the weapons as Uzis, a small and terribly efficient submachine pistol designed by Major Uziel Gal in the late 1940s for the Israeli army. It is now the weapon of choice, all over the world, for close-quarters shooting of a whole lot of bullets in a very short time. I didn't recognize either of the shooters, both Anglos in their mid-forties and kind of generic looking. The SUV was dark, probably black, with tinted windows, with California license plates 6CGI something, something, something, and last seen getting the heck out of there as fast as it could. At lunch hour, this street is usually crowded with pedestrians headed for a quick meal at the local restaurants. Fortunately we were early for lunch, so nobody got shot. Vehicular traffic on the avenue and cross streets was heavy though.

Everything happened so suddenly and so fast, there really wasn't enough time to feel scared while the shooting was happening. The part where my hands shook and I suddenly became aware of my own mortality came afterwards. The adrenaline finally started pumping as we stood up and brushed ourselves off. From the outside Vincent looked cool and calm. I suppose I did, too. Speaking for myself, on the inside I was frightened and angry. I made a mental note if I ever had any opportunity to meet either of those two bastards again neither was going to get away with this kind of casual disregard for human life and potential collateral damage. I could sense Vincent was thinking the same thing.

I got up and brushed myself off. "Thanks, Vincent. I owe you one. You just saved my life."

Vincent looked at me and smiled. I can tell when he's rattled since he tends to sprinkle his sentences with occasional Spanish words. "Claro. De nada. That's what partners do. I think we're safe for now, but we should probably get off the street muy rapido, in case they come back."

We walked quickly over to the restaurant and ordered burgers and beers. I called the cell phone number of a detective I knew from the local police precinct named Hawthorne. We reported the attempted shooting let him know we were OK, where we were now, and where we'd be later for interviewing. He was already en route in response to the first 911-call the police had received from a bystander. He would catch us at the restaurant in 5 minutes, and told me to stay where we were until he had a chance to interview us both.

"What do you think that was all about?" Vincent asked.

"Obviously someone doesn't like one or both of us. Equally obviously we have to start being a lot more careful since there's a good chance we'll see those guys again, probably sooner rather than later. And finally, somebody bad just made a big, big mistake."

Detective Oliver Hawthorne was about my age and height, 6'2", but heavier at about 220 pounds of bone and muscle. He had a soul patch beard and broad sideburns on his otherwise clean shaven, handsome, dark ebony face. Hawthorne had made the rank of Lieutenant fast enough that he was obviously smart and competent. We were not really friends, but knew each other professionally, dating back to when we both started out on the LAPD as rookie cops. I knew him well enough to order a fresh cup of coffee, which was delivered to him as he sat at our table.

"Tell me about it," he said looking directly at me as he picked up his coffee and nodded his thanks.

I introduced Hawthorne to Vincent then answered his question. "There's not much to tell. Two white guys, both mid-forties, and two Uzis, in a black SUV, California license 6CGI something, something, something, doing a drive-by shooting that was obviously aimed at us. It was very professional, very quick. I'm alive and talking to you, because Vincent reacted more quickly than I could and saved us both."

Detective Hawthorne looked at Vincent. "Do you have anything to add to Roger's succinct summary?"

"Yes, I do. The SUV was General Motors manufacture, a Cadillac Escalade I think. The license plate was 6CGI436."

Hawthorne smiled, grabbed his cell phone, speed dialed a number, and requested an APB for the car.

He looked back at me. "I thought you were cool under stress, Roger. Your colleague here makes you look like a rank amateur. OK, I know you well enough to fill out the reports. Your colleague here needs to tell me a bit more about himself."

Vincent described himself as my partner in the detective agency, gave his PI license number plus his business and home addresses, and sat back to wait for additional questions. There weren't any for him.

Hawthorne finished sipping his coffee and looked back at me. "Are you working on any cases that might have gotten somebody upset enough to want you killed?"

This was almost certainly neither the time nor the place for the truth. "Not that I know of, but who knows what it takes to get a criminal scared enough to overreact like this?"

He stood and shook hands with both of us. "I doubt if we're going to find that SUV with people or forensic evidence in it, but we'll try. In the meantime be careful and call me if anything else I should know about happens."

And that was that for the moment. We headed back to the office.

Chapter24.Dinner with "Dirty Steve"

The phone call I was expecting came on my office line at about 3 PM. It was a potential client named John Smith, who wanted to see me immediately. I told him I was available and to come by. He promised to be there in the next half hour. I hung up, noting the strong smell of fish, or maybe fishy manure, coming through the telephone line.

I called Vincent into my office and told him what just happened. "I think it's show time shortly. That call was from a new potential client with urgent business, named John Smith. How do you think we should handle this?"

"If there aren't any guns showing as they come in, let's just beat the crap out of them, inflict some severe pain, and see what we can find out. If they come in with guns blazing I think we should just take them out and not waste a lot of time talking about it."

He checked his pistol, a 9mm Glock, made sure the magazine was full, and racked a cartridge into the chamber. I took my own 9mm Glock pistol out of the gun safe, hidden behind a cleverly hollowed out filing cabinet, and did the same. I slipped the gun into a cross-draw belt holster, which was completely concealed by my sport jacket. Then we waited, me at my desk facing the open door leading from my office into our tiny client's waiting room and Vincent in his office, strategically invisible behind the half-opened door.

About twenty minutes later, there was a knock on the outside door to the waiting room. "Come in," I called out as I stood up behind my desk to be polite. Standing also facilitated drawing my pistol from its holster on my belt and/or diving for cover if it looked like I had to.

The same two men from the SUV walked in, stopping just outside my office doorway. The one in the lead was medium height, medium weight, short dark hair, wearing a sport jacket over a clean shirt and tie with nice slacks. The second man was similarly dressed and similarly unremarkable physically with lighter hair, worn somewhat longer. The two could be told apart mainly by the different colors of their slacks and hair. No guns were showing, but both wore jackets that could easily conceal a weapon. "Are y'all alone here?" asked the one in the front.

"I have a partner, but he's out on a case. I expect him back in less than a half-hour," I replied helpfully. It was a little disconcerting to realize how convincing I could be when I was trying to sound really, really dumb.

The two continued into my office. The one in the lead extended his hand toward me in the universal handshake gesture, saying in a soft voice, with a slight residue of inflections from a Texas upbringing, "Ah called you earlier Mr. Bowman. Ah'm John Smith."

I wasn't sure what the rules of the game Mr. Smith was playing were supposed to be, but it seemed the perfect time to rewrite them. I took a stride towards him with my left leg, as I extended my right hand and grasped the hand Smith had offered as a manly handshake of greeting. Continuing my forward movement and shifting my weight, I pulled hard on his hand, pivoted on my left leg, and launched the hardest sidekick I could generate, directly into his solar plexus. As he doubled up in pain and astonishment, as well as in a serious attempt to breathe, I pulled him towards me in case he needed a hand strike as a calming influence.

In the meantime Vincent screwed his pistol into the second man's ear to encourage him to relax and stand still. Smith was too engrossed in trying to breathe to present any problems. I let go of his hand and tweaked his jacket open. Surprise! The butt of his Uzi was tucked into his belt. I relieved him of the extra weight, carefully avoiding leaving any fingerprints, frisked him for other weapons (there weren't any), and took his wallet, handling just the edges to avoid leaving my fingerprints on it either. A short hard chop to his right shoulder temporarily paralyzed the nerve plexus on that side. A second chop to the left shoulder replicated the injury on the other side. I shoved Smith to the floor, as he moaned pitifully, and gave him a warning.

"Stay right there and don't try to get up or make any noise unless you want me to inflict some permanent damage and really hurt you. Just nod yes if you understand."

He nodded. Vincent hit the second guy directly behind the ear, as hard as he could with the edge of his rigid hand. The second gunman dropped in his tracks like a pole-axed steer. No bump, no telltale bruise, but he was unconscious for the foreseeable future. Vincent removed the second Uzi from his belt using a handkerchief to avoid telltale fingerprints. No other weapons showed up when he was frisked, except for a nasty switchblade knife, which Vincent admired and kept. Another wallet joined the collection on my desk, also handled carefully to avoid fingerprints.

I sat down at my desk while Vincent remained standing on alert. These two might have picked up some friends since this morning that might show up unexpectedly. Or either of them could have remarkable recuperative powers. You can never be too careful in situations like this. "Let's see who Mr. Smith and his nameless friend are when they show their I.D.," I suggested, donning a pair of latex gloves from a convenient desk drawer.

The first wallet was brown leather and well worn. It contained a treasure or two. "Guess what, Vincent? John Smith isn't his real name! He's Elliot Harkins, a DEA agent with a Texas driver's license and a home address in one of the border towns near San Francisco de Texas. It looks like he kept the Harkins family tradition of crooked law enforcement alive for another generation. What would you like to bet sleeping beauty over there is his partner?"

The second wallet was black leather, containing a second set of DEA I.D. and a Texas drivers license in the name of James Corley, home address San Francisco de Texas.

"What next, el jefe?" Vincent asked. "I think we'll be a whole lot safer if neither of these guys is in a position to harm us."

"We completely agree. Please stand over here, directly behind me." I double gloved with another pair of tight latex gloves, pulled out of my desk drawer. Lifting Harkins up to a standing position, I leaned his limp body against the wall facing towards Corley, balancing it carefully so he remained upright. From the pile on the desk, I took Corley's Uzi, checked the safety lever, and carefully placed the machine pistol in Corley's right hand. It took all my strength to lift Corley's limp body up into a standing position to get the angle right, press tightly enough on the grip to override the grip safety, and carefully fire a burst from across the room. The bullets hit directly into Harkins' upper torso, centered on his heart. With my help, the unconscious Corley also sprayed bullets in a random pattern around the office, consistent with the relative positions of Corley and Harkins. Then, I picked up the other Uzi from my desk, admiring it while not putting a set of my own fingerprints on it, and tucked it back into Harkins' belt. I placed it carefully where it wouldn't interfere with the nice pattern of 9mm bullet holes I had created earlier in Mr. Harkins upper body.

Finally I took the Uzi out of Corley's hand, stood him up again and leaned his limp body against the opposite wall. I removed the gloves from my right hand, pulled out my own Glock, and shot Corley three times. I fired the classic two taps to the chest and one to the head, as I stood in front of him. The trajectory would be consistent for all three shots to have hit him as if both of us were standing. I stood far enough away to ensure there wouldn't be any gunpowder residue on his clothes or his body, which fell forward from the wall onto the floor.

I removed the second set of latex gloves carefully and handed all four of them to Vincent. "You're not going to be here when the cops come. Your job is to make these gloves disappear so they can't ever reappear in a CSI lab. Get going now; I'll call Hawthorne in five minutes. Take your Glock. They're going to confiscate any guns they find here as evidence. I think you'll have to meet Callahan's flight and bring him to the house. I'm going to be tied up down here for a few hours."

I described Callahan to him, so he'd know whom to meet, and gave him the flight information.

Five minutes later, I called Hawthorne and told him there had been a couple of killings, one by me in self-defense, and the two dead guys were almost certainly the two men who shot at Vincent and me earlier.

"Stay put," he told me, "there'll be a lot of police in your office very soon." His prediction was perfectly accurate.

I told my story a dozen or two times to a dozen or two police persons. Hawthorne was very unhappy that I was involved with the death of two DEA officers. He was ready to arrest me, but the preliminary forensic evidence supported my version of the story. The local patrol cars found the black SUV parked on the next block, exactly as we had described it, but with a new set of license plates. Hawthorne bagged and tagged all three guns, my Glock and the two Uzis, and kicked me out of my office. It was now officially a crime scene. Eventually he cut me loose, with dire warnings of the consequences if I was involved in any more gunplay in his precinct. I arrived back home just in time to meet Vincent and Steve Callahan arriving for supper. We agreed not to talk business until everyone was settled at the dinner table.

We all sat down to discuss the case at one of Bruce's better dinners. Over roasted rack of lamb, mint jelly, roasted garlic, garlic toast, quinoa with a great sauce, dessert, and a very nice California Zinfandel, we updated each other about the case.

"You first, Steve, and remember, I haven't had a chance to update Suzanne and Bruce yet."

Callahan finished chewing on a large chunk of lamb. "OK. As I told Roger earlier, we arrested the Schaefers this morning at a dog show in Bakersfield. The local police CSI unit did find forensic evidence tying their RV to the two dog show murder victims. We can at least prove both of the dead judges had been in the RV and the Schaefers owned show leads identical to those used to murder the two judges. That's a good start on proving our case. They'll have a preliminary hearing in front of a judge tomorrow afternoon in San Francisco. The DA will charge them with first-degree murder and ask they be kept in jail because they are a flight risk. That should get them held over without bail, at least until they get a high priced lawyer to start shopping for judges that might be willing to issue a writ of habeas corpus.

"Meanwhile, back at the DEA, former San Francisco agent-in-charge Nappeli was arrested by federal marshals in Washington, DC. He is currently in jail, charged with aiding and abetting, as well as criminal conspiracy. Rumor has it he's trying to make a deal in return for his testimony. If that's true, I'm really disappointed in him----it seems like just yesterday he was 100% in favor of law and order. The FBI put together a task force out of El Paso, to investigate municipal and federal law enforcement agency corruption in West Texas. They've already arrested Sheriff Harkins and Deputy Hawks, who are in jail charged with criminal conspiracy, accessory before and after the fact to several murders, and drug dealing. Neither of them is going anywhere for a long time."

Callahan sipped some wine. "That's pretty much all of what I told Roger and Vincent this morning, except I've updated the story a bit. The rest of this has happened since then. With Vincent's help, we participated this afternoon over the phone in a bit of investigative journalism. The story broke in the local newspaper, detailing all he found out in West Texas, which establishes life-long links between the two murder victims and the Schaefers. That's another nail in the coffin for the defense, when this case comes to trial. It wouldn't surprise me too much if our former DEA agent-in-charge for San Francisco also has roots in West Texas. That's going to be up to the FBI to investigate. It's out of my hands now. How about you guys? Anything new from your end, Roger?"

I made a production out of clearing my throat and drinking some wine while mentally formulating how much I actually wanted to reveal to our friend, who was still a working cop. "We had an exciting and reasonably productive day. A couple of guys tried their luck at a drive-by shooting in front of our building when Vincent and I were on our way to lunch. Thanks to Vincent, there wasn't any damage. They really hadn't chosen the right time of day for it. Someone called in a 911. There was enough traffic going by that there wasn't any way they could come back and make a second try without taking two or three minutes to drive around the block. By that time, they'd have been caught. We had plenty of time to get to a safe place after they missed us with their first try."

Suzanne gave me a look saying loud and clear I hadn't heard the end of this discussion and there'd be more to come later.

"The same two guys came by the office later that afternoon, pretending to be clients. I was ready for them this time. When the first one tried to pull his gun, a very illegal Uzi fully automatic machine pistol, I shot him. Three times. He got off a wild burst of shots, which made a mess of the office and of his buddy. Since both of them were dead, I called the cops. Guess who the two killers with Uzis turned out to be?"

Nobody guessed. So it was still my turn. "We had found the two crooked DEA agents from West Texas, agency I.D. and all,

or they found us. One of them turned out to be named Harkins.
He was the right age to be Sheriff Harkins' son or nephew.
There's another connection for your case, Steve. The DA can
suggest they were there to keep Vincent's mouth shut,
permanently."

Suzanne had been listening to all of this and analyzing the
information. She drank a bit of wine and jumped into the
conversation.

"Do we have a lot of coincidence going on here or is there
some way that everything we've seen and heard is
interconnected? This all began when the AKC hired Roger and
Bruce. The idea was to investigate whether there was criminal
behavior going on at the dog shows here in the western United
States, and to check whether the integrity of the judging process
had been compromised. I picked up a stalker at about the same
time Roger was interviewed for this job in New York. Roger and
Bruce had just started this investigation, when the first judge,
Orval Krause, was murdered here in San Francisco. That's when
Detective Callahan came into the picture. The next big event was
the second murder, this time of another judge, Jorge Guerrero, in
Vallejo. While all of this was going on, Bruce was showing Juliet
quite successfully and discovering a whole lot of recreational
drugs were being sold at these dog shows. Have I got it right so
far?"

Bruce and I both nodded yes.

Suzanne continued, "I'd like to suggest a complex, but I
think plausible, hypothesis that connects all of the stuff going on.
If you agree, it not only makes a little sense out of a whole bunch
of seemingly isolated incidents, but points to what we have to do
next. My theory turns out to be an interesting example of how
the scientific method can take us from bits and pieces of
seemingly unrelated data, to a testable hypothesis, to a proof of
our hypothesis. Let's start with a simple statement of
hypothesis: There's a mysterious Mr. X we haven't thought about,

who is pulling the strings on several puppets behind all of these events, and each of these events are related. I think we have one more criminal to root out, and I think I know where to look for him."

Steve Callahan looked and sounded very skeptical. "This is beginning to sound like a bad British mystery novel, Suzanne. Why confuse things that are already pretty complicated without a mysterious super-criminal in the background?"

It seemed a good time for me to jump back into this discussion. "Relax Steve. We've learned through the years to listen to Suzanne's analyses. Whether it's intuition or just raw smarts, she can see what's going on from the perspective of the big picture a lot more clearly than I do, and probably than you do, too."

Suzanne cleared her throat elaborately before continuing. "Let's assume the drug business at the dog shows was organized and orchestrated by our mysterious Mr. X. He recruited the help of two very dishonest and now very dead DEA agents. Let's further assume he's the one who corrupted, if that's the right word for recruiting a couple of long-time drug dealers, the Schaefers. Their job was to supply and sell drugs at the shows so he could develop a highly profitable business on the side. He ran into a problem when judging improprieties became apparent at the dog shows, which he didn't have anything to do with. He was afraid the fixed judging might result in an investigation that could upset his lucrative drug business. He had the brilliant idea that if he instigated the investigation, he could control it by pointing his chosen private detective in the directions he wanted. Especially if the AKC hired a private eye who wasn't too bright and whose loyalty could be bought for a bunch of money and a few additional perks. Apparently Roger was able to convince him, during his interview in New York City, he was that guy, with some cogent suggestions from Sherry Wyne that helped give the right image of being just a little greedy. In this scenario Roger was supposed to stop at identifying the two fixed judges, report back to the AKC who would fire them, and everything could go back to business as usual. Are you with me so far, Steve?"

"It's still a bad movie script as far as I'm concerned, Suzanne, unless you have any real evidence I haven't heard yet. Do you know who your mysterious Mr. X is?"

Suzanne looked directly at Callahan. "Take another sip or two of wine, Steve, and be patient. I'll get there in another minute or two. Hunter Lodge's loose screws were not in the plan when the AKC hired Roger. By coincidence the corrupt judges were personally involved with the drug dealers. I suspect the murders were unplanned accidents in the context of Mr. X's plot. That's what happens when your partners in crime are low-life drug dealers. Put together a random drug war between two Mexican cartels and the two killings of the judges and Roger's simple investigation, as planned by Mr. X, quickly spiraled out of control. Orval Krause, from all we know about him, was an opportunistic wheeler-dealer. I imagine he realized the Schaefers had a lucrative drug dealership operating out of their RV. He had the poor judgment to try to blackmail them into sharing the wealth. Albert responded impulsively, in what we now know was his typical fashion. Jorge Guerrero may have guessed who killed Krause and why. He also tried to shake down Albert and Sadie, with predictable, similar results. Or, maybe Guerrero was just affiliated with the wrong cartel, and conveniently happened to be in the wrong place at the wrong time.

"Hunter Lodge's stalking of me was another attempt to get Roger off the case, but this time it wasn't about drugs, it was about fixed judges. Lodge somehow must have caught on those two judges could be bought. Perhaps he had some inkling their backgrounds weren't pure. Maybe he checked them out a bit more thoroughly than the AKC had when they became licensed judges."

Vincent had told Callahan about the details of our relationship with the AKC, on the way over from the airport, including Hunter Lodge and his floral arrangements. Callahan started to nod as he thought about what Suzanne was saying. "I'm beginning to see where you're going with this, Suzanne. Do you have anything at all that ties somebody we know, to being Mr. X?"

Suzanne paused dramatically to sip some wine and make Steve Callahan wait a bit longer for the answer. Perhaps it was her punishment for his initial skepticism. "So who is Mr. X? The Schaefers and the two murder victims weren't smart enough or well organized enough to put all of these pieces together and herd all of the cats involved in this mess. Neither was Hunter Lodge. Any of the rest of the AKC executive staff could certainly have been involved, but Harold Carswell has to be, by far, the most obvious suspect. He has the managerial skills and was most directly responsible for hiring Roger to investigate the integrity of the judging at the dog shows in this region. He had no idea Roger was as independent and as competent as he is, or he never would have interviewed him in the first place. Carswell assumed Roger would report regularly to him and he'd be able to keep him on track to do his job as Carswell envisioned it."

Suzanne took another sip from her wine glass. "Instead of receiving the regular updates he expected, Carswell had no idea what Roger, Bruce, and Vincent had learned was going on at the dog shows, until he received their first report some time yesterday evening. The report not only identified Hunter Lodge as being involved in crooked judging, but also indicated Roger planned to continue an already active investigation into who was selling drugs at the dog shows. Carswell obviously didn't want this to happen. Reading Roger's report woke him up to the unpleasant news he'd hired an extremely competent private detective, probably the last thing in the world he wanted to find out at that point. When he did receive the report, and the timing here is critical, he panicked and ordered his two crooked federal agents to kill Roger. It had to work this way. For the two DEA agents from West Texas to get to Los Angeles in time to try to kill Roger and Vincent at 11:30 AM local time, they had to start out long before Vincent missed his interview at the El Paso airport before his 10 AM flight that same morning. What could have provoked such an overkill response besides the report Roger sent to Harold Carswell?

"I don't think we'll ever be able to prove it, but I suspect that Carswell's links to the Texas drug scene and the Mexican cartels go all the way back to his Vietnam service in the army. Killeen, Texas is a long way from West Texas, but Carswell may have seen the possibilities of being on a military base. There was a constant transfer of troops to and from Viet Nam, where the drugs came from, and a constant transfer of men and materials by truck and plane off of the base. He may actually have sought out his cartel connections back then."

Of course, Suzanne had hit the nail on the head. A lot of law enforcement agencies in California, Texas, and New York City had a lot of work to do in the following weeks. From our point of view, things finally settled down. Detective Hawthorne returned my Glock to me with his thanks. He actually suggested that I offer to use it on the DEA staff in Washington. They kept calling him, demanding I be punished to the fullest extent of the law for whatever charges he could dream up, as an example to others who might interfere with federal agents in the performance of their duty.

The AKC appointed Stanley Morgan, the corporate lawyer, as the acting CEO on an interim basis. Harold Carswell, was put on paid administrative leave pending a full investigation for alleged criminal activities. Morgan called me immediately after his appointment to thank me on behalf of the AKC, for what he referred to as a splendid job. He told me the check for my promised bonus was in the mail, accompanied by a second check, for double that amount, as an added bonus for the additional services rendered. These additional services included identifying Harold Carswell as a corporate bad apple and solving the murders. He suggested I continue in the employ of the AKC for the rest of the dog show season. I could keep campaigning Juliet on their dime to make sure all of the judging irregularities had been rooted out and the sport was once again clean. He also assured me I'd receive a generous retainer from the AKC in future years in return for keeping the services of my agency available whenever they needed assistance. Carswell was eventually fired with a golden parachute to finance his impending huge legal fees for criminal defense attorneys. After a brief search for Carswell's replacement, Morgan was selected as permanent CEO, which solidified our connection with the AKC.

Morgan eventually explained his visit to LA, several months previously when he called me about having a drink. Even as far back as then, he was suspicious about Carswell and thought about pointing my investigation in that direction. He decided at the last minute not to share his suspicions with me, for fear I'd share this information with Carswell.

A couple of months after I sent Harold Carswell the first report that precipitated so much action, Vincent was back in my office and seemed excited. "Roger, I think maybe we're ready to send the AKC our second, and it should be the final, report. I found a dozen more judges out of several hundred possibilities, who seem to have been picking winners from the wrong end of the leash. They let Hunter Lodge's dogs win too often, as well as a few other owners from other breeds. Interestingly, half of these dozen new judges who've come up on my computer are also from the southwest, one from New Mexico and the others from addresses in Texas. I've got some weasel words in the report, to indicate the methods I used haven't been independently validated. I'd suggest to the AKC they ask the FBI to investigate these possible suspects. The Feebies have the resources to get the truth and should be highly motivated to do so, given the interstate commerce involved in dog shows and the asset forfeiture rules under a RICO prosecution."

I forwarded Vincent's report to Stanley Morgan, now the CEO of the AKC, along with a cover letter explaining what the first report had contained, a copy of the first report, and assuring him the task was now complete from our end. I suggested he request an investigation by the FBI, who had the resources to do it right and the scientists to validate or refute Vincent's statistical methodology. He took my advice.

Juliet continued to overachieve in the show ring with Bruce's handling and their clear bond together. Early that summer, Sherry Wyne stopped by between dog shows to thank us for a job well done. She proudly announced her recent promotion from the AKC as a reward for her astute choice of private detectives. It was the same job title as regional representative, but she had less work to do at the dog shows, more supervision of others, and a sizeable boost in her income.

Sherry, Suzanne, Bruce, and I sat around the patio table sipping fresh made lemonade courtesy of Bruce, while Robert was taking his afternoon nap. Juliet lay in the shade under the table, carefully adjusting her position until parts of her body and legs were simultaneously in contact with Sherry, Suzanne, and especially Bruce. Sherry looked at us for a moment or two and began, "I have an idea I've been working on for a while and would like to hear your reaction to it. Our original arrangement was that you'd return Juliet to me at the end of this case, which is more or less now, and take a puppy from her next litter. I've been thinking of a plan B. It works better for me in a lot of ways, and I do hope you'll consider it.

"If you want to keep Juliet, she's obviously happy here and loves being part of your family. I'd want a formal co-ownership contract for breeding purposes, where I pick the stud dog and get the pick puppy from each of the first two litters. I'll pay the stud fee in that scenario, unless you can still bill the first fee to the AKC. Then Juliet would be yours to keep, with no strings attached. My price for this generous, altruistic act is to have Bruce volunteer to train my two puppies to hunt and show, while he's training the puppies you'll keep from the same litters. I've been totally amazed at how much Juliet has learned from him over the last six months. I thought I was an expert dog trainer until I saw what he could do with her."

Bruce and Suzanne beamed. I thought I saw Juliet smile discretely, but I can't swear to that.

"Thank you, Sherry. I'm too young for you and I'm gay, but otherwise I think I could fall in love with you for keeping us together with Juliet," answered Bruce.

Juliet barked once to remind us she had a vote and it was yes.

Epilogue

Juliet had spent the civilized part of the night in the early stages of labor, producing nothing but a pile of shredded newspaper mixed in with now holey towels. Three exhausted humans gathered outside of her whelping box in a spare bedroom normally reserved for guests near the back of the house. It appeared that Juliet was not totally pleased with her whelping box, nor with Suzanne and Sherry, who kept on insisting she return to it after frequent pee breaks to the back yard. Each outing was a production, with Suzanne hovering nearby, carrying extra towels, in case Juliet chose to present her first pup outside, instead of taking a poop.

"Maiden bitches often can't tell the difference between the need to take a dump and a strong contraction," Sherry had explained, which is why the overly cautious Suzanne brought Juliet's towels with each trip outside.

This was the long awaited first litter for Juliet, who had finally retired from the show ring four months ago with her Silver Grand Champion title. The murders were solved and the AKC bureaucracy was in a bit of an uproar. It seemed like a good time to step back and produce a new generation of Juliet's line, while life was quiet for the whole Bowman clan and the next big assignment was still to come in.

"Having a litter sounded so much less nerve wracking and more natural than this, and a lot less sleep depriving," moaned Suzanne. For what seemed like the hundredth time that night, they stood in the drizzle out in the yard. "I sure hope Roger is getting some sleep – he's getting the early a.m. shift with Robert, if I have anything to say about it. If Juliet ever lets them out, Bruce has no intention of letting the puppies out of his sight for the first week. Do you think we're looking at a C-section yet?"

"Hell, no!" Sherry looked surprised at Suzanne's question. "How many hours were you in labor with Robert? And you only had one! According to Juliet's x-ray, she has somewhere between 10 and 12 puppies in there. That's one very full uterus to get everyone lined up and moved down and out. She hasn't had any really strong contractions yet. Give her time – it could take several more hours before she gets it in gear," Sherry added with a chuckle. She leaned over to feel Juliet's side as Juliet let out a little groan and a strong quiver went through her body. "Then, again, she may be getting ready to do something right now. Let's get back inside."

Sherry and Juliet went on to prove that experience was indeed the best teacher. The first puppy, a boy, popped out within 15 minutes of our return to the spare bedroom, oops the maternity suite, and her whelping box. Juliet alternated pacing the floor and lying on her side in the whelping box, panting until the blessed event. Out came a puppy attached by an umbilical cord to what was left of a placenta. Sherry, carrying the newborn pup in a clean towel, had positioned herself properly to catch the package as it emerged. She quickly opened the water sac surrounding the puppy, and cleaned its mouth and nostrils. Then with a piece of unwaxed dental floss, she tied off the cord and snipped it.

She rubbed the puppy vigorously with the towel to stimulate the first breaths saying, "sometimes this is enough and sometimes it isn't." This was one of those "isn't" times. She carefully supported the puppy's head and neck, while she swung the puppy upside down a couple of times, to help clear the lungs. Her effort was rewarded with an indignant squeal from the puppy, now a free-breathing, healthy firstborn. Sherry had prepared a few breeder essentials for this moment---a pile of template forms for sketching the markings on each pup so we could tell them apart after the event and record vital statistics for each. Suzanne was the designated group scribe. She sketched the spots and recorded time of birth. Sherry weighed the puppy and announced 14.5 ounces for Suzanne to record. Under comments, Suzanne recorded "none". Sherry handed the puppy to Juliet, who had just finished eating the material discharged after the puppy. This discharge, including the placenta, was a rich source of hormones to stimulate her contractions in preparation for the next puppy's birth. Juliet licked and nuzzled the first puppy, stimulating it to start nursing. Then things quieted down for a bit while we waited for puppy #2 to emerge. Based on the ultrasound exams and an X-ray, we had an estimated puppy count of 11 to expect in this litter. It was going to be a long night!

Sherry offered Juliet water and cottage cheese, plus a couple of Tums tablets. She explained, for things to go smoothly during this process, it was important to keep her well hydrated, and, with the cottage cheese and Tums, her body stores of calcium high. Sherry encouraged Juliet to get up and walk around in the nursing suite when she wanted to, which was seldom. All of Juliet's energy was focused on birthing, nursing, and mothering a growing litter of puppies.

Puppies #2 and #3, both girls, came at half-hour intervals and were duly recorded. Everything had gone well thus far and things looked good.

Puppy #4, another boy, decided to make things exciting by demonstrating a classic breech presentation, butt first. Sherry did some reaching around in the birth canal to rotate the fetus into the proper position. Soon another 15-ounce puppy joined the group assembled in the whelping box, nursing, squeaking, and sleeping. Suzanne finally got to make an entry under "comments" on her puppy information sheet.

Juliet was getting a little tired and the gap between births was getting noticeably longer. Puppy #5, a girl, was born while Juliet was walking around the whelping box. Juliet suddenly stopped directly in front of Roger, who was sitting on the floor watching the new pups. Suddenly, a puppy and a pint or so of associated fluids was air mailed directly into Roger's lap. Juliet stepped back into the whelping box, while Roger handed the new puppy to Sherry and excused himself to take a shower.

Suzanne got to make another entry under "comments" on the puppy's sheet.

Puppies #6-11 included another breech birth, a smaller than average puppy, a couple of pups needing more than a simple swing to start breathing, and a progressively more tired Juliet, now taking as long as an hour between puppies.

"That's it," declared Suzanne after #11, another girl, arrived.

"Not so quick," corrected Sherry. "The X-ray isn't definitive. There can sometimes be another pup or two hiding up there. Let's just wait and watch for a bit longer."

Once again, experience was the best teacher. Puppy #12, another boy and the final littermate, was born about 1.5 hours later. We had a healthy, hungry litter of 12 puppies, 8 girls and 4 boys. An exhausted Juliet was impersonating Super Mom and nursing the litter more or less continuously. The next morning Robert had his first visit to the puppies and got to give one a gentle pat-pat under Juliet's watchful, but permissive, eye.

I couldn't resist quoting the famous line that ended "Casablanca", which I had seen about a dozen times. "Robert, I think this is the beginning of a beautiful friendship!"

-----------------------------------THE END----------------------------

NOTE FROM THE AUTHOR

After you finish "The Deadly Dog Show" please take a moment to write a review and post it on Amazon. Amazon makes this quick and easy on the book's home page. Written reviews are important to both readers and authors. Positive reviews sell more books. A few sentences are all that is necessary for a useful review. Of course, I hope you will enjoy this story. But, even if you didn't, please think about providing a review that tells possible readers what you liked and didn't like about the book at http://www.amazon.com/Deadly-Roger-Suzanne-Mysteries-ebook/dp/B00E25BM3I

All of the Roger and Suzanne mystery stories are available as inexpensive e-books from Amazon Kindle (Free for members to download from Kindle Unlimited). All of the novels can be read in any order, so feel free to skip around. There are also three novellas, an Omnibus volume, and a short story anthology available on Amazon Kindle.

For dog lovers:

(The Deadly Dog Show--This book): In a suspenseful thriller set in the hyper-competitive world of canine conformation shows, Roger and Suzanne have to identify Suzanne's mysterious stalker while they solve the mystery of who is murdering the dog show judges. http://www.amazon.com/Deadly-Roger-Suzanne-Mysteries-ebook/dp/B00E25BM3I

And a sequel to The Deadly Dog Show:

Hunter Down: A high-powered rifle shot rings out in California's early morning stillness launching Roger and Suzanne into another suspenseful mystery thriller. In a complex whodunit set against a backdrop of pointing dogs and canine hunt tests, private detective Roger Bowman has to solve a murder case with no clues, no suspects, and no apparent motive. http://www.amazon.com/gp/product/B016V4GQGA

South and Latin American mysteries:

The Origin of Murder is set in Ecuador's Galapagos Islands. As Roger and Suzanne retrace the path that Charles Darwin sailed and walked more than 175 years ago, the body count increases almost as fast as the clues. http://www.amazon.com/Origin-Murder-Suzanne-American-Mystery-ebook/dp/B00K4KDL3O

Rum, Cigars, and Corpses: Roger and Suzanne have to solve a cold case in a hot climate. Weeks after a suspicious accident in Havana claims the life of a tourist, the detective couple retraces the victim's steps as they try to figure out whodunit and why. Intrigue and conspiracies abound in this international thriller set in Cuba, a tropical island that U. S. citizens have been forbidden to visit for more than half a century. http://www.amazon.com/Cigars-Corpses-Roger-Suzanne-mystery-ebook/dp/B01EZBDCRC

The Surreal Killer is leaving a trail of dead women across Chile, Peru, and Bolivia. The victims all seem to have been murdered in exactly the same way. There may be a link to a small group of scientists who meet annually in different locations in the region. This Indie Book of the day Award-winning psychological thriller is a true whodunit mystery novel set in an unusual and exotic locale, Lima, Cuzco, and Machu Picchu in Peru and Chile's Atacama Desert. http://www.amazon.com/The-Surreal-Killer-ebook/dp/B007H21EFO

The Ambivalent Corpse: Private detective Roger Bowman and his girlfriend scientist Suzanne Foster find themselves traveling through Uruguay and Southwest Brazil, with additional visits to Paraguay and Argentina, to solve a baffling and grotesque murder case. Parts of a dismembered corpse are found on a rocky stretch of beach in Montevideo, Uruguay, apportioned equally between Memorials to a German cruiser sunk in World War II and the Holocaust. http://www.amazon.com/Ambivalent-Corpse-Crime-Meant-ebook/dp/B0060ZFRQG

The Matador Murders, loosely based on Dashiell Hammett's Red Harvest, has lots of action, a suspenseful whodunit storyline, and enough corpses to feed an entire Piranha Farm. The book can be read as a stand-alone introduction to the region (Uruguay, Chile)

and to the series characters.
http://www.amazon.com/Matador-Murders-American-Mystery-ebook/dp/B008QD4BJE

<u>Alaska as a setting</u>:

For a change, the butler didn't do it; a bear did. Or did it? In Unbearably Deadly, Roger and Suzanne visit Alaska to find out the circumstances surrounding their friends' deaths. The vast expanse of Denali National Park creates a 6-million acre locked room murder case for our sleuths to solve.
http://www.amazon.com/dp/B00RAOVJWW